# LEAVING
## MAGGIE HOPE

# LEAVING
## MAGGIE HOPE

a novel by
Anthony S. Abbott

LORIMER PRESS
DAVIDSON, NC

2008

Published in the United States by Lorimer Press, Davidson, North Carolina.

This is a work of fiction and any resemblance to real persons
or events is purely coincidental.

Library of Congress Control Number: 2008932530

ISBN 978-0-9789342-3-1 (PBK)

Cover Photo by Megan Rindoks

*To Nancy*

# CHAPTER
## *one*

$\mathcal{F}$ROM WHERE HE LAY the boy could see the shapes of the trees against the sky. Without their leaves they had all been different, some stretching their arms straight upward in fine long lines, some tilted, some gnarled with the fingers of old men, stiff in the joints. But now, in the summer, they seemed to him like soft green sponges. He could fly into them and bounce off from one to the next in the blue June air.

He liked it here in the cave with its dry dirt floor. He had his food in cans taken from the house one or two at a time over a period of weeks so his mother wouldn't notice. He had the apple crate for his books and the mayonnaise jars filled with water and the flashlight with extra batteries and the sleeping bag he had got for his tenth birthday but never used. It was his place, which he had found in the spring, almost by accident, roaming with the big collie from the Wallace's farm deeper into the woods than usual, following her really, finding himself there on the hillside among the rocks, seeing the opening, too small to notice unless you were there.

He had returned to it only on special occasions, mostly after school in the afternoons when his mother wasn't home and couldn't ask him where he was going. He had to be careful. If they found out about it, they would take it away from him. It was his, and he had brought to it, slowly, during the last weeks of school, the things which he would need when the time came. It was his, and now he would stay there until he could figure out what to do.

Elizabeth would have known. Elizabeth had always handled things before, like the time she had taken him away on the train with her to their grandparents, but she was eighteen and she had graduated from high school the week before and gone to New York to look for a job. The boy didn't like it without Elizabeth. One night his mother was nice, hugging and kissing him, making him sit in her lap, calling him "Toots" and giving him money to go to the store for ice cream and candy, and the next night yelling at him, sending him upstairs to his room so she and Bernie could be alone and do whatever adults did behind the closed door in the living room.

"Jesus, David," she would say. "Go find something to do on your own. I've had you hanging around the whole goddam day. Go upstairs and read a book or something."

You could never tell with grownups. When he was younger, it had been all right with just his mother and himself and Elizabeth, and even with Bernie it wasn't so bad at first, but now with Elizabeth gone and Bernie not getting home until eight or nine and sometimes not at all, he was afraid. His mother was different, and so was Bernie.

He couldn't talk to his friends at school about it. It just wasn't something you mentioned to somebody else. So he lay in his bed awake at night trying to think it out, and that was when he had the idea about using the cave, just in case, and began taking the cans of beans and Spam and macaroni and cheese and the knife and fork from the drawer in the back cupboard. Then the blanket from Elizabeth's room and the pillow from her closet shelf and the mess kit she had used at camp.

It was lighter now. The color behind the soft balls of green was more blue. Maybe his mother would be up, downstairs perhaps, in the kitchen. She would be calling him to come down and eat his breakfast or sitting at the table alone drinking her coffee, smoking her cigarette and working the crossword puzzle. Or, maybe, at this very moment she had walked up the back stairs to his room and found him missing. Maybe she was talking on the phone to the police, to the very same policeman . . .

He stopped, remembering the policeman's face and uniform. A quiet face, clean shaven, a strong chin and blue eyes that had looked at him slowly, without anger. And the trousers, dark blue with a gold stripe disappearing into the shining black boots, and the gun in the holster on his belt, the bullets on either side of it, gleaming like silver. His shirt, a lighter blue with the bright badge over his pocket and the insignia of the eagle on the sleeve. The policeman was sitting at his kitchen table drinking coffee and writing things down on his pad, while in the other room the men from the hospital bandaged Bernie's shoulder.

David glanced quickly at the writing on the pad – his mother's new name in capital letters, MAGGIE HOPE PETERSEN, followed by some scribbling that he couldn't really read.

"Just tell me, in your own words, David, what you saw," the policeman had said, looking at him with the kind eyes.

"He didn't see anything," the mother said. "He was asleep and got up when he heard the shot. He came downstairs and saw the mess and ran back up and hid in his room until I went up to get him just now."

"Why don't you let him speak for himself?"

"He's just a kid. He doesn't know anything. What'ya need him for anyway? I told you, it was an accident."

He could see her pacing, back and forth, back and forth, her eyes red from crying, her black dress torn at the sleeve, her curly, brown hair funny like she had slept on it wrong.

He was frightened, even more frightened than he had been when he woke up and heard them arguing. He had snuggled deep into the covers, under all the way so nothing could come in the windows and no sound from downstairs could reach him, but the air under the blankets was stale, and he woke, sweating and gasping. He pushed his head out and breathed long and deep. Then he heard the crash, like a glass had fallen, and then their voices going back and forth. Loud. He crept out of bed and opened the door. The voices were louder, clearer. Across the hall, then down the stairs halfway where he could see below the ceiling into the living room.

His mother sat on the sofa with the shotgun in her hands. She was pointing it at Bernie. He was laughing.

"Get out of here," she said. "Get out of my house."

"Come on, Maggie. What's this goddam virtue all of a sudden?"

"You stink," she said. "Go on back to New York to your whores. I'm sick of you."

He was standing near the window which faced out onto the street. Next to him was a table with a green lamp on it. David kept thinking about the lamp. If she shoots the gun, the lamp will shatter. He could see it, green pieces of lamp flying in slow motion, the bulb exploding, light then dark. Bernie had his coat off and the top buttons of his shirt were undone. His red and black striped tie was pulled loose. He held a glass in his left hand. He took a step toward her.

"No closer," she said.

The boy wanted to run, to scream, but he was frozen. It was a movie, like he wasn't there at all and it was happening far, far away, and he was in a theatre watching it on a very small screen. Bernie laughed. He raised his arm with the glass in his hand, and at that moment she fired and he fell backward into the lamp and David screamed and tried to run up the stairs, but his feet wouldn't go and he only slipped downward, tumbling head backwards to the bottom.

"Quick," his mother had said. "Get back to bed and stay there 'till I call you."

She stood over him, her eyes red, her mouth hissing like a snake's. "You don't know anything. You haven't seen anything."

Then she was gone to the back somewhere, and he clambered up the stairs which seemed like a tower thousands of feet high and his room swirled around him as he lay in the bed and waited, hearing nothing for a long time, and then the sound of sirens and the flashing red lights outside his window and the blue lights also, and then his mother coming to the door and calling him, quietly this time, in pain, begging him almost – "Please, remember David. . ."

Then the policeman at the table writing.

"Tell me in your own words, what you saw."

He looked at his mother and then at the policeman.

"I'm not here to hurt anyone, David," said the policeman. His voice was calm, easy. "I just need to know the truth."

"I told you . . ." his mother said.

And then the boy, trying to stand up, to run. . .

"I feel sick," he said, and he was sick, his head spinning and the sound of the shot coming back, the green lamp exploding, the pieces floating in air and the blood from Bernie's shoulder blooming like a flower.

"I saw it," he screamed, standing and looking at his mother. "You did it. I saw it!" and then her hissing at him.

"Little Judas, stinking little Judas. Traitor. Telling on your own mother." And the boy running up the stairs into his room and closing the door, waiting and watching from the window until the red light and the blue light were gone and thinking I can never sleep in this house again and his legs slipping into the familiar blue jeans, his feet into the old high top sneakers, his brain feverish as he crept down the back stairs into the black silence of the now empty rooms, into the pantry for the flashlight which hung on the rusty nail over the potato bin, outside under the steps where he dug with his hands for the sock of nickels and dimes he had taken one by one from his mother's purse. In case I needed it, he thought, and then across the field, the briars ripping at his bare ankles, to the edge of the woods, where he waited, breathed, before plunging into the dark, weirdly lighted by the flash which only made darker shadows, until he thought he was lost. By the time he found the cave, it was almost dawn.

Now he lay there on the sleeping bag reading the Bible verses over and over. She had called him Judas. He had told, and she had cursed him, and he looked at the sock of money in the dirt next to him and back at the verses. With a cry he seized it, crushing it in his fist, feeling the coins digging into his fingers. Stumbling to the mouth of the cave, he swung his arm round and round in an arc and hurled the sock into the trees, where it caught on a hanging branch and bobbed slowly up and down.

Then the tears came, horrible choking tears that scalded his eyes and ran down his cheeks in dirty streaks. He could not stop them.

Afterwards he slept. And when he awoke the sun was shining in his eyes, gold rays slanting through the arms of the trees into the mouth of the cave. Suddenly he was hungry and thirsty. He hadn't eaten since sometime the day before. He opened a can of beans, folding the top back with care, spooning small mouthfuls onto his tongue and chewing them slowly, letting the taste settle before he swallowed. He sipped water from a mayonnaise jar between bites, and he saw in his mind's eye the children from the German prison camps he had seen in the newsreels standing in the lines for food and holding their bowls of soup with both hands, their eyes upturned in fear and wonder. And for the first time, he knew them.

He looked around the cave, at the cans so neatly stacked and the twin jars of water, the utensils in Elizabeth's old mess kit and the brown army blanket against the wall. Then he heard outside the sound of footsteps in the leaves — not near yet, but near enough to find him if they kept on. And he knew that he must go home. That this place was too precious for him to lose, that if they found him here he would never have himself again. He still had time to circle over the top and down to the road on the other side. He would call from the Wallaces' farm and say he had been lost. He would take nothing except the flashlight. And if she asked where he had been, he would say he had wandered into the woods, that he had been afraid, and that he had called her as soon as he found his way out. And, after all, he thought, that is true enough.

# CHAPTER
## *two*

$\mathcal{D}$AVID LAY ON THE SOFT GRASS in the back yard, and the dog, Gretel, lay next to him. He was going to a new school, a boarding school called Lowell in Southborough, Massachusetts. He would live there, sleep and eat there with other boys from all over the country.

"But why?" David asked. "Why can't we stay here?"

"We can't afford the rent, David," his mother had said. "Bernie and I are getting a divorce, and your old mom has to go to work. I can't work and take care of you, Toots. It's better this way. You'll see."

Bernie was gone, and Elizabeth had come home to collect her things. She and his mother would take David to the train in Bridgeport, and the train would take him to the school. Then they would pack up their belongings, sell their furniture and the green Plymouth and go to New York. In New York you didn't need a car. There were no places to park, and people went everywhere on underground trains called subways. It was decided. That was the thing. They had never talked to him about it or asked him what he wanted. When he got back from the cave, Elizabeth was there, and she had hugged him until he thought he'd break in two. She would take care of him while "Mommy went to sort things out." And when she got home, it had been decided that he would go to boarding school.

No one ever talked about the shooting. Bernie had just gone

away, that's all, vanished into the streets of New York, and Elizabeth had come home, and no one ever said anything. David wasn't going to ask. Asking could only cause trouble.

He rubbed his hand along Gretel's back. She was old now, with a white muzzle, and she slept most of the time. He could remember when she was the sleekest, blackest dog who ever lived. She was a dachshund, but the word had been too hard for David, and so he called her a hot dog, a wiener hound. There was a war on against Germany, and the neighbors laughed about having a German dog in the house at such a time. She had marvelous light brown spots over each eye which David loved to touch with his fingers. And when she ran with her short, stubby legs, it seemed as if her long stomach would scrape the ground. She was a ferocious mouser, and the two of them had hunted together, when he was little, the dog sniffing the baseboards of each room with her ears pricked up and her tail wagging, the boy on hands and knees, dragging behind him the plaster casts on each leg from calf to heel.

It seemed to him that he had always had casts when he was little. He had been born with what was called "bilateral club feet." His Achilles tendons were too short, and he couldn't walk, because he couldn't put his heels on the ground. He could only walk on his toes. So they did operations. They spliced the Achilles tendons, and then reconnected them. Each operation made the tendons a little longer, but after each operation he had to wear the casts, and so he crawled, more dog than boy, following Gretel from room to room, then seeking out her favorite napping places, curling up with her under the dining room table or in the corner of the living room next to the phonograph.

Now he was better, not perfect but better. His mother had taken him to the doctor, because the Lowell School required a physical examination. For a long time, David had refused to go.

"Suppose he makes me have another operation," he had argued.

"Don't be such a worry wart, Toots," his mother had said. "You're a little old man. Just relax and be a boy. When I was a little boy..."

David laughed. "You couldn't be a little boy."

"I could too. I was a little boy before I was a little girl."

"Could not."

"Could too. Now go get your shoes on. It's O.K."

"But what if he finds something."

"Trust me, Toots."

So they had driven in the green Plymouth to the brick building at the bottom of the hill, and even at that distance from the hospital, which towered like a dragon guarding her hoard of gold, he felt sick. Even at that distance he smelled the ether and felt the hands of the doctors and the nurses on his body like clamps holding him, and the hot, scalding tears as the round piece came down over his nose. Even after all that time, he trembled as he walked into the examining room, and his fingers shook as he unlaced the shoes and took off the socks for the doctor to see. The doctor pushed and pulled and kneaded and turned his feet this way and that. He made David walk and then jump, first on one foot and next on the other. He made him run and hop. Then he took the form which the school had sent to his mother and wrote for a long time. He had thick glasses and hairs coming out of his nose. David tried to read what the doctor was writing, but he couldn't make out the words.

The doctor looked up and smiled. "You're O.K., David," he said. "Your feet will hold up. Wear the high shoes until your heels develop enough to hold the low ones on without rubbing. You'll be fine."

But he wasn't so sure. It wasn't a question of the feet working. It was more than that. It was the shoes, which were different from the ones which anyone else wore, and his legs, his tiny birdlike legs, with no muscles below the knee. He had crawled for so long he had developed strong arms and shoulders, but the leg muscles had — what was it the doctor said? — "atrophied" and they would take a long time to develop. David knew what children were like and what they would do and say, he knew their cruelty and the way they could use words to hurt. "Twinkletoes, twinkletoes," he had heard in the hallways of the school and on the playground.

"He's got funny shoes."

"Hey, kid, how come you got funny shoes?"

"He looks like a fairy when he runs."

"Twinkletoes, run for us."

"Just ignore them, David," his mother had said. "They're no better than you are. You have a hundred times more character than they have. Don't let them suck you in."

But she didn't have to go to school, and she didn't have to go outside for recess. It was all right during classes, sitting at your desk, but at recess there were no teachers, and David was always the last one chosen in kickball or red rover, and sometimes he just said he didn't want to play, because it was easier, but if you didn't play, you got teased too, and there was nowhere to go, because you couldn't go inside during recess.

Every morning for as long as he could remember, his mother had come into his room and stretched his feet. She had held the balls of his feet in her hands and pushed and pushed, first the left and then the right, pushed until the pain came.

"No pain, no gain," she said.

Then she kneaded the muscles of his calves and turned his feet to the left and to the right as far as they would go. When he stood up in his bare feet, his heels didn't touch the floor unless he bent over. That was why he had to wear the high shoes, because the heels were too small.

"You'll never get any better, Toots, unless you work at it," his mother said. "I'm not going to be there, so you'll have to do this yourself. Just lie on your back and pull your knees up to your chest. Then grab the ball of your foot with both hands and pull. Don't jerk it. Just pull slow and steady."

She bent over and kissed him.

"I'm on the wagon now, Toots," she said. "I'm not going to let this thing lick me. Don't give up on me. I couldn't stand it if you did."

She kissed him again, and he could feel her dark curls on his cheek.

"Am I still little Judas," he asked.

"Oh, Toots, I'd forgotten all about that. My God, that was the liquor talking. You're my sweetheart."

She tickled him under the ribs.

"You're my sweetheart. Now, get dressed and I'll take you and your big sister to the beach one last time."

# CHAPTER
## *three*

*I*T WAS DUSK when the train arrived in Framingham, and David could barely make out the green letters against the dirty white background. A funny name, he thought. Framing a ham. Why would you frame a ham? Who would name a town that?

"Framingham! Framingham! The station stop is Framingham! Stay in your seats till the train stops, boys." The voice of the red-faced conductor boomed from behind him, snapping him back to what was going on inside the car. Motion everywhere, blurs of blue and gray, browns and tans, reaching for hats and coats, small bags.

"Come on, David," said the boy next to him. "Let's go."

"But the conductor said to stay in our seats."

"Nobody cares about him. He's not a master. Come on."

"You go ahead," said David. "That's all right."

The boy was gone, shooting toward the front of the car under the shoulders of a couple of taller boys wrestling in the aisle. David watched as one pretended to hit the other, and the victim, holding his chin with one hand and feigning great pain, crumpled backward over the chair arm into a seat occupied by another, smaller boy. Suddenly the train lurched to a stop, and what had been an act became real. Like dominoes, bodies one after another fell backwards until all the boys in the aisle lay laughing on the floor.

David liked watching. He liked the sounds they made – the gurgles, the shrieks, the groans of pain. He liked the way you couldn't tell sometimes when they were pretending and when they were really mad or scared. One by one, the boys picked themselves up and moved toward the front of the car, some of them mooing like cows, others neighing. David waited until the last of them had gone by, and then stepped carefully into the aisle himself. His legs were stiff from the long train ride and his feet sore in the new black shoes. He tried to walk as normally as possible, placing each foot heel down and toe out carefully in front of the other. Stay off your toes. Stay off your toes. The doctor's words echoed in his ears, and he could feel the doctor's fingers on his ankles. The doctor's hands twisting and turning his feet. You'll be all right, lad. Keep the heels down.

"Watch your step going down, boy."

Down was harder than up. You didn't want to catch the heel on the step above, and if you got the heel too far out you could lose your balance. The thing was to act normal.

"What's the matter, kid? Got a wooden leg?"

He heard the voice behind him, and the laugh from next to the voice. Two more steps, then the ground. He was fine. Walk, he thought, walk and don't look back. If you look back you're lost. They work all right. They're not great, but they work all right. He could raise his head now, and see ahead of him the crowd of boys pushing to get in the door of the bus that would take them to the school, a couple of them still mooing and someone else saying, "All right, Satchel Ass, it's not funny any more," and everybody laughing and the two masters from the train standing off to the side smoking cigarettes and talking as if nothing was happening. The bus was white, with the words LOWELL SCHOOL printed on the side in red and black letters. The driver greeted all the boys by name. "Hi Willie, whatcha say Mike, hey Buddy Roll, evenin' Satch, what say new boy. Hey new boy, gimme your name."

As David got closer, he could see the man's wide, smiling face, the black mustache, and a few curls of black hair under his driver's hat.

"Hey new boy, mine's Frankie, what's yours?" he said to the boy in front of David.

"Sebastian," said the boy.

"Saint Sebastian," said the driver. "All full o' arrows. O.K. next."

"David."

The smile grew wider. "Good boy," he said, extending his hand and shaking David's. "Davido. You go to Florence some day and see the great statue of Michelangelo. The greatest statue ever made. He's called Davido. O.K. next."

David edged slowly down the aisle, looking for a seat, trying to figure out what Frankie was talking about.

"Hey, Davido."

The voice came from the back of the bus. It was Allie, the boy he had sat with on the train.

"Come on, sit with me, Davido." He smiled, and David smiled back.

"What's going on?" David asked.

"This is great," said Allie. "Frankie does it every fall. He's got a bet with the masters he can name every boy when he gets off the bus. He's figuring out a way to remember the names of the new boys. You wait and see. When you get off, he'll remember that statue."

"How does he know anything about statues?"

"'Cause he comes from Italy. That's where they made the statues."

Soon the doors closed, the lights went out, and the noise which had seemed to come from everywhere grew quieter. Maybe the dark does that, thought David. In the dark you go somewhere else. His eyes wanted to close and he would have leaned his head on the headrest if there had been one on the old bus, but it was just a school-bus repainted. No place for heads. Allie looked out the window and David thought about Elizabeth, his sister.

His mother had said good-bye to him the day before and had left for New York. It was Elizabeth who drove him to the station at Bridgeport in the Green Plymouth.

"You're scared, aren't you?" she said.

"I guess so. I mean, it seems so weird."

"Like a dream," she said.

"Yes, like a dream."

He watched her driving and smoking like their mother. He would smoke when he got older, too. She told him that he was better off at school, that she had to begin a new life, that Mommy needed to get some help for her problem. "She's always going on the wagon, but how long does that last? The first crisis, and she's off again. You're better off without us."

"Look, David, there it is." Allie nudged him on the shoulder, and Elizabeth's face disappeared. "The School, there it is."

The bus was quiet except for a loud moo from the boy everyone called Satchel Ass. David craned his neck to the window, but it was too dark to see more than a large yellow building with a sign in front that said LOWELL SCHOOL 1866. A tall dark-haired woman with her hair pulled back in a bun smiled and waved at the boys.

"Who's that?" David asked.

"That's Mrs. Armbrister. She's real nice," said Allie.

The bus stopped, the door opened, and one by one the boys filed out past Frankie. "See you, Allie," said the driver, as David and Allie passed by, and "you, Davido, don't take no wooden nickels." Two more boys passed by behind David. "Sebastian, with the arrows in him," Frankie said, "and last of all, me, Frankie."

"O.K., Mr. R., I got 'em all. Five bucks you owe me."

"You did it again, Frankie," said the master, pulling out his wallet and taking a bill from it. "One of these years, I'll get you."

The boys cheered, Frankie stood, made a mock bow, closed the doors and drove off. Then the boys turned and marched through the open door of the yellow building, inside across the hall and into the schoolroom, where each one was assigned a desk, alphabetically by form, the older ones in the back the younger in the front. Forms were like grades, Allie had told David on the train. David was a third former, which meant the fifth grade. The highest form was the sixth form, which meant the eighth grade.

David was assigned to D7. That meant row D, the seventh desk from the window. When he reached it, he could see his name, David J. Lear, on a piece of paper taped to the desk. He sat down and looked around. It was the largest room he had ever seen. In the front was a huge, square desk where he had gone to find out his number. This was the master's desk, and you could not, he learned, come up to the master's desk without first raising your hand and getting permission. There were desks like the one he was sitting at for every student in the school, with tops you could lift up to put in books and papers and pencils. He started to count, but lost track at thirty-four, and looked instead at the walls. Two walls, the back one and the one on his left were almost all windows. The third wall, the one on his right, was the most interesting. There were two doors in it, one in the front where they had walked in from the bus, and one in the back where the lady called Mrs. Armbrister stood and greeted the older boys. Next to the back door was an organ and over the organ a huge rectangular banner, white with red borders and in red lettering the words POTERIS MODO VELIS.

Suddenly the master at the front desk shouted, "Attention!" and all the boys who had been standing in the back moved quickly to their desks. David looked around. Everyone was sitting straight, eyes in front of him, hands folded on the desk top.

"Eyes front," said the master sharply.

David blushed and looked straight ahead. Just at that moment, a tall husky man in a gray striped suit marched forcefully through the front entrance. The master stood up, then all the boys stood by their desks.

"Be seated, boys," said the man, motioning with his hand.

The man began to talk. He took his glasses off, wiped them with a pocket handkerchief, and put them back on. He seemed to see everyone. This was the Lowell School's seventy-eighth year, he said, and there were one hundred and sixty-eight boarders and twelve day boys. There were thirty-four new boys — often first formers, sixteen second formers, and seven third formers. The man began to read their names. Anderson, Buchanan… David drifted. He could feel it by the C's, the soft pull of Elizabeth's face and the pricked up ears of his dog, Gretel. Where was Gretel? What was she doing? Was she under the dining room table or nosing near his empty bed? Was she?

"David Johnson Lear."

A pause, then again, louder, "David Johnson Lear."

David came back with a start and stood, jolting his hip against the corner of his desk, causing a titter to run through the room. He turned red.

"Keep alert, boy," the man said.

When he had finished the list he spoke: "Each of you will want to learn as quickly as possible the rules of the school, which your dorm master will teach you. The more quickly you learn them, the happier you will be. Lowell is not a place for laggards. It is the philosophy of this school," and he pointed to the flag over the organ, "that You Can If You Will — Poteris Modo Velis. Your masters will do everything in their power to help you, but you must give your very best. Let us stand and sing the school hymn, 'Fight the Good Fight,' Number 560."

Desk tops opened, and the boys drew from inside the red hymnals with Lowell School stamped in gold on the front. David quickly followed what he saw the others doing, standing on the right side of his desk, his book open to the words he had never seen before — "Fight the good fight, with all your might." He had never heard such singing. The voices soared and swelled, "Run the good race, through God's own grace," and then, when the hymn was over, form by form they marched in twos, the older boys out the back door and the younger out the front, from the schoolroom to the dining hall.

There was so much to learn. Where to stand, how to sit, what the rules were. Where was his trunk and his suitcase? Where would he sleep? Someone was asking for his name.

"David," he said.

"Last name," said the man.

"Lear."

"Lear. Table twelve — Mr. Mulligan."

"I don't know where table twelve is."

"You can read, boy. Now move along."

David looked up. It was so hard to be new. They told you what to do, but not how to do it, they told you...

"Come on, David, you're at my table." It was Allie. David had never been so glad to see anyone in his life. He followed his friend up the center aisle, watching the numbers as he went. There it was, twelve, up in the corner. The man at the head of the table was the curly-haired man who had been checking off names in the schoolroom. That must be Mr. Mulligan.

"Just remember," said Allie, "to always say `Sir.'"

"What?" asked David.

"Never mind," said Allie. "I'll explain later. Let's get there before the gong goes."

When they got there, boys were standing behind every chair except the two farthest away from the master. That suited David fine. Farther seemed safer. He stood like the others, waiting for the next move. From the table behind him came the sound of a gong. Everyone sat down, except the boy next to Allie who walked as fast as he could without running toward the kitchen door.

"What's he doing?" David asked.

"He's our waiter. He brings the food and carries off the empty plates," said Allie. "You'll have your turn."

The waiter came back with two bowls and a platter of some kind of meat. David watched as Mr. Mulligan served the food and passed the plates down each side. Green beans, boiled potatoes and the meat, brownish-gray it seemed and a little green on the edges.

"Mystery meat," whispered Allie. "No one knows what it really is. The food here stinks, but it'll be better when the war's over."

David remembered. On the train the masters had come by to collect a ration book from each boy. You couldn't buy meat or sugar or butter without a ration book because of the war. You couldn't buy gas for the car, because the gas was going overseas to Germany or to the Pacific where the Marines were making their way, island by island, toward Japan. And in France the Allies had landed on the beaches of Normandy. They were making their way across France, and when they got to Berlin the war would be over. David had learned about the war at his old school. There was a map on the wall in his room with flags sticking out of each country — American flags and British flags, German and Japanese flags — to indicate who had control. In art class David liked to draw airplanes and tanks with insignia on them.

"Lear," came a voice from the top of the table.

"Yes?" said David.

"Say 'sir' when you're spoken to boy," replied Mr. Mulligan.

"Yes, sir," said David, angry that he had already forgotten what Allie had told him. Why did they have to be called sir? In the middle ages knights were called sir. There was Sir Lancelot and Sir Galahad. In England, Elizabeth told him, there were still knights and a king and queen. But, in America, there were no knights, so why did you call a master sir? Besides, what did the man want? Did he call him just to see if he would say sir? Maybe that was the game.

"Lear?"

David looked up. "Yes, sir?" He wouldn't be caught again.

"Eat your beans, boy. They're good for you."

"Yes, sir."

David hated beans and peas and brussels sprouts, especially brussels sprouts. He couldn't see how anybody could eat brussels sprouts, but beans weren't too bad, so he ate three beans, and when the waiter cleared, he took David's plate even though he wasn't finished and Mr. Mulligan didn't say anything. For dessert there was apple pie, and David began to feel better. The dining room was bright. Chandeliers hung from the high ceiling, and a huge, blue marlin had been suspended over the doors leading in and out of the kitchen. David tried to imagine the marlin fighting. Did he stab other fish with his sword? Did marlins fight each other with their swords?

The gong rang again, but this time it was not just a single note. It was Yankee Doodle. David turned around to watch. The man playing was the same man who had talked to them in the schoolroom. Sitting next to him and smiling was the dark-haired woman. When he was finished, everyone at his table applauded. Then he stood up and spoke: "You will now go to your dorms and unpack. Please remember there is no running inside the school buildings. And that means also no sliding."

There was a great laugh.

"What are they laughing about?" David asked.

"No talking during announcements, Lear," said Mr. Mulligan.

The man paused and spoke again. "For you new boys, I have a word or two of caution. There are some troublemakers among the older boys. Don't make these boys your models. And don't think it's funny to imitate them. My name is Mr. Armbrister, and my wife's name is Mrs. Armbrister. We would prefer that you learn it correctly, rather than that other version which passes among some of you. Learn our names correctly, gentlemen, and the names of all the masters. That is all. Dismissed."

David was dying to talk to Allie. There were so many questions he wanted to ask. What was the other name? Who were the troublemakers? What did they do?

"We're waiting for you, Lear," said Mr. Mulligan.

"How is that, sir?" said David. Then he looked around. Everyone at the table was sitting at attention with his hands folded on the edge of the table in front of his place. Quickly he assumed the proper position, and the table was dismissed.

"This is what everyone was laughing about," said Allie, as they turned to walk down the narrow corridor which led back toward the schoolroom. The floor was slick and polished, and the distinct downhill slope made it a perfect sliding course. "If you take off your shoes and get a running start, you can slide almost to the bottom," Allie went on. "Of course, if you get caught." He smiled and shrugged his shoulders.

"If you get caught, what happens?" asked David.

"If you get caught, you get marks."

"What are marks?"

"They're kind of like points against you. You can get points for good things like grades and sports and neatness and stuff like that, and you can get marks for bad things. Every week, they add them all up, and at the end of the term they give ratings."

"Oh," said David. He wanted to ask what ratings were, but he didn't want to look stupid. He'd just have to spread his questions around a little. It was like a game. The old boys knew the rules and the new boys didn't, and you just had to learn them as you went along. The new boys who learned the rules quickly would be better at the game than the others.

They were back in the hall outside the schoolroom now, and David noticed, as he had not when he first came in, that there were pictures everywhere. Groups of boys stopped to look at different ones, some down on their hands and knees to see the ones closest to the floor, others stretching to see the high ones. There was the football team, the soccer team, the hockey team and the baseball team; there were pictures of the sixth form and the casts of the operettas, and all of these pictures went back for years and years. David wondered when his picture would be on the wall, and where the pictures would go when the walls were full.

"Come on, David," said Allie. "I'll show you your alcove. You've got to be unpacked by eight o'clock."

"Alcove" was another new word. What was an alcove? It must be a kind of room, David thought. He followed Allie up the stairs opposite the front entrance to the schoolroom, and then they turned into another large room, painted light green. Right away, he knew what an alcove was. There must have been twenty of them, ten on either side. They were rooms without ceilings or doors, spaces divided by partitions with a curtain in front of each one. In each alcove was a bed, a bureau with a mirror over it, a chair, and hooks on the walls for hanging up good clothes.

"See you, David," said Allie. "My dorm's upstairs just above this one. Knock on the ceiling if you need something. By the way, in case you didn't realize it, I'm your mentor. Every new boy has a mentor, and you're stuck with me."

Before David could say anything the other boy was gone. David turned and looked around the room. His trunk was there, and the brown leather suitcase with his mother's initials, M. H., on it. He opened the trunk and took out a picture, which he placed on the bureau. He sat on the bed and looked at it. There was his mother seated at the piano, and Elizabeth standing next to her, one hand on her mother's shoulder. David was seated on the piano in a little sailor suit, his bare legs hanging down, and on the floor next to the piano bench was Gretel. It was an old picture — David couldn't have been more than three and that would make Elizabeth twelve — but it was the only one of the four of them David had.

He began unlacing his shoes, high shoes which came to the tops of his ankles to keep his heels from slipping out. In a year or two, maybe, he could begin to wear regular shoes, as soon as his heels had developed enough to hold them on. But he had to do his exercises.

"Every morning and every night," his mother had said, "sit on the bed and lean forward. Take both hands and grasp your feet, first one then the other, and pull gently toward you, stretching the Achilles tendon."

It was a funny name, Achilles. He remembered asking his mother about it, and she had told him the story of Achilles' mother holding the baby by the ankle in the water of the river — the name, he couldn't remember — to make him immortal. He thought of the arrows bouncing off Achilles as if he were made of iron or gold, and then the last arrow, the poisoned arrow that cut the tendon where his mother had held him. David could feel the pain of the cut like the pain of the knife where they had operated. He didn't like to think about the operations. He focused on the picture, making his mind come back to Gretel and Elizabeth.

"Lear."

A man stood in the entrance to his alcove, a short muscular man in a tweed sport coat and gray trousers, with black hair tight like the hair on a brush. He smoked a pipe. "I'm Mr. Richardson," he said. "I'm your dorm master. We'll have a meeting down at the end of the hall where the leather chair is in about ten minutes. Get your pajamas on and see if you can get your bed made.

David hurried, pulling the sheets and blankets out of his trunk. He had practiced at home, but this was the first time he had to do it on his own. He tried to remember what Elizabeth had told him. You tuck in the bottom first, and then pull the sides down tight and tuck them in. It's called a hospital corner. But it wasn't so easy to get both sides the same and have enough sheet left to fold down over the blanket. He liked the blanket, dark blue with his name tag, David J. Lear, in the corner, but he wasn't sure whether to tuck the sheet and blanket in together or separately.

Out of the corner of his eye he could see boys passing by, some in pajamas, some in bathrobes also. Quickly, he got his pajamas out of the brown suitcase, slipped off his shirt and trousers and put them on. He left his socks on. That was better. Then the other boys wouldn't notice his feet so much. He would finish making the bed later. He would unpack later. He couldn't understand how everybody did whatever they had to do. There just wasn't enough time. He took a glance in the mirror, shrugged, and walked out through the curtain into the center of the dorm. Most of the boys were seated on the floor in front of the leather chair where Mr. Richardson sat and smoked. David slipped in to the back of the group. Over the heads of the other boys he could see the rings of smoke float upward, changing their shapes like clouds.

"Well," said Mr. Richardson. "We all seem to be here. Let's have the new boys each stand up and introduce themselves."

David was glad his name didn't begin with A. That would be awful. He watched as Bailey Abbott, a thin, handsome boy from Marblehead, got up. David thought he was funny. He said "Mabble" instead of "marble" and "had" instead of "hard," but no one laughed. "I'm glad to be heah," he said. He seemed quiet and confident, someone David would like to know. Harold Dickson was next, a short, stocky boy from New York City. He collected toy soldiers, models from different wars. Then it was David's turn.

"I'm David Johnson Lear," he said, looking right at Mr. Richardson, "and I live in Westport, Connecticut, with my mother and my sister, Elizabeth, and my dog, Gretel."

Laughter from behind him, then a stern look from Mr. Richardson for whoever it was. David sat down. He didn't want to turn around and see who had laughed. That would only make it worse.

Terry Roche, a tall, blue-eyed, blond-haired boy, spoke next. He was looking forward to playing football. David could see that he was strong. Griff Ryan, a chubby, wide-eyed boy with a mop of hair that looked like an upside-down bowl, stood up and looked around "I'm from Bermuda, and I hate snow," he said. Then, the little, sandy-haired Ian Stuart, who David remembered because he'd brought his goldfish on the train, struggled to his feet.

"I'm Ian Stuar-rt," he said, rolling the r on the tip of his tongue, and I'm from Aberdeen, Scotland, and my dad has moved to New Yor-rk."

More laughter, and another fierce look from Mr. Richardson. David was glad. At least he wasn't the only one to get laughed at. Then Peter Winemiller tried to get up, slipped, and landed on his seat. "I'm Peter Whoa...," he cried as he slid to the floor. Great gales of laughter, and none louder than Peter. His protruding ears turned red, his black hair stuck straight up, and he just sat and smiled.

"Well," said Mr. Richardson. "With our new seven, that makes thirty-one third formers. Welcome to Lowell, new boys, and welcome back, old boys. We want to make the third form dorm the best in the school. Right, Finch?"

"Yes, sir," said the boy called Finch.

"Right, Abercrombie?"

"Yes, sir," said the boy called Abercrombie.

"Abercrombie and Finch," said the plump boy with the mop, and everyone began to laugh, even Mr. Richardson. David laughed too, but he didn't really know what was so funny about that.

"Remember the rules of the dorm, gentlemen," said Mr. Richardson.

"No climbing the walls of the alcoves," said Abercrombie.

"No talking in the bathroom after lights out," said Finch.

"No visiting in someone else's alcove after lights out," said Terry Roche with a wink.

"You're right, Roche," said Mr. Richardson. "And all you old boys better be careful this year. I'm a much lighter sleeper than Mr. Keith."

More laughter, and then the master resumed. "Rising bell at 7:00, inspection at 7:30. That means dressed, with coats and ties, bed made, standing in your doorway. Any questions?"

David put up his hand.

"Lear?"

"How do you know when it's 7:30?"

"Sir."

"How do you know when it's 7:30, sir?"

"You look up, lad."

"You what, sir?"

"You keep your eyes open, boy," said Mr. Richardson, pointing with his finger back over his head. Behind the leather chair was a fireplace. Over the fireplace was a mantel, and on the mantel was a clock, which said 8:35. David blushed. He would be glad for the day to be over. He couldn't keep everything in his head. As he watched Mr. Richardson, the master seemed to grow smaller and smaller, and the sound of his voice grew faint. The dim laughter of the boys was nothing more than the memory of yesterday's thunder.

The meeting was over. He stood up with the others and walked slowly back to his alcove, pulled back the covers, and lay down on the sheets. He was too tired to finish making the bed, too tired to unpack, too tired to sort out the rules, the points, the marks. He'd do it in the morning.

In the distance he heard a voice say, "Lights out," and then it was dark, except for the glow of the streetlight outside his window. He waited for sleep to take him. After a while he began to rock, slowly at first, his head moving on the pillow from side to side, his brain trying to catch the rhythm of a remembered song, and the the song, the rhythm going faster, until the school was gone, and the rocking swept him into sleep.

He dreamed he was the brave American fighter pilot, Dave Dawson, who flew on dangerous missions over Germany. He soared and rocked through the frenzied air, peering through the orange flashes of the anti-aircraft fire for the German fighters, the vaunted pilots of the Luftwaffe. He flew and dove and spun away and then he was hit and the plane was falling, falling, but never crashing, never hitting the earth, just falling.

The clanging of the bell woke him with a start. He sat up in the bed and looked around. But he wasn't really awake yet and he didn't know where he was. Then it came back — the train ride, the bus, dinner. He drew his feet from under the blankets, and began his exercises. "Don't pull too hard," his mother had said. "Nice and firm, stretch and pull." He could see her face, and for a moment he felt her hand mess his hair and heard her laughter. "Smile, Toots," she would say. "Don't take yourself so seriously."

Now he had to go to the bathroom. He didn't want to walk down the hall without his shoes on. Even after he stretched, it took a while for his feet to loosen up, and he would have to walk on his toes unless he wore his shoes. That was it. He could get dressed. He slipped on his underpants and trousers, then his socks and the high shoes. He took his towel, toothbrush and comb, and walked down the corridor to the bathroom. There were three sinks on one wall, and two stalls and a urinal on the other. A window looked out on the street where they had come in the night before. David used the urinal and waited for a turn at the sinks. He looked around. The three at the sinks had only their pajama bottoms on, but no one seemed to notice that he was different. He was glad he hadn't worn his shirt. When his turn came, he moved up to the sink and looked in the mirror.

His arms and shoulders were fine. They were strong from the years with the casts. And his face was all right. "It'll do in a pinch," his mother had said. He worked the comb through his hair, splashed down his cowlick with some water, brushed his teeth, and smiled. No problems there either.

He was pleased. He would do well today. He would learn the rules, he would say "sir," to the masters, he would be on time. But then the bed had to be made, and his clothes unpacked, and he had to get dressed. He walked quickly back to the alcove and hurriedly pulled the blankets to the head of the bed, stretching the sheets as tight as he could around the sides without redoing the corners. He opened his trunk. That could wait. He would just slide it to the foot of the bed and use it for a table. The suitcase. He pulled out socks and underpants, shirts, sweaters and blue jeans, then stuffed them quickly into the bureau. The good clothes had to go on hangers. First the school uniform — blue suit, white shirt and red tie. Then the gray pants and brown jacket. How strange he thought. It's like we're pretending to be men. Bernie, his stepfather, had worn suits to work, and David remembered meeting him at the train at night and seeing all the men in their suits and sportcoats, carrying their newspapers, coming down the steps of the train, looking for their cars. Why should we wear suits? It wasn't the kind of thing you could ask anybody.

David looked out through the curtain of his alcove to the clock. It was already 7:25. He slipped into his shirt, buttoned it as quickly as he could, and then began on the tie. He stood in front of the bureau, looked in the mirror, and did exactly as his mother had taught him, standing behind him in front of her bedroom mirror at home.

Fat side down to the waist, thin side halfway, then fat side over and around, then up and down through the loop you've made. Tighten, and slide the fat side up by pulling the thin side down. He tried it, but it wouldn't work. It had worked at home, but it didn't work now. The two pieces ended up side by side, and the knot was all crooked. He started again. This time the fat part was too short, and the thin part ended up down to his waist. Finally a third time…

"Well, Lear, having a little trouble?"

"Trying to tie my tie, sir." David turned toward the figure of the master in the doorway. He watched Mr. Richardson's face.

"It's a pretty sloppy bed, boy," Mr. Richardson said. "Look at the way the sheets stick out at the corners. If it's like this tomorrow you'll have to remake it."

"Yes, sir," said the boy.

"Marks start tomorrow, Lear. We want to be sharp. We want no marks against our dorm. Get right up when the bell rings. Don't dawdle."

"Yes, sir."

"Finish dressing and get on down to breakfast."

"Yes, sir."

David sat down on the bed. He could feel his heart beat and his knees trembling. He hated it. It wasn't fair. He had gotten up when the bell rang, and he hadn't dawdled. There just wasn't enough time to do everything. He wanted to tell somebody. Maybe Allie could help him. Yes, he would talk to Allie on the way back from breakfast. He stood up and worked on the tie once more, this time more slowly. "Stay calm, Toots," his mother had said. Good. It was finally right. He slipped on his jacket, spun down the stairs, and walked quickly through the hall and up the corridor toward the dining room.

"Lear," said Mr. Mulligan. "Why are you late?"

David's mind was working quickly. He had noticed on his way into the dining room that breakfast had already started. Except for the waiters and two or three other boys who had come in with David, everyone was seated. He knew Mr. Mulligan would say something.

"Lear," said the master. "I'm speaking to you."

"Yes, sir," said David.

"Why were you late?"

"Mr. Richardson wanted to talk to me, sir." It was a good answer. It was the truth, but it said nothing about feet or ties. Nothing Mulligan could tease him about or get mad at him for.

"Marks start tomorrow, Lear. Don't be late again."

Marks start tomorrow. Marks start tomorrow. The words spun around in his brain, and he saw masters everywhere pointing their fingers at him and laughing. Can't tie his tie. Can't make his bed. Can't get to meals on time. He wanted to melt, to slip under the table like butter.

"David."

It was Allie, bringing him back again. He looked across the table at his friend.

"Eat," whispered Allie. "Mulligan'll make you stay here 'til you finish. Don't let him get you, Dave."

David looked down at the plate in front of him. One egg, sunny side up, with toast for ears, stared back. It would be a challenge. David understood this game from home. He called for the milk and then prepared his egg, smushing up the yolk and white into one light yellow mess. Then he took his fork and placed a square of egg on the piece of toast. Quickly he bit, chewed, then swallowed it down with a sip of milk. Egg, toast, milk…egg, toast, milk. That was the rhythm. It was all right as long as you didn't taste it. He finished quickly, folded his hands and looked up at Mr. Mulligan. "Something you wanted, Lear?" the master asked.

"No, sir," smiled David. "I was just getting in the proper position to be excused."

"Ah," said Mr. Mulligan. "You remember well."

Later, as they were walking out, Allie put his arm around him. "That was great, David. That's the way Mulligan is. He likes to test you. If he can break you, make you cry or mess up, then he doesn't respect you. All the masters are different. Just 'cause you've got one figured out, that doesn't mean a thing. They all think they're the only one."

David felt proud. For the first time since he waved good-bye to Elizabeth from the train window, he felt like he could make it by himself.

"Thanks, Allie," he said. "Thanks for your help."

He walked quickly now through the hall with the pictures and up the stairs to the dorm. He had fifteen minutes before morning assembly, time to finish unpacking and fix the corners on his bed, time to use the bathroom, time to think, well not really time to think. David laughed. Maybe they didn't want you to think. Maybe that's why they kept you so busy. If you thought too much, you would think about things like home. He wondered what Elizabeth was doing, where she was working. She said to write. Where would he get writing paper and stamps? Was there a post office? There were so many questions.

At morning assembly in the schoolroom Mr. Armbrister spoke to them: "At Lowell School we have the rating system. We believe that every boy at this school has it in his own power to control his own destiny. That is what freedom means. You get exactly what you earn. If you work hard, you will earn a higher rating. The higher the rating, the greater the privileges."

He stopped and pointed once again to the banner over the door. "Memorize it, boys. Take it to heart. If you are lazy and undisciplined you will not succeed. If we are to beat the Germans and the Japanese in this war, it will be because we work harder. If you wish town privileges, you must work for them. For a Primus rating, one hundred points, for a Secundus rating eighty points, for a Tertius sixty points, and for a Quartus forty points. You will receive points each term for grades, for neatness, punctuality, and for deportment. Rating badges are to be worn on the breast pockets of sports jackets or blazers, not on school uniforms."

David looked around the room. He could see on the jackets of the older boys small white badges in the shapes of shields, with red borders and red lettering. On each was a numeral — 1, 2, 3, or 4 — and above the numerals the word Primus, Secundus, Tertius, or Quartus. Such strange words, like the words on the banner. Why didn't they just say "one," "two," or "three"? And other words like "deportment" and "punctuality"? What did they mean?

"Points are also given for athletics, for competition on varsity and intramural teams. Every boy will participate in a sport at the level at which he is capable. No one is excused from athletics without a doctor's permission."

David understood that he wouldn't be excused from sports. The doctor had said he was all right. He would just have to try harder to keep up with the others. That's what Armbrister was saying.

"Attention." David could feel his body stiffen even before his mind understood the words. His shoulders straightened and his hands folded in front of him. He was beginning to make sense of this thing. The school was like the army. People had ranks, there were rewards and punishments. You did well, and you got promoted.

The day began with math from Mr. Myers. After math came shop, then English with Mrs. Benzaquin, and then recess. After recess was social studies with Mr. Zachary, and last was science with Mr. Mulligan. Then lunch, and an hour's rest period in the dorm.

David was glad for the rest. His brain was dizzy from trying to find all the rooms and writing down all the different things the teachers said. It wasn't like the school at home where you just went into your classroom and stayed and there was one teacher who taught everything except when the music teacher or the art teacher came in. David tried to remember. Mr. Myers was easy. Straight out of the schoolroom, left past the masters' smoking room, through the common room where the ping pong tables were, and there you were. Then shop. The stairs which went up to the dorm also went down to the basement, and if you turned left at the bottom of the stairs, there was the shop, full of machines and the smell of sawdust and paint and lacquer. Then, Mrs. Benzaquin's room. That was the hardest. You came out of the shop and went as if you were going down to the locker rooms, but you turned right and went down a narrow corridor until you came to another corridor, where you turned again. David didn't think he could find it by himself. He just followed the others.

He liked Mrs. Benzaquin. She was a little old lady with gray hair and square glasses; she wore a long silk dress that rustled. To David she was like a picture from a history book, like someone who really lived in another time.

She walked into the room, slowly like a queen, and wrote her name on the blackboard in block letters — B E N Z A Q U I N. Then she separated it into syllables BEN ZA QUIN and asked everyone to say it, out loud, until they could pronounce it correctly. Then she said that each day when she walked into the room the class was to rise and say, "Good morning, Mrs. Benzaquin," and she would say, "Good morning, class," and then they were to sit down.

"Now we will practice," she said, and walked out of the room, closing the door behind her. Everyone began to talk. Griff Ryan, the boy with the bowl of hair, said something to the boy next to him, the tall blond boy whose name David couldn't remember. They both began to laugh. Then the door opened, and everyone was suddenly silent. Quickly they all stood in their places. David wanted to turn around and look at her, but he was afraid. He could only hear the door close once again and the sound of her footsteps coming toward the front of the room, where he sat. Then he could see her, as she crossed from the side of the room to the desk, smiling. She nodded.

"Good morning, Mrs. Benzaquin," the class said.

"Good morning, class," she answered. "You may be seated." She started to speak. David had never heard anyone quite like her. If you saw her on the street, he thought, she would look just like somebody's grandmother. But when she spoke, there was something magical about her. She read poems to them as if every word was special. "Every word is a miracle, boys," she said. "Don't forget that."

David had always liked words. When he was little, Elizabeth had read him stories before bed. She would snuggle up next to him and hold one side of the book, while David held the other up, and she would read to him. After she had read the book two or three times alone, they would start reading it together. Then David would read it all by himself. Sometimes, when his mother and Bernie had company, she would show off how smart he was by having him come into the living room and sit in the big red chair and read the whole of Ferdinand the Bull out loud to their friends. He couldn't really read, Elizabeth explained to him later. He had just memorized the story and knew by the pictures when to turn the pages.

Ferdinand had been David's favorite book, especially the part when Ferdinand wouldn't fight but just sat and smelled the flowers. David would pause over that and say in a big, melancholy voice, "Ferdinand just sat and smelled the flowers," and the grownups would laugh and clap when he was finished. Later he and Elizabeth would make up words and fool grownups with their learned conversations that nobody could understand.

"Villest dell exeldinkel de venerat?" she would ask.

"Nikalotera nadu," he would answer, gravely.

"Eggoman lets tikelzee," she would urge.

"Vick gothamooer nex," he would smile.

There were no rules except to sound as if you made sense and to listen to the other as if you understood. Elizabeth took drama in high school, and she said this was called "staying in character."

Elizabeth was David's favorite person. He said that Gretel was his favorite person, but then Gretel wasn't really a person, and she was so old now that she wasn't as much fun as she used to be. She slept a lot, and sometimes she made messes in the house, and his mother didn't even punish her because "the poor dog's so old she can't help herself." That scared David, the idea of being so old you couldn't even help yourself. He wondered where Elizabeth was and what she was doing. She had told him at Howard Johnson's that she was going to live in New York in a boarding house with a lot of other girls. That was another funny word, "boarding house."

"Why is it called 'boarding house'?" David had asked.

"Because you board there, silly," Elizabeth had answered.

"But what is board? Is it like a board you build a house out of?"

"No, David. It means an eating house, because you eat there."

"Well, why not call it an eating house?"

"You ask too many questions."

"I know. I'm a pest."

That's what Elizabeth and his mother always said when they got tired of answering his questions. He wanted to know about everything they said, and sometimes he was just a pest.

Elizabeth was beautiful. She had long, blond hair like their father who lived in California. He was dark like his mother. Elizabeth remembered their father because he and their mother had lived together when she was little, but David was just a baby when they got a divorce and his mother had come back East to live. They had taken the train from San Francisco, and Elizabeth had stood in the back and waved good-bye to their father. He just got smaller and smaller until he disappeared. David learned everything from Elizabeth. Her room was next to his, and they shared a bathroom. Their mother lived at the front of the house with Bernie and had her own bathroom and went up and down the front stairs. Elizabeth and David used the back stairs that came up from the kitchen. Sometimes he sat on her bed and they talked while she put on her make-up before going out for a date. She put on lipstick and rouge and did something to her eyelashes.

"Why do you do that?" he asked.

"Because it makes me look pretty."

"I think you're pretty without it.

"I know you do. But you're just a boy. Men like girls to wear make-up."

It was another funny word, "make-up." If you were late and you missed a class you had to go to make-up. You had to make up the work. If you didn't know the answer to a question you had to make up an answer. Make up was like make believe. Superman was made up. So why was what Elizabeth put on her face called make-up?

Elizabeth said that she was old enough to get married, or almost old enough. She would work for a couple of years, and then she would get married when she was twenty or twenty-one. Teenagers weren't supposed to get married. She would wear a long white dress with a veil over her face and a train, and David would walk her down the aisle, where the groom would be standing, waiting for her.

"Why is the man called a groom?" David asked. "How can a dress have a train?" he thought. He tried to imagine a dress with a train on it. He thought about groom. You groomed a horse. A groom was someone who worked in a stable.

"Why is the man called a groom?" David asked again.

But Elizabeth was somewhere deep inside the mirror.

The bell woke him. David rubbed his eyes. He couldn't remember falling asleep. Boys walked past his alcove in blue jeans and corduroys: it was time for sports — football or soccer. Mr. Armbrister had told them at lunch that "a healthy body makes a healthy mind," but what was healthy about football? David could feel the big bodies in their padding pounding against each other. It made him shudder. Soccer was better, but still it was feet and running and kicking. David wished that they had swimming. In the water he felt stronger, pulling and stroking with arms and shoulders made muscular from his years in the casts. His legs were thin and his feet fragile. "Oh well," he thought, lacing up his sneakers. "At least I don't have to wear shorts."

He walked down to the soccer field with Ian Stuart.

"How's your goldfish, Ian?" he asked.

"A bit puny," said the blond boy. "I may have to give him some marks for not eating all his breakfast."

David laughed. He enjoyed jokes. Sometimes, at home, before the bad times, before the fights and the shouting, after he was supposed to have gone to bed, he would sit on the front stairs and listen to the grown-ups talk after dinner in the living room. He could hear their voices if he sat on the fourth step from the top. His mother's voice was easy to recognize, and so was Bernie's. Sometimes Bernie would sound angry or something would break. Then he would run quickly back to his room and get into bed. He didn't want Bernie or his mother coming upstairs if they were in a bad mood. But sometimes his mother played the piano and Bernie told her jokes from the office, and David listened from the fourth step. He didn't always understand what the words meant or why the joke was so funny, but he liked the stories.

As they walked down the hill from the school building, David looked out over the playing fields. To the left, nearest the road, was the varsity football field with its tall goal posts and the lines marked off every ten yards. Straight ahead was the j.v. football field, where the third and fourth formers practiced. David could see Griff Ryan and Terry Roche warming up. They talked as if they were old friends.

"Look," said Ian Stuart. "There's Mr. Mulligan."

David could see him out of the corner of his eye as they passed by on their way to the soccer fields further down the hill toward the woods. He was glad Mr. Mulligan didn't coach soccer. He seemed right for football with his cap pulled down over his eyes, his strong jaw, and his thick, muscular legs. He looked good in shorts.

Mr. Myers, David's math teacher, was the soccer coach. He looked more like a math teacher than a coach. He didn't even wear a red cap with a white L on it or a sweatshirt with LOWELL written across the front. As the boys arrived, he handed each of them a colored T shirt to put on. There were four colors — blue for Yale, red for Harvard, green for Dartmouth, and orange for Princeton. These would be their teams for the season. They would play games against each other twice a week, and at the end of the season an all-star team would play outside games against their big rivals, St. James and Roxbury.

David felt comfortable sitting on the bank listening to Mr. Myers. Most of the bigger, more athletic boys were playing football, and David could see, as he looked around, that the boys sitting around him were mostly third and fourth formers, many of them no bigger than he was. He slipped on his green Dartmouth T shirt and followed the rest of the green and orange shirted boys to the lower soccer field where they practiced kicking, dribbling, and passing. Mr. Myers showed them how to do each thing before he asked the boys to do it, and even if they made mistakes, he didn't yell at them. He just told them what they did wrong and asked them to do it again. "Kick with your instep, David, not your toe," he said, after David had kicked a little dribbler off to one side. Then he planted his left foot next to the ball and brought his right around slowly, catching the ball perfectly off the laces of his shoe and sending it far down the field. "With your toe you have no control." Then he smiled and rolled him another ball. "Go ahead, you can do it."

David watched the ball carefully, then ran toward it and placed his left foot next to the ball just like Mr. Myers had. He swung his right foot around and caught the ball right on the laces. The ball soared straight ahead, not very far, but straight ahead, and David ran after it to dribble it back for the next boy to kick. The sky was blue and the air crisp and nobody knew he was different. So far it was all right.

The shower-room was something else. There were five showers, and the older boys moved in and out easily, laughing, talking, punching each other, squeezing the soap out of their hands as if it were a fish. Two or three would share a shower, bumping each other in fun, giggling and pointing to parts of one another's bodies. David tried to act casual. He had never had to take a shower in front of anyone before. In fact, no one except Elizabeth and his mother had ever really seen his legs. He knew it was important not to act scared. He could feel his heart pounding, but he walked from the locker room to the shower, towel around his waist, trying his hardest to look just like everyone else. No one seemed to notice him. Then he tripped over the tile partition that kept the water from running into the locker room — not a fall, just a trip, the kind he was used to at his old school. He caught his balance and went on, but the other boys were looking at him now, and in the shower next to the door Griff Ryan and Terry Roche started talking.

"Man, those sure are funny looking legs," said one.

"Where'd you get those gams, man?" said the other, laughing.

David walked away from them to the far end of the shower room. He would ignore them, just as his mother had told him. "Don't lower yourself to their level," she had said. "And when you start feeling mad, just remember Hubert Green."

David could see the playground at his old school and Hubert Green, fat Hubert Green leaning against the jungle gym or the slide and looking for someone to pick on. David was his favorite target. "Twinkle, twinkle little toes," he would say, or "whatcha got on under them shoes?" He liked to stand in the doorway when recess was over and bump the younger kids he didn't like. David hated him.

One day when Hubert Green stuck out his foot to trip him as he went by, David struck. His right fist went straight into Hubert Green's stomach, and his left to the older boy's nose. David struck and struck, blindly swinging, driving his shoulder into the fat stomach of his enemy, grabbing the surprised bully around the legs and wrestling him to the ground. He was Gretel tearing at the mouse, he was Dave Dawson protecting America's honor. He would kill Hubert Green. He sunk his teeth into the flesh of the bigger boy's belly, flailing with his fists at anything he could hit. But Hubert Green was too strong. He rolled David onto his back and sat on his stomach, pinioning his arms to the ground. David could only see the face of Hubert Green and the string of spittle in Hubert Green's mouth growing longer and longer. He closed his eyes and felt it catch him on the cheek. He wanted to be gone, to be far away, to lock himself in the bathroom at home and scrub his cheek until it hurt. He could hear Hubert Green's voice saying "Do you give up?" but he would not open his eyes and look. If he looked at the face above again, he knew he would scream or cry, so he shook his head back and forth, eyes closed, and felt the knees of Hubert Green pushing the air out of his lungs and the hands of Hubert Green pressing down harder on his wrists. Then everything was far away and nothing hurt any more.

When he opened his eyes, he was on the couch in the principal's office.

"Are you all right, David?" the principal asked.

"Yes," said David.

"What happened out there?"

"Nothing," said David. He didn't want to talk about it. It wouldn't make any sense to a grownup.

"The boys say you started it. Is that right?"

"Yes."

"But, why?"

David wouldn't talk. He couldn't. He knew if he tried to talk his voice would break and he would start to cry. He hated Hubert Green and he could not talk about it. And later when his mother took him home, he would not talk about it to her either.

"Go to your room, then," she said, "and stay there until you're ready to talk. You're not a baby, David. You can't just avoid things you don't like. Now go think about it."

In his room he got very, very angry, and he took his crayons and began to draw on the wall. He took blue and red and yellow and black and began to draw. First he made a body and colored it blue. Over the blue he drew red trunks, and on the chest a gold seal with a bright red S. Then the hair, black, carefully combed, and the face strong, with a straight, square chin. Then he drew Hubert Green, fat Hubert Green with his stomach hanging out of his purple shirt, and his big ears like cauliflowers. And then Superman smashing Hubert Green with his fist, and stars and x's coming from Hubert Green's mouth.

When his mother came in, she cried and got angry and made him take soap and water and stay in his room until he got all the crayon marks off the wall, but they wouldn't come off, and the next day the marks remained on the wall, so he had to stay home from school, and the day after that was Saturday, and he was not to go out and play until the wall was clean, but no matter how hard he scrubbed, some of the lines stayed on. Even Elizabeth couldn't get them off. Finally his mother came back and sat on his bed and stroked his head with her hand. She loved him, she said, and she was only punishing him for his own good. She understood why he had hit Hubert Green, but she wanted him to learn not to lose his temper. "Someday your temper will hurt you badly, Toots, if you keep on like this," she said. "It's your demon."

So he turned his back on Griff Ryan and Terry Roche, and he washed himself quietly and walked out of the shower room, stepping carefully over the tile partition as if nothing had happened. Then he went upstairs to his alcove and changed his clothes for dinner, tied his tie and smoothed out the wrinkles in his bed before he walked back down the stairs to the schoolroom. He opened his desk and looked inside at the books which he had brought back from each of his classes, the pads of paper, and the yellow pencils with Eberhard Faber written on the side, the pencil sharpener and eraser, the hymnbook for evening prayers, and the dictionary Elizabeth had given him as a going away present. Inside the dictionary was a note from Elizabeth:

*Dear David —Just because we're far away from each other doesn't mean we aren't still friends. If you want to ask anything or say anything, I'm still there. Just write to me — 27 Barrow Street, New York, New York. I'll write you back. Love, Elizabeth.*

There were x's and o's next to the love, which his mother said meant kisses and hugs, and he couldn't figure out which was which, but he certainly was not going to ask anyone. Not even Allie.

David got up from his desk and walked to the master's station at the front of the room. There was a different person there tonight and David felt less afraid to ask a question.

"Excuse me, sir," he said, "but I would like to write a letter to my sister, and I have no writing paper or stamps."

The man opened a drawer in front of him, reached into it, pulled out two sheets of paper and an envelope, and handed them to David.

"Will that be enough for now?" he asked.

"Oh yes, sir," said David, "but what about stamps, sir?"

"When you're finished, bring your letter to this desk and the school will mail it for you."

"Yes, sir, thank you, sir," said David. He walked back to his desk and sat down. For a while he just looked at the paper. It was white, with no lines on it, and at the top of each sheet was a shield with the words Poteris Modo Velis written under it. Beneath them was printed LOWELL SCHOOL 1866. He thought hard, and then he began to write:

"Dear Elizabeth, It is almost the end of my first day at Lowell School. I met a nice boy named Allie. My soccer team is Dartmouth. Mr. Myers is nice, but Mr. Mulligan is mean…"

Then he thought some more, and erased, "Mr. Mulligan is mean." Suppose someone saw him writing that and told Mr. Mulligan. Suppose the school looked at the letter before they mailed it. But they couldn't open it if he licked it and sealed it tight. He would wait and write during rest hour in his alcove. That was it. There were too many people in the schoolroom. He put the writing paper back in his desk and closed it. He looked around the room. Mrs. Armbrister was standing at the rear door talking to the older boys coming in.

"Attention," said the master at the front desk, and Mr. Armbrister marched in through the door at the front. Everyone stood up and sang Hymn 542, "Eternal Father Strong to Save." David sang with them.

# CHAPTER
## *four*

*I*N OCTOBER THE LEAVES began to change, bursting into orange, yellow and red like balloons at birthday parties. On Sundays, if it wasn't raining, the boys were allowed to walk down the road past the football field, across the reservoir, into the woods behind to play capture the flag. The dirt path that led from the paved road into the woods served as the center line, as Reds divided against Whites and plotted their strategies. For David it was strange and wonderful to be off the school grounds mixed in the colors of the turning trees. Sometimes he would stand for five minutes or more watching one tree, waiting for one leaf to fall so that he could follow its crazy zig zag path to the ground. He wanted to climb the tree and be high, high above where he could see the faster boys racing to grab the enemy flag before they were caught, racing to free their friends from prison. Nobody seemed to care much whether he played or not. That was the nice thing. He could play if he wanted, but if he wandered off to the place where the three cedar trees made the fort it was all right as long as he came in when the whistle blew. It made him think of his cave. He wondered if anyone had found it and what they must have thought crawling in to see the boxes and the food and the mayonnaise jars of water. He had brought the Bible to school with him, but the rest he had left just as it was. And now he would never see it again.

One Sunday Mr. Mulligan came, and it was all different. There was to be no shirking, he said. He stood on the center line, Reds on one side, Whites on the other, and he shouted at both teams. "I hear the stories about this sissy game and how half of you are off in the woods telling dirty jokes or sitting on your asses. We'll have none of that today. You play or get your butts kicked." He laughed and blew his whistle. "Five minutes to hide your flags and set up your prisons. Then move! And no dancing back and forth across the center line like a bunch of fairies."

David hated Mr. Mulligan. He hated the way Mr. Mulligan would catch boys running in the halls and squeeze the backs of their necks until their faces turned red. He hated the way Mr. Mulligan made fun of the way Ian Stuart talked, but most of all he hated the way Mr. Mulligan looked at him. At least he wasn't at his table any more. They changed tables once a month, and David had switched to Mr. Melvin's table down near the door. But he still had to go to science class every day and sit in the middle of the second row right in front of Mr. Mulligan's desk. Mr. Mulligan liked to surprise people. He liked to walk to one side of the room or the other and suddenly turn around and ask a question to see if you were awake. One day they had been studying the solar system and Mulligan had flashed around:

"What color is Mars, Lear?"

"I don't know, sir."

"I don't know, sir," mimicked Mulligan. "What kind of an answer is that? Pretty witless, don't you think?"

"I don't know, sir."

"I don't know, sir," mimicked Mulligan again. "For Christ's sake, Lear, can't you read?"

"I don't know, sir," came a voice from the back of the class, followed by laughter.

"How many moons does Jupiter have, Lear?" Mulligan continued.

"I don't know, sir."

"Did you do your homework, Lear?"

"Yes, sir."

"Then why are you so witless, Lear?"

"Because we didn't read that far, sir."

"What do you mean, didn't read that far?"

"We only did Mercury, Venus and Earth for today, sir."

"Nonsense, boy," the teacher said, but suddenly he turned away from David and started down the line to the other end of the room where Terry Roche sat smiling, with his long legs crossed under the desk. Everyone knew Terry, even though he'd only been at school for a month. He was the best athlete in the third form, and when the j.v. football team played Latin School, he ran all over them with his long, loping strides. Terry was the most popular boy in the class.

"What's the closest planet to the sun, Roche?" Mr. Mulligan asked.

"Mercury, sir," said the blond boy.

And nothing more was ever said about it. Only after that Mr. Mulligan would look at David, arching one eyebrow and saying nothing.

English was his favorite subject. The class had to memorize poems and recite them. David picked "Barbara Frietchie" and "Old Ironsides." "Shoot if you must, this old gray head, but spare your country's flag, she said." David could see Barbara Frietchie sticking her old gray head out of the second story window, shaking her fist at the retreating Confederate soldiers, and he could feel the great frigate sailing through the seas, guns blazing, to protect America against the British:

*Oh better that her shattered hulk*
*Should sink beneath the wave.*

*Her timbers braved the stormy deep*
*And there should be her grave.*

Mrs. Benzaquin said he read beautifully, and gave him 100 for elocution.

"Oh better that her shattered hulk," said Terry Roche.

"Should sink beneath the wave," said Griff Ryan.

"She's old Ironsides," said one.

"She's a shattered old hulk," said the other.

"Her breath smells," said Ian Stuart, rolling his r's.

David didn't like this talk; it made him feel uncomfortable like he was doing something dirty. It was even worse the day of the strike. Terry and Griff decided it would be funny if Mrs. Benzaquin walked in and nobody stood up. David was against it, but he knew it was no use to fight. Everyone wanted to do it. So on the day that Griff and Terry chose, she marched in the door as usual and the whole class sat there silently like stones. She looked at them, and David watched her look, and he felt like garbage. She did not speak for a long time. Then she said, "I am going to walk out of the room, and I am going to walk back in again. I shall assume that this never happened."

And she did. She walked out and came back in and everyone stood up and said, "Good morning, Mrs. Benzaquin," and it never happened again.

Another day she was reading a poem and stopped:

"Can anyone tell me the meaning of the word 'gossamer'?"

Silence.

Then David raised his hand. "It means 'thin,' I think," he said.

"It does, indeed," she said.

"Teacher's pet," said Terry Roche after class.

"Very good, David," mimicked Griff Ryan in Mrs. Benzaquin's voice.

In the dark corridor leading from English to social studies they bumped him, bouncing him with their shoulders from one to the other. David tried to ignore them as he had tried to ignore everyone who made fun of him. He smiled and bent over to pick up his books from the dusty floor as the others walked away. He listened for his mother's voice. "You're different, Toots," she had told him, "and there are lots of kids like that Hubert whatsisname who will try to make you feel bad because you're different. You just have to be stronger. Don't give them power over you by being a baby, and don't lose your temper. That way they gain what they want."

But it was lonely. Sometimes when there was no work to do, he wanted to go talk to someone or just mess around, but he didn't know how to begin. There wasn't anyone he could go and talk to, except maybe Allie, and he hadn't seen much of Allie since they changed tables. The whole thing was so stupid. He loved school as long as there was something planned. Classes, except for science, were great, and soccer wasn't bad. Even meals were all right, now that he was at Mr. Melvin's table. It was free time he didn't know what to do with, like evenings in the dorms after study hall or Saturday afternoons. Sometimes he would read, and sometimes he would stand at the window of his alcove, watching the boys with Primus or Secundus ratings walk down to the village for ice cream and comic books.

He wrote to Elizabeth: "I miss you. What are you doing? Will I come to your place for Thanksgiving? We get four days. I need to talk to you about how to make friends."

A week later he got a letter from his mother:

*Dear Toots,*

> *Here I am in New York City working as a waitress (at my age) in the Victory Hotel on Madison Avenue. I help out at the desk sometimes, and the people here are real nice. I think you'll like it. I got you a little room right next to mine for Thanksgiving, and we'll have a good time. Your school wrote me, and I'll be waiting for you at Grand Central Station on Wednesday. Maybe Elizabeth, too, if she can get off work. I'm better now, Toots. So don't worry. Don't wrinkle your handsome face up in that frown you get when you're scared. I didn't write you sooner because I couldn't. But now I'm fine. The school says you're doing well, and I'm proud of you. I'm always proud of you.*

*Love, Your Crazy Mom*

*P.S. By the way, Gretel died. I forgot to tell you. She was very old, over a hundred years old, I guess, in dog years.*

He could feel the tears coming, and he hated it. You couldn't cry, or even start to cry, because someone would come along and see you. They might stick their head in your alcove, and the next thing you knew it would be all over the dorm. Even sitting on your bed with the curtain closed you were never safe. He would have to rock it out. Yes, this was a real rocker. David could feel it coming on. It was risky to rock at rest time, because Mr. Richardson might walk by and see him as he made his rounds to check if everyone was "in or on his bed," as the rules stated. Night was safer. Sometimes Mr. R. would walk by and check the alcoves with his flashlight, but only if he heard a noise, and then usually David would hear him coming and stop. The dangerous thing about rocking was that once you went too far, you couldn't hear anymore. But that was the point, really, to rock away from there until you slept and the sleeping took the pain away. Otherwise you just lay awake, like a soldier at attention, staring at the ceiling and listening to the sounds coming from the alcoves on either side.

That night he began with music. You could begin with music or pictures. The music set the beat, and you made the music in your mouth, like an orchestra playing, only softly so only you could hear. Then the pictures of where you wanted to go — this time the house in Westport with the green shutters and the lawn rolling away from the road down to the brook in back and the long grass behind where he and Gretel had played. He could hear the sniff of her nose, and see the tail like an antenna sticking up in the long green grass. He saw the driveway on the other side and the fence that separated their yard from the McCarvers next door and the McCarvers' apple tree that bent over the fence and gave them free apples in the fall, and he saw the apple crates he borrowed from Mr. McCarver for his games. He saw his room and the books on the shelf by his bed — Dave Dawson, Bomba the Jungle Boy, Robin Hood and the story of Homer Price and the Doughnut Machine. And it was bad, seeing all these books, because he did not know where they were now and he didn't know where Gretel was, so he rocked harder and the rhythm of the song took him to Elizabeth sitting at her dressing table putting powder on her face and lines under her eyes and lipstick on her mouth. Usually she was happy when she did this, humming to herself or singing, but tonight she was stern.

"You going on a date, Elizabeth?" the boy asked.

"No, sweetheart, I'm not."

"Where you going?"

There was no answer. David started to sit down in his usual place on her bed, but there was a suitcase in the way. It was open, and her clothes were inside, her white nightgown and the blue bathrobe, her slippers and a skirt and sweater she usually wore to school. David was scared.

"What's this for?" he asked.

"I'm going to New York."

"Where in New York?"

"To Grandma and Grandpa Sampson's."

"Can I come too?"

"No. You're too little."

"But I don't want to stay here alone without you."

"It's all right. They won't hurt you. They aren't mad at you."

"Who?"

"Mommy and Bernie."

"Why are they mad at you?"

"Because I told them off about their drinking."

And suddenly he could feel the tears coming. "Take me with you," he tried to say, but the words never came out, only the beginning and he reached to her with his hands and put his face hard against the softness of her sweater and sobbed. For a long time she held him, and then "O.K.," she whispered. "Get your coat and boots, and be very quiet. They don't know we're going."

And they went, two frightened children, down the kitchen stairs out into the dark while the lights blazed in the living room, and the sounds of laughter came from behind the closed door. By the time they got to the station David was feeling better. He had never been to New York before. Of course he had been, Elizabeth told him, when he was real little, but that didn't count. They had lived in New York with Grandma and Grandpa Sampson when their mother had brought them East, but David didn't remember that. He didn't remember anything before the white house in Westport with the green Plymouth that his mother drove to the beach in the summer like a crazy racing car driver, her left arm hanging out the window and a cigarette dangling from her mouth, and so for David it was like his first trip to New York.

It was late and the ticket office closed, so when the train came like a great dragon cutting the black of the night with its single eye, they had to buy their tickets from the conductor, who punched holes in a long piece of paper and gave it to David to hold.

"You're traveling late for such a young man," said the conductor.

"I'm seven," said David proudly. "That's not so young."

Elizabeth counted her money, and said something about a taxi.

David watched the conductor walk down the aisle, and thought of his grandfather, who had white hair, lots of white hair neatly combed, and red skin. He wore suits, blue suits and gray suits in the winter, and white suits in the summer. His grandmother smelled like perfume and called David her "little man." Sometimes they came to the house and brought him presents, and once they took him in their car to the beach.

He tried to look out the window, but he could only see the reflection of his own face unless he put his hands around his eyes and placed them tightly against the glass. Even then there wasn't much to see, so he closed his eyes and went to sleep against Elizabeth's shoulder.

When he woke up, all the people were standing and putting on their coats and getting their cases down from the overhead racks.

"Come on, sleepy," said Elizabeth. "We're there." She took down her suitcase, and he held her hand tightly as they walked out of the car onto the platform. He couldn't believe what he was seeing. The whole station was indoors. There were lights and platforms as far as he could see, and trains everywhere.

"Is this the biggest station in the world?" he asked.

Elizabeth wasn't in the mood for talk.

They walked out into a huge room with stars on the ceiling and signs everywhere telling you to "Smoke Luckies" or "Drink Seagram's." He wondered if that was what his mother drank.

"Stop gawking and come on, David," Elizabeth said. "It's late, and I'm tired."

He followed her across the room and up some stairs and out a door onto a kind of street with a roof over it where there was a line of taxis in all different colors — red, green, yellow, orange, and checkered. Everything was magical. He loved New York.

But his grandfather was not at all happy to see them.

"What do you mean, bringing a little boy like that all the way into the city at this hour of the night? Anything might have happened." His grandfather's face was very red, and Elizabeth looked like she was going to cry.

"Come on, sweet boy," said his grandmother quickly. "Let's get you to bed. I don't see any point in my little man standing in the doorway all night." She led him by the hand through the living room and into a bedroom. She turned down the covers on the bed and began talking:

"You go wash your face, honey, and then climb right into bed. I'll get you a little fresh air. I just can't understand the world these days."

From the bathroom he could hear the sound of a window opening, and then the click of a door closing. Quickly he went to the bathroom, flushed the toilet, ran water on his face and hands, dried them and hurried back out into the bedroom. He could hear Elizabeth and his grandfather arguing in the next room, but he couldn't make out the words. He stood next to the door:

"I couldn't stand it any more," he could hear Elizabeth say. "They're drunk every night. It's no place for a child to live. I can't do my schoolwork. I can't bring my friends home. We don't eat properly."

"Now, Elizabeth, you exaggerate," his grandfather said.

"No, I don't. I'm afraid something will happen. They argue and fight. You have to do something."

Then she began to cry, and David ran for the bed and jumped under the covers. It wasn't long before the door opened and Elizabeth came in. David could hear her blowing her nose in the bathroom, then the sound of water running, toilet flushing, and a body next to his in the bed.

"David," she said. "You've still got your clothes on."

"I know," he said. "I was listening at the door."

"You little devil."

He laughed and got out of bed. "I don't have any pajamas, do I?"

Then she laughed. "No," she said.

He took off all his clothes except his underpants, and got back into bed. Elizabeth held him, and her nightgown felt smooth and clean against his skin.

"Will they make us go back?" he asked.

"Yes," she said.

"Will they punish us?"

"Not you."

"Will they punish you?"

"Yes, probably."

"Why?"

"For running away and taking you."

"But I wanted to come. I asked to come."

"I know. But they don't understand that."

"I'll tell them I wanted to come."

"Hush, David. Go to sleep. I can't think anymore tonight."

She turned away from him, and after awhile he could hear the deepness of her breathing. But he could not sleep. He was cold, and he wanted to close the window, but he could not make himself get out of bed. His grandmother had opened the window. She would be mad if he closed it. So he watched the curtains billow, breathing like spirits in and out, and he thought there was something behind them in the window, something that would take him away, outside into the blackness, and he put his head under the covers, where they couldn't find him. He made himself small and tight like a fist against the dark.

When he woke in the morning, Elizabeth was gone, the sun was shining, and the fears of the night before seemed foolish. He was very hungry, and when he burst, face washed and hair combed as well as he could with his hands, into the dining room, the others were seated at the table. If anyone was mad, nobody showed it. The table was set with a white linen cloth, and in front of each place was a linen napkin in a silver ring. There were eggs and bacon and tea and marmalade all the way from England, where Christopher Robin came from. And he sat down and put his napkin carefully in his lap and ate with good manners, because his grandmother was from the South "where people still have manners, honey," and she was not going to have her grandson and granddaughter growing up "like two Yankee hellions in the wilds of Connecticut."

David laughed. He hadn't heard his grandmother speak much. She was funny. When she said, "wilds," it sounded like "walds."

"Grandma, why do you talk like that?"

"He's off again," said Elizabeth. "Why, why, why…"

"That's all right, honey," said his grandmother. "You just ask away."

"Well," said David, "why do you say your words different from Elizabeth and me?"

"Differently," said his grandfather.

"Differently," said David.

"Because I was born and raised in Georgia, honey, and that is the way people speak there."

David thought the "there" sounded like "they ah," but he wasn't going to say anything about that. "Was my mother born in Georgia?" he asked.

"Yes, but she ran off with a Yankee scalliwag when she was nineteen, and forgot her heritage."

"Oh, you mean my father who lives in California."

"That's right, honey. But we do not speak of him in this house."

"Oh," said David.

After breakfast Elizabeth took him to the Central Park Zoo. There were elephants and brown bears and polar bears and seals swimming and diving for fish and baboons with red behinds and a black gorilla who looked like he could bend the bars of the cage if he tried. There were black panthers and a spotted leopard, but no tigers.

"Why aren't there any tigers?" he asked.

"This is just a small zoo," said Elizabeth. "They have the lions and tigers at the Bronx Zoo where they have room to run. It's too crowded here."

"Oh," he said, and then, after a pause, "you know what, Elizabeth? I think I would like to live here. Why can't we just stay with grandma and grandpa?"

"Because you wouldn't have any friends, and besides grandma

and grandpa are too old to have us around all the time. You would wear them out."

"So what will we do now?"

"Bernie's coming by to pick us up after work. We're going home."

"And then what happens?"

"I don't know, David. Just stop asking me questions. I really don't know. Come on, sweetie, let's go get some ice cream."

"All right," he said. He liked New York. Maybe they would come back.

∞

So now he was coming back, but it didn't seem as exciting as it had then. What would he do? He couldn't just sit in a hotel room all day. There was no yard, no Gretel to play with. Suppose he wanted to see Elizabeth? How would he get there? Where was Bernie living? Why didn't Bernie want to stay with his mother anymore? He knew it had something to do with the drinking and the night she shot him in the shoulder. But why? Why did she do it? What did Bernie do to her to make her so mad?

He couldn't concentrate. He tried to do his homework, but the time would go by and he hadn't finished. It was like he was somewhere else and when the time was gone, he couldn't remember where he'd been. One day Mrs. Benzaquin asked him to stay after class.

"You don't seem yourself, David," she said.

"No, sir, I mean no, ma'am," he said.

"Look at me, David," she said.

He tried to look at her, but it scared him. He wanted to get up and leave.

"David, I'm not going to bite you. You're a wonderful student, but your work has been very careless lately. There must be something troubling you. Would you like to tell me about it? Maybe I can help."

Something in him wanted to tell her about it very much, but something else in him would not speak. Saying things was dangerous. Suppose he told her and she told everyone else. Suppose Mr. Mulligan found out and told Terry and Griff. No, it was safer to be silent.

"My dog died," he said. The rest was too complicated, too hard.

"That is sad," she said. "But don't become obsessed by it. You are too good for that."

He got up and started to leave.

"David," she said. "We adults are not as foolish as you think us. Come to me, if you wish, some time."

"Yes, ma'am," he said, and moved quickly into the safety of the dark corridor.

On the train to New York he sat with Ian Stuart. When they stopped at Bridgeport and David didn't get off, the blond boy said, "I thought you lived in Westpor-rt."

"I do," David lied. "I'm going to visit my sister Elizabeth in New York. She works there now."

"I see," said the blond boy.

The lie made David uncomfortable. It wasn't completely a lie. At least that was better than a whole lie, but it still made him feel bad. He looked out of the window. The stations were coming closer together now, coming every few minutes — Norwalk and South Norwalk, Stamford, Rye, Mamaronek, Port Chester, Mount Vernon, and then nothing but buildings and streets as if the world were one big city for as far as the eye could see, and more train tracks coming in and joining the one they were on, and then a river and the conductor saying, "The station stop is 125th Street, 125th Street." Outside on the streets there were brown-skinned people everywhere.

"It's called Harlem," said Ian Stuart.

David didn't answer. He watched, fascinated, out the window as the train began to move, watched the faces in the streets and laundry hanging on lines from the windows of the apartment buildings, watched as the wall beside the train grew higher until you couldn't see and then darkness.

"It's the tunnel," said Ian.

"What tunnel?" David asked.

"A tunnel under Par-rk Avenue. It r-runs all the way from 96th Street to Grand Central Station, over fifty blocks. Fifty blocks is two and a half miles."

David didn't remember the tunnel, but he did remember the platforms as he carried his brown suitcase with the letters "M.H." on it up the long ramp to the big room with the stars on the ceiling and the signs on the wall. He saw his mother immediately, standing with the other parents behind a rope to let the passengers out. He waved to her with his free hand, and they met where the rope ended, her eyes smiling and her curled brown hair shining.

She kissed him on the cheek, and laughed.

"Don't you look a sight with lipstick all over you." She took out her handkerchief and wiped the spot. "Let's have a look at you, Toots," she said. "You're kind of pale. What are they feeding you up there?"

"Runny eggs and boiled potatoes," he said.

"Well, come on, let's get something good," she said.

She took his hand, and they walked through the huge room with the stars on the ceiling. "They're called the signs of the Zodiac. Each constellation makes the shape of an animal or a person. See? There's Taurus the Bull. And over there is Pisces, the Fish. That's your sign."

"There's a crab," said David.

"The crab's called Cancer. That's my sign."

"Hey, watch where you're goin', lady," growled a passerby.

David laughed. This was fun. He had forgotten about school already. They walked from the big room past the Translux Newsreel Theater down a long hall with a ceiling that looked like a church. David saw shops on both sides and newsstands bright with magazines, comic books, candy bars, and chewing gum. At the end of the hall was a sign which said SUBWAY.

"Stay close and hold tight," his mother said. "This is what they call rush hour." She started down the steps with David close behind, weaving in and out of the crowds coming up the stairs. David had never seen so many people. They put nickels in the turnstile and clanked through, then plunged into another mass of people waiting for the Uptown Express. You didn't walk into the train. You were pushed. You were part of a wave. You didn't stand in the train.

You were somehow suspended, held up by the people on either side and rattled against them by the motion of the train. The lucky ones with seats clung tightly to their bags and briefcases. No one looked at anyone else. Then the train stopped, and they all poured out and up the stairs into the blessed space of the open air.

They were on the corner of Lexington Avenue and 86th Street. David had never seen such a corner before. There were three movie theaters, an R.K.O., a Loews, and a smaller one next to it called the Grande. It was dark, and the lights sparkled white and red and yellow against the black of the sky and the shadows of the buildings. He tried to read the titles.

"Can we go to the movies?" he asked.

"I knew that was the first thing you'd want to do," she said, laughing. "Maybe tomorrow night or Friday. But not tonight. Come on."

They crossed Lexington and Park Avenues, then turned at Madison and walked up five blocks. The Victory Hotel didn't look like much to David.

"It's not a regular hotel, Toots," his mother said. "It's what's called a residential hotel. People live here for a year or two. It's their home. They give me my room for free and I can eat in the restaurant when it's not busy."

She took him up a flight of stairs from the lobby and showed him her room, a long dark room with a window at one end but no windows on either side.

"Well," she said. "How do you like it?"

David wasn't sure he liked it at all. A double bed with a table next to it stood against one wall. Next to the bed, close to the door, a wardrobe bulged with clothes. On the opposite wall a sink, a refrigerator, and near the window a bureau. In the middle a table, a couple of straight chairs, and a sad burgundy couch. Nothing really matched, David thought. It was like they just gave her whatever was leftover.

"Hey, gloomy face," his mother said, "what's the matter? I know. You need a drink, and so do I."

She kicked off her shoes with a sigh, walked to the sink and took two glasses from the cabinet. Then she sat down and began to rub her feet. "Bring us some ice from the old ice box, sweetie, would you, and grab yourself a coke. And bring me that little bottle over there on the bedside table. My feet are killing me. The trouble with waitressing is you have to stand up all day. I'm no spring chicken."

David brought the ice tray, the coke and the little bottle and watched as his mother poured some of the liquid from the bottle into her glass and the coke into his.

"Bottoms up, sweetie," she said, "and here's to us. Somebody up there better be watching out for us, 'cause we're sure not doing so hot on our own."

She drank quickly, easily, then poured another and sighed. "Wow," she said. "That feels good. Now tell me about that school of yours."

So he told her about the school and the ratings and how the points worked, and about Mrs. Benzaquin and how much he liked English, and while he talked he watched her bottle, which was not Seagram's but something called Old Forester, and saw her tip a little more into her glass.

"You know," she said, smiling. "It's so damned funny about this family. We're what's known as genteel poor. Champagne tastes and beer budgets. Your father loved to read. And your grandmother. And me. Look at me." She held up her hands. "I used to play the piano every day. And Elizabeth, little Liz. My God, she saves every penny to go stand behind the back row of seats to see a Broadway play. We've got lots of culture in this family."

"I'm going to be in a play," said David. "An operetta."

"Is that right?"

"I'm going to be a girl. There are no girls at school, so the younger boys with high voices have to be girls. It's Gilbert and Sullivan. The Mikado. Do you know it?"

"No, sweetie, I don't, but I bet you'll be cute." She leaned over and kissed him. "I'd like to see you in it."

"Why don't you? Please. Come and see it."

"Are you kidding? You think these bozos would give me three days off to go see an operetta? They don't even know what the word means. Come on, Toots, I'll show you your room. You can change or whatever, and we'll go eat."

She fished around in her purse and pulled out a key with a green plastic tag on it that said 21. "It's right next door," she said. "You go on in there and wash your face. I've got to change my dress and fix my face. Unzip me before you go, will you?"

He got up and walked around behind her. He wanted to put his arms around her neck and his head next to hers, but he didn't. He just unzipped her and took his bag and walked to the door.

"Hey, Toots," she said.

"What?"

"You know what 'M.H.' stands for?"

"No," he said.

"It's me. That's my old leather bag. Maggie Hope. Margaret Hope. It's a great name. I had that bag in California, when I was married to your father. It's seen a lot of places."

But he was tired and did not care right now about the bag. He walked into the hall, closing the door quietly behind him. Then he turned the key in the door marked 21. It was a small room, much like his alcove at school, except that there was a sink. A towel and a small piece of soap wrapped in paper lay on the bureau. He put down the bag, took off his coat and tie and rolled up his sleeves. He unwrapped the soap and turned on the water, cupping his hands under the spigot, splashing his face over and over. Then he soaped and rinsed it and dried it with the towel, which he then folded and placed carefully on the rack next to the sink. He lay down on the bed to wait for his mother and fell fast asleep.

In his dream he was at the beach, he and his mother and Elizabeth, and they lay in the sun on brightly striped blankets. They put suntan lotion on themselves, and then David stood up and said, "Good-bye" very politely, and began walking into the water. When he reached the waves his mother screamed and Elizabeth came running toward him, but he smiled and kept walking right into the waves and underneath, farther and farther until he was walking on the bottom of the ocean, and he could see their arms and legs kicking and splashing and their faces anxiously peering down into the water searching for him. He was happy underwater, and he breathed quietly and looked for crabs and snails.

"Hey, silly, you planning to sleep through dinner?"

He rubbed his eyes and looked up. It was Elizabeth.

"Wow," he said. "Elizabeth. I thought you weren't coming."

"Just wanted to surprise you."

She reached out and he tunneled his head against her and let her hold him. The tears ran down his cheeks onto her sweater.

"I didn't cry once at school," he said.

"I know," she said. "It's hard to be strong all the time, isn't it?"

"Sometimes you just want to pop somebody good," he said.

"Whack 'em in the nose," she laughed.

"And make the blood run all over."

"Like Captain Marvel."

"Yes," he said. "Boom, Pow, Zap."

"Do they tease you very much?" she asked.

"Not too much," he said. He told her about the shower, and about Mrs. Benzaquin, and her face went all sad when he talked, and she pulled out a Kleenex and began to wipe her eyes.

"Now look what you've done," she said, sniffing. "You've made my eyes run."

David laughed. "Serves you right," he said. And they bumped and hugged and she gave him some gum, and they went to get their mother from the next room.

On Thursday they went to their grandparents for Thanksgiving dinner, and afterwards David and Elizabeth walked in the park while their mother and a cousin who worked at Hattie Carnegie's played bridge with their grandparents. David wanted to go to the zoo, but Elizabeth said she had a surprise for him; she wanted to take him for a ride on the carousel.

Before he saw it, he could hear the sound of the calliope in the distance. It was like the Pied Piper of Hamlin, and all the children came from east and west, north and south. You couldn't not come. You heard the sound and you walked toward it and saw the other children walking toward it, and then you saw the roof with its flag and the popcorn sellers in the booth next door, and then the horses, going round and round. David had never seen anything so beautiful. Black horses with white manes, white horses with golden manes and bright red saddles, and all of them going up and down with their mouths open. They were crying, he thought, crying to be free.

They rode and they rode, and David closed his eyes and flew through the dark night over the waves of the sea into the lands of the past. He was Sir Lancelot searching for the Holy Grail. He was Richard with the heart of the lion. Up he would go and out into the sky with each thrust of the horse, and Elizabeth with him riding sometimes in front, sometimes in back, out in the sky to do battle against the Saracens, to recover the holy city of Jerusalem for the Christians.

Afterwards they sat on a bench, eating popcorn and watching the others ride. It was cold but bright and they snuggled against each other to keep warm.

"Do you remember when we ran away?" asked David.

"I remember," said Elizabeth.

"I thought it was fun," he said.

"Fun for you, maybe, but it was pretty rough on me."

"Why?"

"Bernie was awful. He took away my allowance and would hardly speak to me for a month."

"I wonder where he is."

"He's living in the Village, not too far from where I live."

"Oh."

"Do you want to see him?"

"I don't know."

David had liked Bernie at the beginning, when he had come to the house in his army uniform with silver bars on the shoulders and red and green ribbons over the pocket. He was a hero, and the neighborhood had a big party for him. They sang and danced and his mother played the piano in the living room, while David and Elizabeth sat at the top of the stairs and listened. If someone came out they would scuttle back to their rooms like squirrels. Later, Bernie brought presents like the wind-up tank that shot sparks from its gun and the plane that you could launch from a ring. He talked about the war and the Germans and the Japs and said things like "slanty-eyed bastards." David thought he was neat.

He went away for a long time, and when he came back, he wore a blue suit with a white shirt and a striped tie. He had been wounded, his mother said, and received an honorable discharge. David remembered going to meet him at the station in the green Plymouth and how all the men on the train had suits like Bernie's, and they all had gray hats with little feathers on them.

"Why do they all wear the same hats? I think they look stupid," he whispered to Elizabeth in the back seat of the car, while his mother kissed Bernie on the station platform.

They all had dinner together, and then David and Elizabeth went upstairs. After a while his mother came. Her eyes were shining, and she held out her hand toward David. "Look, Toots. Bernie's proposed. We're going to be married."

And then Bernie and his mother went away, and Mrs. Mc-Carver from next door stayed with them. She let David drink tea with milk and lumps of sugar in it. Then his mother and Bernie came back with lots of big, brown suitcases, and Bernie picked David up and laughed and scratched him with his beard and promised to be great friends. And he moved all his suitcases into the house, and Bernie and his mother went upstairs and closed the door and didn't come out for a long time.

After that his mother didn't read to him any more. Elizabeth read to him, and they had their dinner early in the kitchen because Bernie didn't get home from New York until late, and David would have his pajamas on when Bernie got home, and Elizabeth would take him upstairs, and then grownups would come in and they would drink cocktails and eat dinner in the dining room. David and Elizabeth would sit on the stairs and listen, and sometimes the grownups would talk about her and sometimes about him. David didn't like it. They called him "poor little chap" and felt sorry for Elizabeth because she didn't get good grades at school. Sometimes they sang and talked after dinner like they had before, and sometimes there was only his mother and Bernie and sometimes the sound of their voices, shouting at each other and then something breaking.

One night Bernie caught him on the stairs and sent him to his room. "If I catch you eavesdropping again, young man, it'll be a good paddling for you."

He went into Elizabeth's room. She was sitting at her desk.

"Why did Bernie have to come and spoil everything?" he asked.

"It's no good for a woman to live alone, David," Elizabeth said. "A woman needs a man. That's what Mommy told me."

"But why?"

"To love her and take care of her. To keep her company."

"But we do that."

"It's not the same," she said. "Now go on to bed. I've got work to do."

Elizabeth touched him on the arm. He was back in the park.

"Where have you been, silly? Daydreaming again?"

"I was thinking about Bernie."

"Don't bother," she said. "Come on, we better get back."

It was getting dark, and by the time they had walked back across the park to their grandparents' building, the bridge game was over and the teapot out. They all sat together and drank tea and talked about Elizabeth's job and David's school, and David's grandmother gave him a present.

"Wow," he said. "A watch. I've never had my own watch before. How did you know how badly I needed it?"

"Oh, a little bird told me, sweetheart," she answered, winking.

He put it on his wrist and displayed it proudly for everyone.

"Now I won't have to worry about being late," he said, and he put the watch to his ear and listened to the sound of the mechanism going back and forth, back and forth. He loved it, and he kissed his grandmother on the cheek and hugged her.

On Saturday he went to the movies. His mother walked him down to 86th Street and bought his ticket for him. At the Saturday matinees there was a woman called a matron who watched the children in a special section of the theater so those under twelve could stay by themselves. He would walk back to the hotel afterwards.

He came out of the theater when the show was over and consulted his watch. It was 4:45. Three older boys came out with him.

"Say, that's a nice looking watch you've got there," one of them said.

"My grandmother gave it to me," said David proudly.

"Can I see it?" the second boy asked.

David held out his wrist for them to admire the watch.

"I'm gonna get me one like it," said the third boy. "What kind is it?"

"I don't know," said David.

"Take it off and look on the back," said the first boy.

David untied the strap and turned it over, but he could not see any place where…suddenly the watch was out of his hand the boys gone, running down the street, around the corner, out of sight. He ran after them as fast as he could, but when he turned the corner he could only see the three of them what seemed like miles ahead already across Park Avenue. With every step he only got farther behind.

When he got back to the hotel his mother asked him what time it was.

"I don't know," he said.

"Where is your watch, then?" she asked.

He sat in stony silence, staring palely at the floor.

"David, look at me. What happened to your watch?"

"I lost it," he mumbled without looking up.

"Look at me," she said, "and tell me what happened."

He could feel himself beginning to cry. He did not want to cry. "Some boys," he said, "took it."

"Come on, David, how can someone take a watch off your wrist."

There was nothing he could say. The shame burned him, and the tears came.

"Oh, for God's sake David, don't be such a baby. If you can't take better care of yourself, you just can't go out alone. Now what happened?"

"They said…they wanted one just like it…and wanted…to see the back."

"So you just took it off and showed it to them."

David nodded.

"David, sweetheart, this is New York City. This is not your snooty school where everyone has everything. People steal things here."

He knew now and he would remember.

"Well," she said, "you'll just have to be without a watch. There's no money to be buying you watches every three days."

# CHAPTER
*five*

FTER CHRISTMAS IT SNOWED, coming down at first in big wet flakes sticking to the pavement and then dissolving. But during the night the temperature dropped and the flakes grew smaller. By morning the road was buried, and the sound of laughter in the dormitories could be heard even before the rising bell. At breakfast even Mr. Armbrister had to concede. He played a rousing chorus of jingle bells on the official gong and declared a holiday. Several of the masters were unable to make it to school, he said, and therefore, classes would be "temporarily suspended." Boys of all shapes and sizes shed coats and ties and plunged down the stairs to the locker room. There were socks and sweaters, mittens and boots, hats and jackets — the armor of a winter field day — to put on. There was to be a snow war between the Reds and the Whites. The older boys had talked about snow wars at color meetings, but this was David's first experience of one.

The rules were simple. The upper soccer field was divided in half, and each color was given half the field from which to draw its snow supply. You had until lunch time to build your forts. After lunch the fight itself would begin. According to the rules anyone hit by a snowball was officially "dead," and had to go to the prison under a master's supervision. Each team built forts, behind which they hid to make their snowballs and from which they emerged to throw them. Not even the forts were safe unless you stayed right against the wall, because the other team could lob high fly balls up into the air, and they could land on you when you weren't looking. You had to cover the whole field. If you didn't the enemy could sneak around the side and come up from behind and pepper you with balls. All morning they worked, rolling big snowballs through the long grass, rolling them farther and farther until they became the base of the wall. Everywhere Reds and Whites alike scurried like ants, packing the walls solid and high, building up stores of ammunition and holding councils of war.

David was a scout for the Reds. His job was to carry ammunition and messages from one fort to the next. He wasn't strong enough to be a thrower or fast enough to be a torpedo, but he was quick and small enough to duck low in the open spaces between the forts. At lunch they marched into the dining room to stoke up with fuel before the battle. The forts were finished, the strategy planned. You couldn't build any more after lunch, and if your fort was hit by a human torpedo, you couldn't rebuild it, so the torpedoes were the big heroes, zig-zagging across no man's land, trying to reach the wall of an enemy fort before being struck by a snowball. Sometimes they would send two or three torpedoes in the hopes that one would make it. "Remember, David," said Allie as they walked back from lunch to take their positions, "if the Captain yells 'torpedo,' stop whatever you're doing and start throwing at them."

David could feel his heart pounding under his shirt, and he watched with pride as the red flag was raised on the central fort. "Are the judges ready?" shouted Mr. Armbrister.

"Judges ready," answered Mr. Parilli. Harold "Hank" Parilli was tough as nails. He coached football and taught science and was so strong he could climb the rope in the gym all the way to the ceiling without using his legs. He scared David. The whistle blew, and the war began. David and Ian Stuart packed snowballs as fast as they could in the protection of the central fort, then took off, one to the right and one to the left, to carry their piles to the throwers on the wings. For awhile the battle was even, with only the foolish and the slow being picked off. Then there was a silence, as if everyone had become suddenly tired or bored. Then from the Reds' right wing a shout and a charge.

"Torpedoes," yelled the Whites, and fired a volley of balls.

"It's a trap, it's a fake," David heard someone yell, and then from the left corner a whir of red bodies hurling themselves toward the white flag. David stood to watch, mesmerized by the speed of the runners, the rain of snowballs and the cries of the judges as each runner was hit. One made it through, hurling himself against the White fort, but the fort held and the flag stood, and the runner returned dejectedly home. Now the Reds were in serious trouble. They had lost ten of their best runners in the rush.

Then the Whites rushed, and David rose to his feet, throwing as hard as he could, but they seemed to be everywhere.

"Left!" shouted someone, and David ran with a supply of balls to the left wing. Quickly the bigger boys threw at the oncoming figures, and one by one they fell, sprawling dramatically in the snow when they were hit, but the Reds had committed too much to the left, and as David turned to run back to the center, he saw three of the fastest Whites only yards away from the flag. One was hit, a second was hit, but the third, ducking behind the second for cover suddenly leaped for the fort and landed high on the wall taking the wall and the flag with him into the bowels of the red fort. It was Terry Roche.

The whistle blew and the Whites dashed across no man's land, lifted Terry onto their shoulders and carried him up the hill toward the locker room.

All winter they played in the snow, trudging to the woods for snow-ball-capture-the-flag, and gathering around the hill to the north of the dining hall for skiing. They skated on the flooded and frozen football field and made snow sculptures and igloos from the masses of snow piled up on the sides. At night they studied and rehearsed for the operetta and slept hard and deeply, worn out by the day's play and the night's work. David was happy with the rhythm of school life, with the mornings in class and the afternoons in the snow and the evenings rehearsing and trying on costumes in the dressing room under the stage in the gymnasium. Most of all he loved singing in the church choir on Sunday.

He didn't really talk to anyone about it. It was hard to talk about the things he really loved. When he sang in the choir, he felt different. It was as if he had traveled to another country. "Dona Nobis Pacem" they sang, and the notes took them, hair combed and clean in their red robes, to where God lived.

He thought about God, how God was in the music, in the harmony they made with their different voices, the young sopranos like David and Freddie Felton, who had, Mrs. Rossiter said, the most beautiful voice of all — the altos, and the older boys, whose voices had changed, the baritones. When they sang right, when they got just the right notes, David could feel his skin tingle, and God was there, somehow, under the tingling.

And God was there in the Bible stories Mr. Armbrister read at evening prayer in the schoolroom. During the week before Christmas he had read the stories of the birth of Jesus, the one from Luke about the shepherds and the one from Matthew about the three kings following the star. In January he started reading the parables. David loved the parables — the Good Samaritan and the treasure in the field and best of all, the talents. The parable was like the school motto — Poteris Modo Velis. If you got five talents, God expected you to take your five and make five more. If you were given three, you had to make three more. The servant that got one dug a hole and hid his talent in the ground. He didn't make any. "You can if you will, gentlemen," said Armbrister, wiping his glasses. "But for those of you who don't try," he grimaced, "there will be weeping and wailing and gnashing of teeth."

Everyone at Lowell School knew about that. They had seen in the shower room the bruises, the purple welts on the buttocks and thighs of the boys who had felt the wrath of Armbrister. They knew of the famous wooden paddle and the even more terrifying "Flexible Flyer," a leather strip attached to a wooden handle. David had seen the faces of the boys returning to the schoolroom from the secrecy of the headmaster's study.

David understood this, and he printed carefully on the blank page inside the cover of his Bible, Matthew 25:14-30, Parable of the Talents, so he would not forget it. Ian Stuart said that you weren't supposed to write in the Bible, but David didn't care, and he carried the Bible with him to the church across the street so he could follow the lessons.

"Goodie-goodie," said Terry Roche one Sunday as they walked back to school.

"My, isn't David a sweet boy," said Griff Ryan in the voice of Mrs. Benzaquin.

The words echoed in David's ears all day, and as he lay in bed that night he thought he would have to rock. But then this was not a rocking thing. It was a thinking thing. It was a matter of figuring things out. If you were good and did what all the masters asked, then you got good grades and high ratings, but the other boys didn't like you. If you wanted to be popular and have friends, then you had to be like Terry Roche and Griff Ryan, making jokes and bathroom noises and running in the halls, climbing the walls after lights out, and passing notes behind the teachers' backs. He would be bad, then, if he had to, because he was tired of being picked on and called "goodie-goodie."

The next day in class, when Mrs. Benzaquin asked a question, he stayed silent, and that night in the dorm during free time, he got in the large wicker laundry hamper and let Harry Dickson and crazy Peter Winemiller push him up and down the hall. When Mr. Richardson caught them, he got out red-faced, but smiling. They were sent to their rooms, and he had to miss the bedtime story hour. The following morning at breakfast he let his shirt tail hang out and was sent from the dining room to tuck it in. At recess Terry Roche and Griff Ryan were teasing Ian Stuart about his accent. Ian began to cry.

"Only babies cry," said Griff Ryan.

"Snot nose," said Terry Roche.

Ian swung at them and missed. Then he turned and ran away, and his tennis shoe came off. David grabbed the shoe and threw it in a mud puddle. Terry laughed. Ian looked at David. "Fine friend you are," he sobbed, then ran to recover his shoe. David shrugged. If he was going to be bad, he would just have to be bad.

That evening, during study hall, David was called into the headmaster's study. He was terrified. He could feel the crack of the Flexible Flyer already. He knew the system. "Assume the position," the headmaster would say, and then the victim would kneel on the floor, placing his head and arms and upper body on the cold leather couch.

He knocked on the door.

"Come in."

The headmaster sat behind a large mahogany desk smoking a cigar. He flicked ashes into an ashtray made from a horse's hoof. David had heard about the cigars too, how Mr. Armbrister had made boys who were caught smoking puff on one of his cigars until they were sick. Then they would never want to smoke again.

David stood in front of the desk trembling.

"Sit down, boy," said the headmaster without looking up. He was reading through some papers. David sat in a chair opposite the headmaster and waited. He thought of the parable of the talents.

"Remember boys," the headmaster had said, pounding his fist on the desk in front of the schoolroom, "that God requires no more from us than the use of the talents we have been given. The one-talent man is not required to get five back. But woe to the man who buries his talent in the ground. God has no love for shirkers."

David could feel the blow coming. He had been a shirker. He had buried his talent. He would receive his punishment.

"David," said the man. "Do you like to be called David?"

"Yes, sir," said the boy, trembling. This was strange.

"David," said the headmaster. "You're a pretty remarkable young man."

"Yes, sir," said the boy.

"And during the first semester you had the finest academic average in the third form. In fact, you had the highest general average in the third form. Punctuality, neatness, deportment all perfect."

Silence, a puff on the cigar.

"Now I have in front of me a report from Mr. Richardson about last night, a report from Mr. Langdon about breakfast this morning, and a report from Mr. Myers that you and Roche and Ryan were bullying Ian Stuart. It doesn't make sense."

He looked up and caught the boy's eyes with his own. For David this was new territory. He felt like a bird that has fallen from the nest and hurt its wing. He needed help.

"David," said the headmaster. "I'm not going to hurt you. Why did you do these things? They're not like you. What's happening, son?"

It was a different voice David heard, a voice kinder than the one that spoke in assemblies or the dining room. He would take a chance.

"If you're good," he said slowly, "nobody likes you."

"Ah," said the headmaster, "so that's it." He smiled, and all at once David felt better. He knew it was all right to talk, and the words began tumbling out.

"When I worked hard," the boy said, "I didn't have any friends. People teased me and called me teacher's pet and stuff like that. I don't know. I mean, it wasn't any fun."

"And now?"

"Now what, sir?"

"Is it fun now?"

"Kind of."

"Are you happy? Do you like what you're doing now?"

No answer.

"David," said the headmaster, "Mrs. Benzaquin says you haven't answered any questions in class for two days. Do you like that, not answering questions?"

"No. She kind of looks at me and then I feel guilty. So I look down at my books and then it isn't so bad."

"Why don't you answer questions?"

"Because Terry and Griff wouldn't like me if I did."

"Do they like you now?"

"Yes."

"Do you know why?"

"No."

He paused, flicked his cigar and leaned toward David. "Because they can control you. They can make you do what they want and they like that. You, my lad, are a very bright young boy. They want to drag you down to their level. I'm going to tell you something, and I want you to remember this the rest of your life. You'll never have a real friend if you sell yourself. They've got to take you the way you are. If they like that, fine. If they don't, you've got to find other friends that do. You're selling your soul. You're destroying yourself to be popular. Don't do it. You're too good for that."

"Yes, sir."

Then Mr. Armbrister did something that completely surprised David. He got up from the desk, walked around to where David was sitting, pulled up a chair, sat down beside him and began to talk like a — David didn't have one, but it seemed to him that Mr. Armbrister was talking to him like a brother. "You're a good one, David. You've got talent. You're gentle and wise. You'll have something to teach them someday. Don't forget it. Now, go on up to bed."

David hesitated. "Mr. Armbrister," he asked, "will I be punished?"

"You have been," said the headmaster. "Two marks for the dorm incident, one for coming to breakfast with your shirt tail out, and three for Ian Stuart. We don't tolerate bullying here. I think that's enough." Then a pause, and he added, "this time."

When he came out of the office, study hall was over and he slowly climbed the stairs to his dorm. He was very tired. His head ached and his legs felt heavy. He undressed and got into bed. He didn't want to see anyone or talk to anyone. Later, after the lights were out and Mr. Richardson had walked by, he began to rock, but he couldn't get the tune, and as his head went back and forth, back and forth there was no rhythm he could catch, only the darkness and then light as if a searchlight were shining on his face. He opened his eyes. Mr. Richardson was standing there and with him, Mrs. Armbrister.

"Are you all right, David?" she asked. "Are you sick?"

She was tall and pale in the dark there with her black hair pulled back, her eyes puzzled in concern. He remembered her smile by the door on the day school had opened. She touched his forehead.

"He doesn't seem feverish," she said.

"I'm all right," said David.

"Why were you tossing your head back and forth?"

"It helps me to get to sleep. It makes me tired," he said. He didn't want to talk about the music, the rhythm. They wouldn't understand.

"I don't think it's good for you, David," she said. Then she tucked in the covers, kissed him on the forehead and went away. Where had she come from? Why? Had Mr. Armbrister told her about their talk? Had Mr. Richardson called her? Had she gone back to Lowell House or was she in Mr. Richardson's apartment? He liked her. He would like to talk to her, but he didn't know how. Could he get up and call her back and tell her he was sick? It was too complicated. He lay in bed and waited for sleep to come. There would be no more rocking tonight, and he was too tired to think about what Mr. Armbrister had said. He would wait until morning.

In the morning he felt dizzy, and at breakfast he could not eat.

"Eat your eggs, Lear," said Mr. Langdon.

"I can't sir," said David. "I feel sick."

"Nonsense, boy."

He looked at the egg on his plate. The yolk was runny and the white had clear places where it had not been cooked. He could feel his stomach turning.

"Eat, Lear," said the voice, and he could feel the food rushing upward, and the tears, and then darkness.

When he woke up he was in the school infirmary in white pajamas with a red L on the pocket. Mrs. Armbrister was sitting by his bed smiling. "Well," she said, "it's nice to see you awake, David. You gave us a little scare."

David smiled back weakly. He looked at himself, at the bed and the white room. "How did I get here?" he asked.

"Mr. Langdon carried you up the stairs after you fainted."

He thought about being carried and how strange it was that he had been undressed by someone when he was asleep. He closed his eyes and felt the smoothness of the pajamas with the tips of his fingers. It was nice to do nothing, to be taken care of. After a while the door opened and a doctor came in to listen to his heartbeat and look at his throat and ears and take his blood pressure. He could feel the band tighten around his arm and the blood pumping fast and hard then more slowly as the band loosened.

"Am I all right?" he asked.

"You look pretty good to me, young fellow," said the doctor.

"Just tired and overwrought, I'd say. You just rest for a day or two before they send you back to the trenches."

The doctor left and Mrs. Armbrister kissed him on the forehead. "You just push that little button on the table if you need anything," she said. "Miss Lindsay is right outside. I'll check in on you later."

David closed his eyes. He hadn't been in a hospital for a long time, not since he was five. He didn't like to think about that time or the times before that when his mother had taken him to Norwalk to have his feet fixed. But lying here in the white bed in the quietness of the white room, he could not keep his mind from drifting to the long corridors and the doctors holding him down on the stretcher while they wheeled him into the operating room. "You promised," he heard himself saying. "You promised," and his mother's voice in the distance saying, "I'm sorry, Toots, I didn't know." He was high, high on a hill, and down below Gretel, wearing a pointed party hat, stuck her head out the window of the Green Plymouth. Elizabeth floated up toward him on angel wings, and his mother stood on the street corner in white overalls selling hot dogs.

He woke up in a sweat and for a moment he did not know where he was until he saw the church across the street and the town hall next to it. He pushed the button, and Miss Lindsay came in. She was short with glasses and frizzy black hair.

"I need to…" David had trouble getting the words out.

"To urinate or evacuate?" she asked.

"What?"

"Number one or number two?"

"Both, I think."

"Well, let's get out of bed and see if we can walk."

He put his legs tenderly on the floor, and she led him, one arm around his waist, out the door and across the hall. He felt better after a few steps.

"I'm all right now," he said.

"Well, don't go fainting again on us," she laughed, and let him go in the bathroom by himself.

Later she gave him juice and pills. "Drink it all down," she said. "You need your liquids. You boys just don't know how to take care of yourselves. What they need is some mothers around here."

By supper time he was hungry, but all she would give him was soup and crackers and more juice. "No solid food until tomorrow, the doctor says. That tummy of yours is a little tender right now." After supper Mrs. Armbrister came in and sat with him and talked about Lowell School. She had children, too, she said, a son who went to the school and a daughter who was just his age, and she knew how children needed mothering. She brought him playing cards with pictures of the Empire State Building on them and taught him how to play solitaire. When she left, she kissed him again, this time on the cheek.

It was hard for him to go to sleep. He was tired, but when he closed his eyes he would see long corridors with nurses and doctors rushing up and down and feel like he was falling. He didn't want to dream the hospital dream again, and he didn't want to think about his feet. He opened his eyes and looked out the window. It was dark. Under the streetlights near the town hall he could see some parked cars. A car came slowly toward him, the headlights making him close his eyes until it had passed. At the same time he heard the sound of a car door closing and the click of a woman's heels on the sidewalk. He opened his eyes, but he couldn't see anyone. She must be right next to the building, he thought. The sound stopped, then continued directly underneath him. A door opened and closed. His heart began to beat fast. Maybe it was his mother. They had called her in New York and she was worried. Or Elizabeth had come. Maybe they thought he was really sick and she was told to come right away. He lay down and listened for the sound of footsteps outside his room. It wouldn't take her long to get up the three flights to the infirmary. He waited. Five minutes. Still no sound.

When he was sick after the operations she always came, tearing into the parking lot of Norwalk Hospital in the Green Plymouth, cigarette hanging from her mouth. Sometimes he could see her from his window, and he would wave to her and she would hold up the bag with Howard Johnson ice cream, one of the thirty-eight flavors he had to guess before she would let him eat any. She was fun then and joked with the nurses and doctors. She tickled him and made him laugh and read him stories and lay on the bed beside him and said, "When I was a little boy..." And he would always fall for it, again and again.

"You couldn't be a little boy," he would say.

"Oh, yes I could," she would answer. "I was a little boy before I was a little girl."

"Oh," he would say, not quite believing, but never really sure she couldn't have been.

He slept long and hard. When he woke up it was morning, and he was hungry. His head felt clear, but when he got up to go to the bathroom, his legs were wobbly, "like a baby deer's," Miss Lindsay said. The doctor told him he could go back to classes in two days, but that he would be excused from sports "until you get your strength back, lad." David liked "lad." No one had ever called him "lad" before. The doctor ruffled his hair and told him not to worry so much. "Be good to yourself, lad," he said. "I'll see you tomorrow." After lunch Mr. Richardson came to see him and later Mrs. Benzaquin brought him a book called The Man in the Iron Mask which he read straight through from beginning to end, and when the time came for him to go back to classes he felt sad to leave the peace, the whiteness of the place. As he dressed to go, he could see out the window the boys with Primus ratings walking down to the village for ice cream. He would like that, a Primus rating, and weekends and trips to the village. He would work toward that.

He hadn't thought much about what Mr. Armbrister said, but now the headmaster's words came back to him clearly. If he was going to get a Primus, he had to do what Mr. Armbrister said. But that wasn't the point, was it? The point was that he had to do what he knew was right. But doing what he knew was right wouldn't get him any friends. So he would have to do without, at least until he could figure out how to do both, and that he couldn't do. It was too complicated.

For a week he was excused from sports, and he was glad for the chance to catch up on his work and read. One afternoon, while he was in the library, Mr. Hackett, the librarian, asked him if he'd like to play chess.

"I've never played, sir," said David.

"Well come on, then," said Mr. Hackett, "I'll teach you."

He was a funny little bald-headed man with a big mustache that twitched when he talked. The boys called him Rabbit.

"The thing about chess, my dear boy," he said, mustache twitching, "is that it is supremely logical. Nothing happens by chance. Lady Luck has no role in this game. Every move is calculated by the mover, and then counteracted by the next move of the antagonist. The winner is he who thinks farthest ahead, just as in battle, my dear boy."

Mr. Hackett taught history, had an apartment in Back Bay, and went in the summer to England, "the cradle of our culture, the nurse of our civilization, dear boy. We are all but Englishmen in exile." He would look sad and pretend to cry, then place his hand over his forehead for melodramatic effect.

David enjoyed both his conversation and the competition of the chess games. Their games continued even after David resumed sports. With a slip from Mr. Hackett, he could do his homework in the library instead of the school room. Chess was good for him. It gave his mind something to figure out, and he learned chess the way he learned mathematics, carefully, logically, and thoroughly. He learned what each piece could and could not do, and he learned how to work them together, castle and knight, bishop and queen, covering the diagonal squares from great distances to trap the fleeing king. During hobby time on Thursday evenings, he went to the chess club with Ian Stuart and began playing against the older boys. He learned from his mistakes and found that a move one boy did on him he could do on someone else.

He studied hard and stayed out of the way of Terry and Griff. For some reason they didn't bother him any more. No one really did. It was funny. Could Mr. Armbrister have said something to them when he was sick, or Mr. Richardson? He wondered.

He apologized to Ian Stuart. That was the most important thing, he thought. He went into Ian's alcove one night, and just said, "I'm sorry for what I did." Ian Stuart said nothing, but two days later he fell into step with David, and they walked to the gym together for operetta practice. Both of them were girls, chorus girls in flowered kimonos and black wigs. When they walked, they had to take tiny little steps, because that was the way Japanese girls were taught. He loved the rehearsals.

"It's because of Mrs. Rossiter," said Ian Stuart. "I've seen you looking at her."

David blushed. He did like her more than any other teacher. She was the choir director and the music teacher, and she was different from the others somehow. She was softer. Something about her made David want to go home with her. He thought of her at night before he went to sleep.

David wrote to his mother and to Elizabeth, asking them if they could come to the operetta. It would be in April, he said, as part of Founder's Day Weekend, when the students who had graduated from Lowell came back to visit. But they couldn't come. They had to work, "to make a goddam living," his mother had said once over Christmas vacation.

At school all the talk was about the war and about baseball. At the Saturday night movie in the gym there was always a cartoon and a newsreel before the picture. The war was almost over. The Allies were advancing into Germany, and soon the troops would be coming home. The great ballplayers — Williams and DiMaggio — were in the service, but they would be home soon, maybe even before the end of the season. Mr. Hackett was a Red Sox fan, and he promised to take David to a game at Fenway Park when Williams came home. He was the best hitter in history, Mr. Hackett said. He could see the stitches on the ball as it came up to the plate and knew whether it was a curve ball or a fast ball by the way that it spun. He had hit over .400 in 1941 and then gone off, like the others, to serve his country. He was in his absolute prime, and gave up his best years for the war effort. So did DiMaggio, the Yankee Clipper, the feared enemy of the Red Sox, the fisherman's son from San Francisco whose long beautiful strides covered the spacious outfield of Yankee Stadium like the ship he was named after. "Oh, what a rivalry that was," said Mr. Hackett, "and they'll be back soon."

Secretly, David liked the Yankees best, but he would never say that to Mr. Hackett. He had read Lou Gehrig: Pride of the Yankees and he had seen in the newsreels the part where Gehrig, who was dying of some disease David couldn't say the name of, stood on home plate in Yankee Stadium and said, "I consider myself the luckiest man on the face of the earth." He was dying of some strange disease, and he didn't even feel sorry for himself. He considered himself lucky. That made a great impression on David. He would never be a ballplayer like Gehrig or Ruth or the terrible Ty Cobb, who slid into second basemen with his spikes flying. But he could have character, like Gehrig, like DiMaggio. He could learn to stay calm and controlled and not throw his bat in disgust after he struck out. He could, in Mr. Armbrister's words, "develop character."

And one day the year was over, the whole school marching in their blue suits and white shirts and red Lowell School ties in the order that David knew so well now — from the schoolroom out the front door and across the lawn to the gymnasium to take their places in their designated rows, the same rows that they had filed into every Saturday night for the Saturday night movie. It was time for Prize Day Exercises. They stood at attention, hair combed, cow-licks plastered down with water or hair cream, shoes polished, handkerchiefs folded, listening and half-listening as Mr. Armbrister spoke the opening prayer. Then they sat down one final time on the brown benches to hear his words of wisdom to the graduating sixth formers and listen as the names of the prize winners were called out and the boys walked forward and up the stairs to shake the hand of the headmaster. It was his show, and he ran it with precision. Awards were given for neatness and punctuality, for athletics and for scholarship. "At the Lowell School," said Mr. Armbrister, "we give books rather than trophies. You can't read a cup."

"And for the highest academic average in Form Three — David Johnson Lear."

His heart beat so fast he could hardly walk, and he wondered if all the parents were watching his feet as he clumped down the aisle and up the stairs to the stage to receive the book from Mr. Armbrister. He beamed as he took his prize from the headmaster's hand.

"I see you followed my advice. Keep it up, lad. The Founder's Medal may be yours one day."

The words echoed in his head all the way to the station. It sounded wonderful. The Founder's Medal. To the Sixth Former with the highest general average. Yes, that was something to work for. He would like that very much, the gold medal hanging from the red and white ribbon around his neck.

"Well done, David," said Mr. Langdon, and handed him his envelope. That was the system. You got on the bus for the station, and were given your traveling orders. He opened the envelope, and read, "To be picked up at Bridgeport by grandparents." That was a new one, but it wasn't bad. It might even be fun.

And it was. They tucked him into the back seat of their sleek, white Chrysler and drove him down the Merrit Parkway over the Whitestone Bridge to Queens, then all the way out Long Island to Southampton, where they had rented a house at the beach for the month of June.

He showed his grandfather the book with the inscription inside the cover. "That's just fine, boy, fine," said the white haired-man, admiring the book. "Yes, indeed. That's the way to do it. Be number one. There's only one place that counts and that's first place. Number two is nobody. Remember that."

His grandfather was the sort of person who let you know where he stood. "Don't put too much salt on your food, boy," he would say at dinner. "You'll get hardening of the arteries when you're my age.

"When I was a young man, eighteen years old, my father gave me 25 dollars and told me to go make my living. In those days you had to work. Work, boy. None of this giveaway stuff by the great FRANKLIN DELANO ROOSEVELT."

He fairly boomed the words out. More than anything else David's grandfather hated Franklin Delano Roosevelt. "New Deal, shmew deal," he said. "Don't let anybody tell you different."

His grandfather was a Republican, and Republicans, David gathered, were for hard work. The Democrats, they were for giving everything away to everybody.

"Welfare, shmellfare," he would say, "It's just throwing money down the drain."

At breakfast they ate boiled eggs in egg cups. You clipped the top off the egg with a special pair of scissors, and then ate it with a very small spoon. They ate toast with English marmalade, and drank tea. It was the only place he was allowed to drink tea.

"Close your mouth when you chew, boy," his grandfather would say. "Don't they teach you any table manners at that fancy finishing school of yours?" And then before David could say anything he would answer, "No. They just let the pigs come up to the trough and slop it in with their hands." And he would laugh and laugh, and his face would turn red.

Every night, David and his grandmother would meet his grandfather at the train station, and sometimes they would drive to the club for cocktails and dinner, or maybe they would go back to the house for supper, and afterwards his grandmother and grandfather would go to the club to play bridge. David could stay home alone. He was old enough, and if he had a problem he could telephone. David loved to be alone in the house. Sometimes he would wander through the rooms, just touching things. He felt free when he was alone. He could sing songs from the operetta or make up plays, or he could listen to the radio. There was the Lone Ranger, with the galloping hoofbeats of the great horse Silver. "High-ho, Silver, away," shouted the masked-man with his deep voice, and you could picture the stallion thundering through the deep canyons of the old west. There was Jack Armstrong, All-American boy, which David didn't like nearly as much, because he didn't know what All-American meant. It was a funny word-all. You couldn't live in all America. And there was Henry Aldrich who was always getting into trouble, and Fibber McGee and Molly and Fred Allen and Jack Benny and Amos and Andy, which he didn't like because half the time he didn't understand what they were saying. And there were the mystery stories. Sometimes, he would lie in bed with the lights out and the covers tucked around his neck. "What evil lurks in the hearts of men? The Shadow knows." That was a good one, the Shadow, and the Thin Man, but the best was the Green Hornet. Maybe it was the music that he liked. Mrs. Rossiter had told him that the music was called "The Flight of the Bumblebee" by Rimsky-Korsakov, but it sounded like a car to him, and when he heard the music he could see the car, spinning at top speeds around dangerous curves on spine-tingling missions.

His favorite time was the time on the beach. He loved the ocean, the great curl of the waves coming in and in, always in, the wave going out being sucked up by the next wave coming in. He wondered what made waves and why they didn't stop, run down like a clock or something. He liked to walk out through the waves and then float there, waiting for a big one to pull him in and down, down into the sand while he held his breath and waited for the wave to release him. There was a lifeguard where he swam, and his grandparents let him go to the beach by himself as long as he stayed in the roped off area where the lifeguard sat in his high white chair.

One weekend his mother came, and on another Elizabeth. These were the best of all. They would ride the waves again and again until they were exhausted, and then lie together on the big orange and yellow beach towel. His mother or Elizabeth would put lotion on his legs and back and rub it in with their long, soft fingers. It was like old times, and he would forget for a while that they had moved to New York.

"I wish I could go back with you," he said to Elizabeth.

"I wish you could, too," she said. "But you're better off here. It's hot and sticky in the city, and I have to work all day and go back to a muggy room at night."

"Let's build a castle, Elizabeth," he said.

"Come on," she said. "You're too old for sand castles."

"No I'm not. Why is anybody too old for sand castles? Don't be a dumb grownup."

"What do you mean, dumb grownup?"

"You know what I mean. Grownups are always telling us to grow up, and look what they do."

She looked at him. "I guess you're right. Why should anybody be too old for sand castles?"

So they sat there in the wet sand near where the waves were coming and made turrets and bridges, a moat all around with tunnels for the water to go through into the inner moat and in the middle a huge tower like a birthday cake with a window for the princess to look out and down below a drawbridge with popsicle sticks for the prince. But as they finished, the waves came near, and David said, "The princess stood in the tower, looking over the depths of the sea…"

"And the great ocean waves came," said Elizabeth,

"And swept away the walls of the castle," said the boy, as the first wave hit the outer walls of the castle and splashed over them into the inner moat.

"And the prince came riding," said Elizabeth, "and took the princess away to higher ground, and as they stood and looked down, a wave came…"

"And buried the tower under its force," said David, and they watched as wave after wave leveled their work.

Then she said, "You know, you're going to camp in July."

"Nobody told me," he said.

"Well, you are. It'll be fun. They've got baseball and swimming and tennis and horseshoes and all sorts of stuff."

"Why do I have to go to camp? Why can't I stay here?"

"Because Grandma and Grandpa only have the house for a month. They can't afford any more. They have to go back to New York."

"I'd still rather go with you."

"I told you. You'd be miserable. You'll see, you'll like it."

He didn't.

It was called Camp Saugatuck, and they all had to pretend they were Indians. Meetings were called Pow-wows, and the head of the camp was called Big Chief…There were four houses with twelve boys in each house, and every house was called a wigwam, and each wigwam had the name of a tribe — Sioux, Cherokee, Iroquois, and Apache. Because David was new and one of the youngest boys he didn't have any feathers. You earned feathers by doing things, and as you got older and older and bigger and bigger you got more and more feathers, until, if you were real lucky, you could be a junior chief. That took forty-four feathers. His counselor was a junior chief named Tom Forrest, and he went to a college in New Jersey called Princeton. His Indian name was Runs-like-the-Wind, because he was the fastest runner of the counselors.

David could never seem to get any feathers. He got a white feather for chess and a green feather for swimming. He figured at that rate it would take him twenty-two years to become a junior chief, and he'd look kind of silly (he added it up, 22 plus 11 equals 33) going to camp at thirty-three even as a counselor. They wore their feathers at Pow-wows. During the day they wore blue shorts and red undershirts with a blue S with an arrow through it on the front. Once a week at Pow-wows around the campfire they wore their Indian leather vests and their headbands, and the Big Chief awarded the feathers of the week. Every boy had an Indian name, given to him after two weeks at camp. If you were an old camper, you kept your name from the year before, except if you didn't like your name, you could ask your tribe to change it. If the tribe voted in favor of the change, then you could get a new name given to you by the Big Chief. You would kneel down in front of everyone and the Big Chief with his headdress going down his back and his robe on would pass his wand over your head and pronounce some Indian lore and then give you your new name. David's name was Wooden Face, because no one ever saw him laugh or cry during the first two weeks. He didn't mind; it wasn't a bad name, and at least they didn't make fun of his legs or give him some sissy name like Bird Who Walks.

David thought all the Indian stuff was pretty corny, like calling the doctor the Medicine Man and the Big Chief's wife the Great Squaw, but it was all right. What he really hated were the rules. If they had eggs for breakfast, you couldn't leave the table until you finished your egg, no matter how awful it was. Sometimes they had fried eggs that were all runny on top like the one David had gagged on at school, and sometimes they had Cream of Wheat with big lumps in it. There were days when he would be sitting in front of his bowl or his plate in the dining hall long after everyone else had left, and it was only the kindness of the dietitian that got him out at all. After breakfast they all had to go back and make their beds and then go to the outhouse. They didn't have bathrooms. Each tribe had two outhouses, and every boy had to have a bowel movement after breakfast. If he didn't, then he was sent to the Medicine Man for a spoonful of Milk of Magnesia. It was humiliating; the counselor came and stood by the door and asked you if you'd done anything. David couldn't lie, because he'd turn red, and it was so obvious that he gave up the idea of even trying to lie after two times. There were rules about dress and where you could go and what you could do. There never seemed to be any time you could just relax. It was like walking on glass: one tiny mistake and you were cut.

Late in the summer they caught a snapping turtle in the lake and brought it to shore, the jeep dragging it by a great thick rope up to the square where the Pow-wows were held. The chief cut off its head with a great axe, chopping again and again with the axe almost bouncing off its thick rubbery skin. Before the head was gone, David had watched, fascinated, as the great turtle snapped sticks in half with its deadly jaws. The thought of a turtle like that lurking in the depths of the lake bothered David; what if it came into the swimming area? For days afterwards he watched for shadows in the deeper water as he swam carefully in the roped off area. He wished he were brave. He knew it was good to be brave, but he felt the clutch of fear in his stomach and he could not drive it away.

When the day came for camp to end, there was a grand final Pow-wow, and all the parents were supposed to come to watch the Great Feather Ceremony. David had won the camp chess championship and was to receive his red and blue feathers, and he sat in the Apache circle watching for his mother and Elizabeth in the rows of parents who gathered in the outer ring. The ceremonies began, and still they were not there. David continued to hope, but as each tribe rose to receive its final feathers, he grew less and less confident. The ceremony ended, and the young braves ran to join mothers and fathers, aunts and uncles. Then they walked to the softball field where the cars had been parked and loaded their duffel bags and bats and balls and rackets in the waiting mouths of the car trunks. The Big Chief told David that someone would come to get him the next day. It was Friday, and no one could get off work, so he watched the dust from the wheels and tried to memorize the numbers on the license plates as the cars wound their way down the dirt road toward Danbury and Hartford, Westchester County and New York. By supper time the camp was silent, and at dusk a water moccasin snaked its way across the beach, reclaiming the world for itself.

When someone did come to get him it was not his mother or his grandfather. It was Bernie. David was shocked. He hadn't seen Bernie since the summer before. What was he doing here now?

"Where's my mother?" asked David.

"She can't make it, Tiger," said Bernie, smiling. He was wearing shorts and tennis shoes and a Hawaiian shirt. His hair was cut short. It was like he wanted to dress for camp or something.

"Where's Elizabeth?"

"She can't make it either."

"Where's…?"

"Your grandad?" he interrupted. "I know. I sound like a crummy broken phonograph record. But he can't make it either. So get in the cab and I'll tell you on the way to the station."

Bernie put David's duffel bag and the suitcase with the "M.H." on it in the trunk of the cab, and they got in.

"Listen, David, I know you don't love me, and I know I was the last person you expected to see, but well, I'm going to be in charge of you for awhile, you know, until your mom and Lizzie get straightened out."

"What do you mean, straightened out?"

"Your mom's in the hospital having an operation."

"What kind of operation?"

"It's a woman thing."

"What kind of a woman thing?"

"Christ, you always did have to know everything. All right, it's called a hysterectomy. It's when the tubes, the uterus, you know the stuff you use to have babies, when that stuff gets bad and they have to take it out."

"Where is she?"

"She's at Bellevue Hospital in New York."

"Can I see her?"

"Not yet. Maybe later. You gotta be thirteen to visit in the hospital."

Another stupid grownup rule, David thought. The cab dropped them at the Wesport station, and they rode the local to New York.

"So what'd you think of the camp?" Bernie asked.

"Not much," said David. "Who picked it out?"

"Me and your mom. A lotta kids from here always went there."

"So where are we going now?" asked David.

"To my place."

"In Greenwich Village?" asked David.

"How'd you know that?"

"Elizabeth told me. She said you lived near her."

"Near where she used to live," said Bernie.

"What do you mean, 'used to live'?"

"She moved."

"Why didn't she tell me?"

"She asked me to tell you."

"Why didn't she tell me herself?"

"'Cause she's not around to tell you. She's in Georgia, at some island, on her honeymoon. She got married."

"When does school start?" the boy asked suddenly.

"What?"

"When does school start?"

"Tuesday."

"Good," said David. "Boy, will I be glad to get back to school."

He was mad, not so much at her doing it as her not telling, as her not asking him to come and be ring bearer. She promised. She had promised in the spring when she took him to her friend's wedding in the Village during spring vacation. She had promised when he watched the bride all in white walk down the aisle and her little brother following after with the ring on a cushion. She had promised, and he had dreamed of seeing her all in white with him standing next to her. It wasn't fair. For a long time he just stared out the window and didn't say anything. Then he turned back to Bernie, who was sweating even in his shorts and his Hawaiian shirt.

"Bernie? Where's my grandfather?"

"I don't know. In Saratoga Springs, maybe, or Vermont. Somewhere cooler than this."

"Bernie? Are you and my mother still married?"

"Nope."

"When you left, did that mean you weren't married any more?"

"You gotta wait a year."

David counted months. "Oh, I see." Then, "Well, if you're not married any more, why are you…"

"Doing all this?"

"I dunno. You might say, just for the hell of it."

David looked out the window some more.

"Bernie?"

"Yeah?"

"Since we're kinda stuck with each other, we might as well make the best of it, I guess."

"I guess so, Tiger."

"Shake on it?"

"Sure."

Still he was mad. "Damn Elizabeth," he said to the window. "Damn Elizabeth."

# CHAPTER
## *six*

*D*AVID WATCHED OVER Mr. Langdon's shoulder as the master carefully filled in the weekend check-out sheet:

"Destination?"

"New York."

"Mode of transportation?"

"Train."

"Person with whom you are staying?"

"My mother." The boy fairly beamed.

Mr. Langdon looked up and smiled back. "That's wonderful," he said.

"My first weekend," said David proudly.

"You've earned it," said the master. "Have a great time, and don't forget to check out and check in with whoever's on the desk. The school station wagon will take you to Framingham Friday at 12:30 and meet your return train on Sunday at 5:45."

"Thank you, sir," He stepped down from behind the desk and returned to his seat in the study hall. He was a fourth former now, and his seat was almost halfway back, opposite the center of the window that looked out over the playing fields. David could see his reflection in the glass as he sat down, and he smiled at the rating badge newly sewn on his pocket. He had earned a Secundus, and he was entitled to take a weekend. So he had decided to go to New York. He had written his mother telling her what train he would be on, and he had planned the weekend in his mind.

They would walk through the great room at Grand Central and look at the stars on the ceiling, and then he would buy a comic book — Superman, Captain Marvel, or the Phantom — from one of the newsstands on the long corridor that led to the subway. Next, down the stairs and through the turnstiles, and a dash for the front of the train where he could stand looking out the window into the dark tunnel watching the signals turn from yellow to green and waiting for the lights of the next station to appear. Then they would get off at 86th Street, and the three theatres would be there — the R.K.O., the Loews, and the Grand. He would decide which movie he wanted to see, and she would take him, or he would go by himself on Saturday afternoon when they had the matron on duty. He wouldn't talk to strangers. He was tougher now. He had gone to the movies over Christmas the year before and had turned his back and ignored them when some older boys tried to talk to him.

Saturday night they would go out for dinner and have steak and French fries, and maybe she would take him downtown to the Radio City Music Hall to see the Rockettes, like Bernie had when he stayed with him at the end of the summer. Maybe they would go to the arcade in Times Square with the pinball machines and the baseball machine where you could swing at the ball.

"David!"

He felt a hand on his shoulder.

"You better get some work done," Mr. Langdon said. "It's only Wednesday."

"Yes, sir," he said. He pulled out his Latin book. Mr. Langdon was his Latin teacher.

❧

The boy sleeping across the aisle from him on the train was Daniel Humphrey, one of the most popular sixth formers. David liked his clothes — gray flannel trousers, a blue button-down shirt, striped tie, tweed jacket and dirty white buck shoes. David kept looking at the shoes, as Humphrey slept, head tucked against the window, feet against the aisle arm rest. Maybe he could wear shoes like that now. Maybe the doctor would tell him he could wear regular shoes. Yes, he would talk to his mother about that. She could take him to the shoe store, and he would try on some white bucks, and see how badly they slid up and down on his Achilles tendon.

It was his eighth trip on the train, and he was beginning to learn the stations: Worcester, Springfield, New Haven, Bridgeport, Stamford, New York. That was six. He had left one out; there were seven stops. What was it? Oh…Hartford. You could tell Hartford by the big Remington sign; some one had told him that they made Remington rifles there. He loved to look out the window and try to read the names of the stations they passed without stopping. There were strange, hard names like Mamaronek, and easy ones like Rye. Port Chester was where the three gigantic rolls of Life Savers were suspended from the walls of what he supposed to be the Life Saver factory. He remembered Mount Vernon and Botanical Gardens, which was just a fancy word for zoo, or was it something else?

At Springfield, Humphrey woke up, and when the train pulled into Hartford, the older boy got up and sat down next to David.

"Slide on over, Dave," he said. "The train always fills up here, and we'll both end up sitting next to fat old ladies if we don't sit together."

David laughed. He liked Humphrey. He didn't really know him very well, but Humphrey always said hi to him in the halls. He was Vice-President of the Reds and sang baritone in the choir.

"Where you going?" Humphrey asked.

"New York. What about you?"

"Stamford."

"Is that your home?"

"It sure is. It's Homecoming Weekend at the high school, and my brother Jack is coming home, too. We're gonna see some of our old friends, catch the big game, have a good time. What about you?"

David answered him easily. There was something about Humphrey that made him feel at home. Most of the time at school David kept things to himself. It was too hard to explain about his father in California and his mother and Bernie and Elizabeth all living separately in New York. It was easier to be quiet. But somehow on the train with Humphrey he felt safe. He told the older boy his plans for the weekend, and the two of them talked about movies and baseball and girls.

"You ever kissed a girl?" Humphrey asked the younger boy.

"Who me?" The boy looked at Humphrey incredulously. "Oh no, but you have, I bet."

"I guess I have," the older boy said knowingly. "I sure have."

"What's it like?" asked David.

"What do you mean, what's it like?"

"You know, what's it feel like to kiss a girl?"

"Well," said Humphrey, "it depends on whether the girl kisses you back. It's no fun to kiss a girl and have her just stand there with dry closed lips looking at you like you're a jerk. She's got to want it, too."

David wanted to go on, but he didn't know what to ask next. He really knew nothing about girls. He actually didn't know any girls except for Marion Fisher, who had lived across the street from him in Westport. He and Marion had played together as friends, but he had never really thought of her as a girl. He closed his eyes for a while and listened to the click of the wheels against the tracks.

At New Haven "Cashew Nuts," or "Cashews" for short, boarded the train, and his visit was invariably a high point of every trip. Nobody knew or even seemed to want to know his real name. He was a slight, little man with a hooked nose and a gray Union News uniform; the Lowell boys persecuted him mercilessly when he entered the car with his silver basket full of candy and nuts and comic books, but his eyes never ceased to sparkle and his wit was a match for the sharpest barbs. He had earned his name by always ending his spiel with a rousing cry for the purchase of cashews. "Vell, vell, so dey let di monkeys out a da zoo for da veekend. How about some nize cashew nuts for da monkeys?"

"Christ, Cashews," said Humphrey when he heard him. "That joke is as old as Methusaleh, and about as stale as your damned cashews."

David laughed.

"Hey you, leetle vun. Vy you laugh at him? You seenk he be funny to make fun of his elders?"

David's face grew red. He was laughing so hard now that tears began to come from his eyes. He hadn't laughed like this in ages, and he really didn't know what was so funny, but he just couldn't control himself. Cashews and Humphrey continued to talk, but he couldn't really follow what they were saying. Cashews started on down the car with the familiar cry, "Hershey bars, chewing gum, peppermints, cashew nuts. Get your nize fresh cashew nuts." He was marvelous, old Cashews, thought the boy. He was always the same, and he never disappointed you.

Stamford came, and Humphrey had to leave. The two boys exchanged promises to recount their weekend experiences on the return trip. David watched him as he sauntered confidently down the aisle and out the door, then returned to his window vigil. He tried to do what Mrs. Armbrister told him to do. "You're too tense," she had said. "You're a wonderful boy. You work hard and you play hard, and you give a hundred percent effort to everything you do. But there are times when you just have to relax and enjoy yourself, let yourself go." Well, it was easy enough to say it, but it was something else to actually do it. He took a deep breath, exhaled slowly, and began to watch the stations, but already thoughts of Monday's homework assignments began to intrude. He should have brought some books, but when he had packed on Thursday night, he had been determined to make this a weekend of pure enjoyment. If his mother had to work on Saturday, he would read comic books and listen to the radio. He'd show Mrs. Armbrister that he knew how to relax.

"Grand Central Station. Everybody out. Grand Central Station." He was already in line, bag in hand, when the train stopped. He edged his way forward and out the door until he felt the freedom of the platform, then accelerated almost to a trot as he weaved through the crowds of people, up the ramp to the gate, and literally burst from the dimness of the track into the bright light of the waiting room. His eyes swept the area like a camera focusing on each of the women who might be his mother. She would be wearing her beige polo coat. He looked for the brown eyes and the dark hair, curled at the neck.

He sat on a bench to wait. She was not there. He looked at the clock on the far wall; it was a little after 6:30, the height of the rush hour. If she'd taken a taxi it was probably stuck in a huge snarl only a few blocks from the station. She'd had to get out and walk, and would be there in a few minutes. The subway was horrible at this hour. He remembered times when a train had to sit between stations for fifteen minutes. Or maybe someone had been hurt and his mother had to help him. He looked at the clock — 6:45. Then he thought — maybe she is waiting for me someplace else. He tried to remember the wording of his last letter. He had written, "Meet me in the waiting room." That was it. Instead of coming to the track, she had gone to the waiting room, the large room filled with benches upstairs near the 42nd Street entrance. He had walked through that room before; it was filled with cigarette smoke and sleeping old men. He debated. If he went there, she might come to the track while he was in the waiting room; then she might think he hadn't come. He looked at the clock again; it was 7:00, he would have to risk it. He picked up his bag and hurried down the hall under the archway into the big domed, star-covered main hall. He took the stairs up two at a time, then turned left through the swinging doors into the waiting room. He walked down one aisle and back the next, peering anxiously at the figures seated on the benches. God, how he wanted one of them to be her. He had not cried in a long, long time, but he could feel the tears beginning, and he took deep breaths trying to bring himself under control. She was not there.

Now it was 7:30, and David sat on the bench by the same gate through which he had burst so happily an hour ago. He looked at the telephone booths across the hall. Of course, why hadn't he thought of it before; he would call her; she was tied up at the hotel and was assuming that he would call her when he got in. With renewed hope he dialed.

"Good evening. Victory Hotel."

"Is Mrs. Petersen there?"

"Just a moment please." David could hear the voice in the background. "Hey, Harry, you know where Maggie is?" He could not hear the response.

"I'm sorry. Mrs. Petersen is out for the weekend."

"Are you sure? This is her son, David. Isn't there a message for me or something?"

There was no message. He hung up and lay his head against the telephone box: for a moment he could do nothing, absolutely nothing. He neither cried nor thought; he felt only numbness. He got up and walked slowly back to the bench by the gate. At least that was familiar. Humphrey would have said, "Shit," David thought; but he wasn't mad, only sick. Then he remembered Elizabeth.

He zipped open the bag with the familiar "M.H." on it and rummaged through his clothes, looking for the letter. It was in the pocket of his other jacket, laid out neatly on the bottom. He pulled it out. Even the name looked strange. "From Mrs. Philip O'Donnell, 233 W. 115th St., NYC." He read the letter.

> *Dearest David,*
>
> *I know you're mad at me, but I couldn't help it and someday I will explain it all to you, when you're older. Please believe me that I didn't want to go off without telling you. Do you remember Phil from Westport? He's the redheaded piano player that used to come pick me up when I was in high school. The one you used to ask why he had spots on his skin? Anyway, I want you to come see us when we're settled. . .*

He kept reading. There it was, the number. He walked back across the echoing stone floor to the phone booth. He dialed slowly, one eye always on the area around the gate, just in case.

"Hello?" It was Elizabeth.

"Elizabeth?"

"David? My God, what's the matter? You sound awful."

For a moment he could not talk at all. The tears began, and he could not stop them.

"David? Where are you?"

"I'm...I'm...in...Grand...Central." The boy tried to stop, tried to get his voice under control.

"Why aren't you in school?"

"I came...on the...train. Mommy was...supposed to...meet me."

"Oh, Jesus."

"She…she…never came."

"David, just calm down and listen. Where are you?"

"By…Track 32."

"You just stay there, and I'll be down as fast as I can. O.K.?"

"O.K."


Thirty minutes later it was not Elizabeth but her husband he saw walking toward him. Phil was tall and strong and walked with big strides. He seemed angry.

"Let's go, David," he said. "It's getting late."

And they set off, not down the long hall with the newsstands, but in a different direction to a train called the Shuttle which took them to Times Square, and then they followed the green lights to another train called the Broadway Express which took them uptown past 86th Street to 96th and 110th and then 116th. COLUMBIA UNIVERSITY the sign said. They got off, and walked down the hill toward the Hudson River. Then Phil turned into a small doorway on the left-hand side. It smelled of cabbage. They walked up a flight and Phil put his key in the lock of Apartment 2A. They went in.

Elizabeth was sitting, reading a book on the couch by the window. Behind her, through the window David could see only the grimy wall of another building. Her eyes brightened when they came in the door, but she didn't get up.

"Come over here, sweetheart," she said, "and give me a hug. I don't know what's the matter with me. I'm so tired I can't seem to get any energy."

David sat on the couch next to her.

"You like it?" she asked.

It was a combination living room-dining room-kitchen, with a tiny stove, sink, and refrigerator tucked into an alcove against the wall by the door.

"The back room's our bedroom and Phil's workroom. He's got his piano back there so he can do his arranging while I'm out here cooking or reading. When the baby comes, I guess we'll have to move the piano out here."

"You're having a baby?"

"Didn't I tell you? I guess that's why I'm so tired. In another month or two I'll be able to feel the baby kick. When you come down for Christmas, I'll let you feel him too."

David just put his arms around her and hugged her.

"Hey," she said after a while, "I bet you're hungry. I bet you haven't eaten."

She got up slowly like something was wrong.

"I'm so lightheaded, sometimes. I get up and my head just swims. I feel like the baby's taking all my strength."

She fixed him a bowl of spaghetti and meat balls, "Franco American, your favorite," she smiled. He ate it with some bread and butter, while she smoked and talked, and when he was finished she gave him some canned pears and cookies. Phil went in the back room to work.

"I would have invited you, honestly, David, but we didn't even have a real wedding. It was just a justice of the peace. We just decided all of a sudden to get married, and you were at camp, and there was no time to make plans." She took a long drag on her cigarette and tapped it on the edge of the chipped ashtray.

"It's O.K., Elizabeth," he said, but it wasn't. After a while Phil came out from the back room, and then Elizabeth went in there with him, and David could hear them talking. Then she came out with some sheets and a blanket and made up the couch into a bed, while he brushed his teeth in the bathroom and put his pajamas on. He climbed into the bed and she kissed him, turned off the lights, and went back into the other room.

He looked out the window. There was nothing you could see but the wall of the building next door. He wondered what he should do next. It was tricky with grownups. If you said the wrong thing or did the wrong thing then they just got mad and you were stuck. He wondered if he should ask about his mother. Maybe they would telephone her in the morning, and she would come get him, or maybe Phil would take him over there. But they said at the hotel she was away for the weekend. Maybe she had never gotten his letter. Maybe she didn't know he was coming and went away. He wouldn't ask Phil about it. He looked stern, like Mr. Mulligan, like he was busy and had better things to do than worry about David's mother. He would ask Elizabeth, in the morning, when she was feeling better. Things were always better in the morning.

In the morning, when he woke up, Phil was gone and Elizabeth was sitting at the kitchen table reading the newspaper.

"Hi, sleepy," she said. "It's almost ten o'clock."

He got dressed and ate a bowl of Wheaties. On the box was a picture of Ted Williams in his army uniform. He had helped America win the war, and in the spring he would be back in another uniform — a Red Sox uniform. The war in Europe had ended in May, when Hitler had killed himself in his secret bunker. Mr. Armbrister had announced it at assembly, and "in honor of our brave boys," he said, all the churchbells in the town would ring for five minutes. While the bells rang the boys were to stand silently and give thanks. But the war wasn't really over, he had said, because the Japanese would not give up. It was not until August that the Japanese surrendered, and that was only because of the atomic bomb, which had been dropped on the cities of Hiroshima and Nagasaki. David had no idea what the atomic bomb was until he got back to school in September and they had shown newsreels of the explosion, the largest explosion that had ever taken place in the history of the world. Afterwards in his mind he saw over and over the mushroom shaped cloud, growing higher and higher, and the terrible faces of the people whose homes had been destroyed in an instant. Mr. Armbrister said it was good, because it saved thousands of American lives, but Mr. Langdon thought it was wrong.

While David ate, Elizabeth bustled around, taking the sheets and blankets off his bed and sweeping the floor.

"Phil likes it neat," she said.

Then they went walking up Riverside Drive toward Grant's tomb and back down Broadway and through the Columbia University campus. On the steps of a gigantic library they threw peanuts to the pigeons.

"Listen, David," she said. "I called the hotel this morning, and they don't know where Mommy is. I don't know if she got your letter or not, but I think you ought to know that, well, she's sick. She's not always in control of herself. Sometimes she forgets things. I think it's better if you don't do this again. Just write Bernie or me if you want to take a weekend.

"Poor kid," she said, running her fingers through his hair. "I know it's hard to understand. It's just that our lives are a lot more complicated than you think. We don't want to hurt you."

In the afternoon they played Monopoly. Phil was banker, and after about an hour Elizabeth went bankrupt.

"Here," she said, "you take my property, David."

"You can't do that," said Phil.

"I can if I want to," said Elizabeth. "It's my property. If I want to give it to David, I can."

"It says in the rules if a player goes bankrupt, he must return his property to the bank."

"Well, smell the rules," said Elizabeth, and she stood up and threw her property in Phil's face and ran into the other room and slammed the door.

"It's the baby," said Phil and followed her.

For a long time they stayed in the other room, while David picked up the cards from the floor and put all the pieces back in the proper compartments. When they came out they were smiling. They all ate dinner together, and David went to bed early.

On Sunday morning, Phil took him to the train. The subway was almost empty, and as they rode downtown, he talked.

"Look, David, I'm telling you this now, well, because your sister loves your mother so much that she can't see her faults. She isn't going to tell you the truth, because she doesn't want to think about it, but the fact is your mother has a drinking problem and that's probably why she didn't meet you. She just can't be counted on. She is just not the sort of person you can rely on. I know you don't want to hear that, but it's true, and I'm telling you for your own good. I don't want you hurt by her again. Just stay up there at your school. You're better off."

As the train emerged from the tunnel at 96th Street David began to look intently out the window. He watched the apartment houses along the tracks with the laundry hanging out and the brown faces gazing at the trains. He wondered what it must be like to live in a place like that with the trains going by all day and all night and the streets so dirty and the windows broken. It was not until the train was well out in the country that he remembered Humphrey. The older boy would be getting on at Stamford, and he would have to tell him something about his weekend. He could always lie, he supposed, and make up something he had done, but he did not like to lie and he was not very good at it. Usually he blushed or stammered until the other person found him out. He'd just have to wait and see; certainly there was no need to tell everything.

David pressed his head to the window as the train slowed for Stamford. He could see Humphrey just ahead on the platform arguing with a man. The man, tall with graying sideburns under his hat, pointed his finger at Humphrey's chest. Humphrey threw up both arms, turned around and stepped aboard. David looked toward the front of the car; a moment later Humphrey appeared, all smiles. He saw David.

"Hey, kid, how ya doin'?" He yelled down the length of the car. "Man, what a weekend, what a weekend!" He eased himself down into the seat and stretched. "I could sure use some sack, kid." But he was not ready for sleep yet. He began to talk. "You know Jack, my brother. I told you about him, well, Saturday night we went downtown to the flicks and took in a double feature. It must've lasted 'til midnight. You remember that one we had at school where what's-his-name — Randolph Scott — plays the Marine sergeant who steals a steam roller and then comes roaring in and plows through all these bamboo huts, smashing up everything and shootin' Japs with his machine gun? Well, the one last night was just like it 'cept it was John Wayne and 'stead of a steam roller, it was a big caterpillar tractor, and 'stead of Japs it was Germans."

He stopped to take a breath. David loved it. "What was the other one?" he asked.

"The other one was even better. It was about this guy who was hunting, and he ended up in this kingdom called...Zenda. That's it. Prisoner of Zenda. And the king is sick and can't go to his coronation-so this guy who is out hunting has to pretend he's the king so that the bad guys won't take over the country, and he has to play the king, has to, you know, actually be king 'till the real king recovers. There's a great sword fight at the end."

Humphrey was in high gear now. "Then afterwards we went to Sammy's, that's the place where all the high school guys go, for hamburgers and milkshakes; and then we snuck home real quietly and tiptoed upstairs and talked and talked 'till I don't know what time we fell asleep."

David savored the milkshakes and the hamburgers and tried to picture the scenes in the movies and wondered what it would be like to have a brother to talk to.

"What about Friday night?" David asked.

"Oh shit," said Humphrey. "Friday night was great, too. Jack and I went to some girl's house for a party after the game. I saw this girl across the room, and I said to myself, 'I know this girl,' and went up to her and introduced myself and she said, 'Dan, you don't remember me, do you?' And it turned out to be Cindy McGregor, who I'd gone to grade school with, and she'd changed so much I didn't even recognize her. It's like...you know..." and he made the motions of curves with his hands.

"Did you kiss her?" asked David.

"Did I kiss her? 'Course, I kissed her good. Listen, Davey, I'm gonna give you a little free advice. When you kiss a girl, you know when you get a little older, just remember don't kiss her like she was your mother or your sister."

Humphrey made a kind of peck with his lips. "None of that stuff. You gotta open your mouth and kind of taste each other's lips real slow."

That was a new sensation for the boy. Somehow kissing with his mouth open seemed strange, and he wasn't at all sure he wanted to taste someone's lips.

"Now, David," said Humphrey. "Tell me what you did."

"Who me?" said the boy.

"You and your mom have a good time?"

David tried to speak. "I…uh…well, she…"

Humphrey changed his manner. Suddenly his voice became quiet, gentle.

"Something went wrong. Is that it?"

"Yes."

"You want to talk about it?"

"I don't know."

"You don't have to, but sometimes it's better. It's no good keeping it all inside."

"My mother," David began. "She never came."

"So you didn't see her 'till later?"

"I never saw her the whole weekend."

"Jesus. So what'd you do?"

"I stayed with my sister."

"Did you go out or anything?"

"No."

"Nothing at all?"

"Nothing at all."

They did not talk for a long time, but David did not mind the silence. He was trying to think out what had happened, and Humphrey seemed content to close his eyes and doze. Elizabeth said his mother "forgot things." Phil said she was "just not the sort of person you could rely on." She was sick. She had a drinking problem. David knew about the drinking in Westport and he could see the bottle of Seagram's on the little table next to her bed in the hotel. Sometimes the liquor made her voice slur, and sometimes it made her happy and she would hug him and call him "precious baby" and cry and then wipe her eyes and send him out of the room until she could "get herself together." But she wasn't always like that. Sometimes she didn't drink at all, and in the mornings at the restaurant she seemed fresh and happy, and the customers liked her and laughed at her stories. "Maggie Hope," she would say, "that's me. Down but not out. Down for nine, and always up for one more time." Maybe it was the operation that she had. He hadn't seen her since then. Maybe it did something to her. And then there was Elizabeth. She just wasn't the same. Grownups made such messes of their lives.

He looked out the window for a while. Then he had a thought.

"Humphrey, you awake?"

Humphrey grunted.

"Do you mind if I call you Dan?"

"Help yourself," he said, opening his eyes.

"You know what?"

"No, what?"

"I decided something just now."

"What?"

"I'm glad I'm going back. I mean I'm really glad."

"Why?"

"Well, that's what I just figured out. You see, grownups are kind of messed up. That's why we go to school! At school everything's O.K. You don't have to worry. You know when to work and when to do sports. Everything is…well…planned, so you don't have to wonder what's going to happen next. Everything is O.K."

Humphrey opened his eyes. "You're a smart boy, David," he said. "I know I made my weekend sound terrific, but it was only because Jack was home. He kind of looks after me. My mom doesn't care what I do, and I didn't even see my dad 'til breakfast this morning, and he drives me to the station. Big deal! Then he gives me a a lecture about working harder and getting good grades. Hell, he doesn't even know who I am. Why do you think I'm at this school, anyway? They just don't want me around."

There was silence now except for the clack of the wheels on the rails. Then David spoke:

"Hey, Dan, where's Cashews?"

"Today's Sunday. He doesn't work on Sunday."

"Oh." There was a pause; then David spoke again.

"Hey, Dan."

"Yeah?"

"I feel better now."

"Me too."

"You want to play cards?"

"Sure."

"What'll we play?"

"You know how to play poker?"

"No."

"Well Christ, if you're ever gonna grow up, you gotta learn how to play poker. Come on. I'll teach you right now."

# CHAPTER
## *seven*

STAY UP THERE at that school of yours," Phil had said. David took him seriously. He spent Thanksgiving at the school with the handful of other students who lived too far away to go home or who hadn't been invited somewhere. He liked it. There were only a dozen of them, and they sat for their meals at the head table, decorated with paper pilgrims made from magazines in art class and cardboard turkeys with orange heads. Mrs. Armbrister fussed over them and Mr. Armbrister told them stories about the war. He loved to talk about the war, and he almost seemed sorry that it was over. Most of all he loved Rommel and Patton, and he told stories of their tank battles in North Africa and Patton's speed in marching his troops across Germany. "He would have gone straight to Moscow," the burly headmaster said, "but Eisenhower wouldn't let him." Armbrister took the salt cellars and the pepper shakers and forks and spoons and placed them in various positions in front of his plate. He moved them here and there, illustrating first the German tactics and then the American. He showed how Patton had marched his 3rd Army across France fast enough to save the day in the Battle of the Bulge. "One of the greatest feats in military history," said Armbrister, using his napkin to make the bulge that the Germans had poured through.

"Was Patton the greatest general in the war?" asked a small boy in glasses to David's right.

"I certainly think so," said the headmaster, smiling.

"And who was the worst?" asked Ian Stuart, whose family had moved back to Scotland.

"Oh, Montgomery, without a doubt," said Mr. Armbrister. "He practically ruined the whole D-Day invasion."

Ian Stuart blushed, and the small boy in glasses said, "My father told me that Patton slapped a soldier in Italy. He said Patton had a terrible temper."

"Nonsense, lad," bristled the headmaster. "Nothing but a bunch of lies. He was a strong disciplinarian. Slackers always hated him, and made up stories about him."

On Friday night after dinner he gathered the boys by the fire in Lowell House and read them a ghost story. He was a great ghost story reader, and more than once in the library with all the lights off except the one light with its eerie green shade by which he was reading he had made the younger boys scream with terror. This time, as the fire crackled and the wind outside blew, he read "The Monkey's Paw." David would never forget it. It was like you were in the story — the fire and the wind in the story just like the fire in the Lowell House living room, and the lights all out except the small lamp, and the hand, the Monkey's Paw, thrown in the fireplace, and then removed. David could see the hand with its tiny, grotesque fingers, and the wishes, the three wishes, the second one the most terrifying. The son, dead, then resurrected by the second wish, marching toward the house, coming closer and closer to the door. David could see the mangled body of the son in his mind as the mother opened the door — to nothing, just emptiness, because the father had used the third wish to return him to his sleep in death.

That night in the nearly empty dorms it was hard to sleep as the now barren branches of the trees blew back and forth in the November wind, making strange figures against the street light. David kept seeing the paw, crawling out of the fire across the floor of the house as if it had a will of its own, as if no matter what you did to it, it would keep living, keep crawling.

In the morning he played chess with Mr. Hackett, and told him about the story.

"Oh, yes," said the librarian, twitching his mustache like the rabbit he was always called. That part David understood, but the other part made no sense to him. Terry Roche kept calling him "the sick rabbit." Why was he sick? David could see how Mr. Hackett wiggled his nose like a rabbit, but if he was sick, David certainly didn't see what the sickness was.

"It's too bad about that family of yours, Lear," said the librarian. "A lad needs a bit of order in his life. And by the way, watch the white bishop. You'll lose her if you don't."

David concentrated on his move.

"What you need, my boy, is some friends. I mean, after all, a lad can't stick to his mum and his sister forever. He has to have friends his own age."

David knew that. The problem was how to get them.

"The thing is," said Mr. Hackett, "to slow down a bit. Don't be driving yourself so hard. Take time to see people. And by the way," he added with a smile and quick cross of his castle, "Check-mate."

"My mother called it my demon," thought the boy. "Every time I get close to somebody, then I lose my temper."

There had been Bobby Carlton who played goalie for the Harvard soccer team. David liked him. They warmed up together, and when Bobby got tired of playing goalie, David let Bobby kick some at him. They began dressing together in the locker room and walking up after practice and taking showers together. Bobby was nice. He didn't tease him about his feet or make jokes about his family. Then one day in a game David lost his temper. The score was tied 1-1 with just a few minutes to go, and there was a loose ball in front of the Harvard goal. David kicked it, but his aim was poor and he drove it straight into the arms of Bobby Carlton. He was furious at himself. He hurled his body at the goalie, smashing him, the ball, and himself into the nets.

"Goal," he yelled triumphantly, "goal, goal."

He felt a hand on the back of his neck, lifting him up. It was Mr. Myers.

"Get off the field, and stay there until I tell you to come back," he said.

David sulked off and brooded and watched the game end and

the players run up the hill to the locker room. Then Mr. Myers walked over to him.

"You know that was a foul, a deliberate, flagrant foul, David," said the man, "Why did you do it?"

David was silent.

"You know, David, we adults are not ignorant," he said. "You think that we don't understand, but give us a little credit. I know how badly you want to win. I know how important success is to you. I haven't taught you in math for two years for nothing. I also know about your family situation. Look at me, David."

The boy lifted his head and looked at Mr. Myers' face. It was a kind face, and there was no desire to hurt in the eyes.

"If you keep on like this," said the man, "you'll destroy yourself. You'll have no friends, and no one will help you celebrate if you do win."

And so he tried, tried to check the urge to win, the need to be first, but it drove him, and night after night he rocked his head in the dark until the silence came inside and he could sleep. In the morning he was the first one up, the first to the bathroom, the first to be dressed and standing in front of his alcove curtain for inspection, the first down to breakfast. In June, Alden Clifford had won a prize for not being late to anything for three years. David was determined to break his record. He would have a perfect record for four years. All he had to do was be careful. That was the thing. You couldn't be careful and relax at the same time, and if you couldn't relax, you couldn't have friends.

Except for the friend business, things were better this year, David thought. With a Secundus rating you could go downtown on Saturday afternoons and buy candy and comic books at the Southborough Soda Shop. His feet were better, too, and he no longer had to wear the high top shoes which Terry and Griff had teased him so about his first year. He was also in the Student Council, appointed by the headmaster as the representative of the fourth form. There were ten on the Council, the three color officers for the Reds and the Whites and one representative for each of the lower forms. David didn't say very much at the Council meetings — it was mostly the headmaster and the sixth formers who did the talking — but he liked being there in the headmaster's study with its soft leather chairs, its walls of books, and the huge antlered deer head that resided over Mr. Armbrister's desk.

The Council helped plan school events like Founder's Day and Winter Weekend, but most important they helped the headmaster decide on appropriate punishments for those who had been caught smoking or stealing or those who had received more than ten marks in a term. They were also required to witness the punishment when "swats" were awarded. They stood in two lines on either side of the infamous couch, and the victim, who had been marched into the headmaster's office and asked if he had anything to say before punishment was administered (he almost never did), was then asked to walk through the two lines and "assume the position." Mr. Armbrister delivered the swats with gusto.

If the boys were brave, it wasn't so bad, David thought. There was something fine about taking your punishment — what was the word Mr. Langdon had used? — "stoically," that was it. It meant "calmly," "without passion." But the crying, the red eyes, the snot coming from the nose, the screaming and struggling, the color presidents holding the victim down sometimes — that was awful. David hated to see the boys who had been paddled afterwards. He avoided them as if he shared the guilt of what the headmaster and the Council had done.

Then in December, about ten days before Christmas vacation, something terrible happened — Terry Roche was paddled. David admired Terry and Griff. Terry was a great athlete, and Griff was funny. David was neither. He really wanted to be friends with them, but he didn't know where to start, and being appointed to the Council only made things worse. "Ass licker," Terry said under his breath to David one day as they were all walking from math to English. "That's what your damn student council is — a bunch of ass lickers, helping Armbuster do his dirty work."

Another day Terry had whispered, "He likes beating little boys."

So, when Terry was hauled in before the Council, it frightened David. Terry was brave — of course, Terry would be brave. David had no doubt about that, and David only admired him more for his stoic courage. That wasn't it. It wasn't even whether Terry deserved it. He had sassed a teacher, and that was automatic swats. It was afterwards that David was frightened of, because he knew that Terry would say something to him, and he was right.

"Little Judas," Terry said in the hall on Monday morning. "You're going to get yours."

When and where and how, David didn't know, but he found out that night. He didn't know what time it was, but he had been asleep, and before he knew what was happening, there was a hand on his mouth, something over his eyes, someone lying on his chest, another holding his legs.

"Don't make a sound," said Terry's voice, "or you're dead meat."

Someone was pulling his pajamas down, and then he felt something hot, something burning like pepper, on his balls. Then a voice. "If you tell, you'll be punished again. No sound now, ass licker."

And then they were gone, and for a long time he lay silent in the burning humiliation of the pain. He wanted to scream, to strike out, like he had at Hubert Green, but he knew that was wrong. He must bear his punishment stoically, no matter how much it hurt. The night crawled by like a bug with a hundred legs crossing a wide highway. In the morning he looked, but there was nothing to see. Still, it burned, and all day it burned, through math and English, Latin and science and social studies. In the shower, after sports, he saw Terry and Jumbo Jim Elliott, the big tackle from the football team, and he guessed who had lain on his chest, but he said nothing. The soap and water made the pain subside, and he felt glad that he had not spoken. It was something private between him and Terry.

The next day, in English, something else happened. There was a new teacher who had come back from the war. His name was Richard Fourier, and he was very excitable. He was short with a military crew cut, and piercing blue eyes that looked right through you. He read poetry with dramatic flourishes, especially narrative poems with lots of action. On this particular day he was late, and Terry, who was not much of an English student, took it upon himself to mimic the wild gestures of the teacher in front of a delighted class.

He was so engaged in "The Highwayman" by Alfred Noyes that he didn't hear the door open or see the teacher come in.

"I'm tired of your smirking little face, Roche," the teacher snarled. "You think you're so damned smart, making little remarks that you imagine I don't hear and imitating my expressions behind my back. Now get out of here and don't come back into this room until you can shape up."

After class they found Terry sitting on the floor in the hall by the shop.

"Come on, Terry," said Griff, "Let's go to math."

"I'll never go to that man's room again," said Terry angrily.

"Yes you will, Terry," said David. "It's like what happened to me yesterday. I deserved it. I took my punishment and went on. It's O.K. We'll get through this."

Griff was silent. It was clear that he didn't know what David was talking about.

Then David had an inspiration. "Look, Terry," he said. "I know you don't like English, but I can help you." He held out his hand, but Terry stayed, sitting on the cold floor of the dark basement corridor. David went on to math class. It wasn't much, he thought, but it was a beginning, almost a beginning.

The next day, at morning assembly, Mr. Langdon announced that all boys not being picked up by their parents for Christmas vacation needed to check with him to confirm arrangements. Christmas vacation! David had completely forgotten it was so close, and he didn't even know where he was going. He went forward to the master's desk.

"It says here," said Mr. Langdon, thumbing through his index cards, "That you're to take the train to New York and that Mr. Petersen will meet you."

"How about that," said David. "Bernie's pinch-hitting again."

Bernie wasn't a bad pinch-hitter. At least he was fun, and he let David do anything he wanted. That was how David learned to go in the subway by himself. Bernie lived on Christopher Street and he worked in Rockefeller Center, so he taught David how to take the Sixth Avenue subway from West 4th Street to Rockefeller Center and then find the Associated Press Building, the one with the statue of Atlas in front of it. Bernie would go to work and leave David on his own during the day. Sometimes David would just stay in the apartment and read and eat Necco wafers, piled in neat stacks in the bathroom cabinet according to color, and sometimes he would take the subway to Rockefeller Center and watch the skaters and the lights in the big tree and take the elevator up to Bernie's office. It didn't say "Petersen." It said SUTTER, WINSTON, MINTER, AND DONALDSON.

"How come it doesn't say Petersen?" asked David.

"'Cause I'm just a flunky," said Bernie. "I just do their dirty work for them."

"Will you get your name on the door someday?" asked David.

"If I hang around long enough," said Bernie.

Bernie had a girl friend named Sally Dawes. She had short black hair and wore earrings with big loops on them and high-heeled shoes with spikes that sometimes caught in the gratings on the side-walk when they walked to dinner. She had big breasts that jiggled and wore dresses that showed them. At 5:30 she usually came over to Bernie's to "fix a little drink" before dinner, and she would get David to sit with her on the sofa until Bernie got home.

"Ya know, Tiger," she said one day after her second drink, "ya know that school of yours costs a bundle of money."

He knew that.

"Ya don't think Bernie makes that kind of money."

He had never thought about it.

"Ya know who's payin' for you to go to that school? Ya know who's payin' for us to go to Peter's Back Yard for dinner? Ya can bet your ass, excuse the expression, that it's not Bernie Petersen. Bernie's a swell guy, and I love him. He's a lotta fun, and he's pretty sharp for an ex-Army lawyer, but he doesn't have that kinda money. It's that lady in California — that Mrs. Ariel — it's her, Baby, that sends the money. Bernie pays the bills, but it's her that sends the money."

She stood up and shook her glass.

"Empty again."

⚘

He told Elizabeth about it.

"I mean," he said, "is it true what Sally Dawes said about Bernie getting the money from a lady in California named Mrs. Ariel?"

"Yes, it's true."

They were lying on the couch in Elizabeth's apartment, and David had his head on her stomach, listening for the baby to kick.

"Who is Mrs. Ariel?"

"Molly Ariel is your godmother. She was Mommy's best friend when they lived in California. She and Mommy and Daddy were inseparable."

"Why didn't you tell me about her?"

"Because Molly wanted to stay out of the picture."

"Why?"

"Why? Why? Why? You haven't changed a bit. Always wanting to know why. Do you remember getting in bed with me during thunderstorms at home? I would try to explain what thunder was and lightning, and you would always say 'why?'. . ."

"I felt one," said David, "a little one."

"I felt it, too."

"Does it hurt?"

"No. It's kind of like something stretching inside."

"This Molly Ariel," said David. "Have I ever met her?"

"Once or twice when you were little. She visited us in Connecticut."

"Was she the lady who came when we had all the trouble?"

"You mean when Bernie left?"

"Yeah."

"She's the one."

His mind was racing from one thing to another.

"What do you want for Christmas, Elizabeth?"

She laughed. "Let's get up. I need to walk. You're supposed to walk a lot when you're pregnant." She walked over to the kitchen table and picked up a package of Pall Malls.

"Let me light it for you," said David, and he struck the match and held it out while she drew in. He could see the tip turn red as she inhaled.

"I'm serious," he said. "What do you want for Christmas?"

"You don't ask somebody what they want, Dummy. Giving is a surprise. If you know in advance, it's no fun."

They walked together up and down Broadway looking in the store windows. Then she left him at the subway. In the daytime he was allowed to go by himself. He took the train direct from 116th Street to Sheridan Square, and didn't have to change. Now he knew two trains, the D train which took him from West 4th Street to Rockefeller Center, and the Broadway local which took him from Sheridan Square to 116th Street. He studied the maps in the subway cars, and memorized the stops along the way. He liked knowing where he was and where he was going.

He got Sally Dawes to help him with Christmas. She was fun to shop with.

"So, who you gonna get presents for?" she asked.

He thought a moment. "Elizabeth, of course, and my mother and Bernie and maybe…"

"Maybe who?"

"Phil."

"Why maybe?"

"Should I get Phil a present?"

"If you want. You don't hafta."

"I don't think he likes me. I feel like I'm kind of in the way."

"Newlyweds are like that. They like to be alone. You know. Get 'em a joint present, something they both would like. Then you don't hurt his feelings."

They walked through the village, and he got a piano record for Phil and Elizabeth, a pin for his mother, and a pair of cuff links with tigers on them for Bernie, "so he'll think about me when he wears 'em," said David. Sally bought a tree, some icicles and lights and colored balls. They went back to the apartment to wrap the presents and decorate. She made herself a drink, and they sat on the floor, cutting and tying and talking. Then she made another drink.

"Why do you drink so much, Sally?" he asked.

"It relaxes me, Sugar," she said.

"Does Bernie drink a lot, too?"

"Oh, yeah, Bernie can belt it down pretty good."

"Does my mother drink a lot?"

"She drinks a whole lot."

"Phil said that she had a drinking problem. What does that mean?"

"That means you can't stop."

"Do you have a drinking problem, Sally?"

"You sure do ask questions," she said, shaking her head. "Maybe I do, Sweetheart, maybe I do."

She went out to the kitchen and came back with her glass half full. "Just a little one for the road," she said.

When Bernie came home, he joined her. They were in a good mood.

"It's real pretty, Tiger," he said, looking at the tree in the corner with the lights and the icicles and the presents wrapped, sitting underneath it. "You and Sally did a good job."

Sally kept whispering to Bernie, "Come on, Bernie, tell the kid."

"Not now, not now," he would say. "When, then?" she would ask. Finally he gave in. "O.K., Sally, I'll tell him."

He turned to David. "Tiger," he said. "You're a super kid. Me 'n Sally think you're great."

"Yeah, kid," said Sally huskily, "we think you're great, and we don't want you to think we're runnin' out on you."

"But it's kinda complicated," Bernie went on. "Sally and me, we'd like to get married and get out of the rat race, get out of this city and start a new life for ourselves. So we won't be able to take care of you after this."

"We're going to Nevada and get married," said Sally, "then we're gonna live in California."

"And what do I do?" asked David.

"I dunno, Tiger. We'll just have to wait and see what Mrs. Ariel says."

It was strange, having this Mrs. Ariel responsible for him, someone he didn't know who pulled the strings behind the scenes like the puppetmaster in Pinocchio. What was she like, he wondered, and why did she take all this trouble for him? She didn't have to send him to school or pay Bernie to take care of him.

On Christmas day he took his presents and rode the subway to Elizabeth's. His mother was there, looking pale and tired with streaks of gray in her brown curled hair and circles under her eyes. She kissed him and held him close.

"I honestly didn't get your letter," she said. "Please believe me, Toots."

"I believe you, Mom," he said, not because he did but because he wanted to. But he also believed that she had gone off for the weekend, forgotten he was coming, and he held back from her in his heart. He would be careful with her from now on. They exchanged presents. Elizabeth and Phil gave him a book, The Stories of O. Henry, and his mother gave him a watch. He laughed and put it on proudly, and when Phil asked if he could see it, he said, "Oh, no!" and held his hand over his wrist. He was not going to lose this one.

His mother had moved to a hotel on Broadway and 111th Street so that she could be closer to Elizabeth and be able to help her with the baby. After dinner he walked her back. She put her arm through his and talked quietly.

"It looks like you're going to have to be the man of the family, Toots. There's not much left inside of me."

He tried to imagine the empty places inside of her.

"I can't work much," she said, "I'm too tired. And so it's pretty much welfare checks and whatever your grandmother sends me."

"Where is Grandma now?" asked David.

"She's in Palm Beach. They always go to Palm Beach in the winter."

"Will they come back this summer?"

"I doubt it. Your grandfather retires from the bank this year, and he won't be able to afford the beach house on his retirement. Those days are over."

"Where will I go this summer?" he asked.

"I don't know, Toots. We haven't got that far yet. I'll talk to Molly about it."

"Molly Ariel?"

"Yes."

"Do you like her? I mean, is she one of your best friends?"

"She was."

"And is she really my godmother?"

"Yes."

"And does she really pay for all my school and my clothes and everything?"

"She does."

"Why didn't anyone tell me?"

"She just wanted to stay in the background."

It was the same thing Elizabeth had said. David liked to ask twice to see if the stories were the same. But all the stories about Molly Ariel were the same, Bernie's and Elizabeth's and his mother's.

The new hotel was much like the old one, but smaller and dirtier. Her room was strewn with clothes and smelled of bourbon and cigarette smoke.

"Sit down awhile and talk to me, Toots."

He sat on the bed by her feet. She reached down and touched him.

"Do you love me, David?" she asked.

"Yes," he answered.

"Say it, then."

"I can't."

"Come on," she coaxed. "Just say, 'I love you, Mom.'"

"I can't," he said again.

"You're still the same," she said. "You just look at me with those big, sad, dark eyes and say nothing. I never could get you to say it, even when you were little."

She sat, her legs stretched out, her head propped up by the pillows, her glass in her left hand and her cigarette in her right, inhaling and blowing the smoke up into the air, her eyes distant.

"I used to be fun. I used to be beautiful. I used to play the piano, and the all the men would gather around and listen. You know that, Toots? I was something, then. You don't understand that, do you? I was Maggie Hope. Your father, he was something, too. We were the bright, young things, and we danced 'till dawn. I had silk dresses and bobbed my hair. We took off our shoes like Scott and Zelda and walked in the fountains."

"And Bernie?" asked the boy.

"Oh, Bernie, he was later. He was cute. He saved me from boredom. I picked him up in a bar one night when he was still in the Army. He looked sexy in his uniform, and he started coming out to the house. We had fun."

"Why did he leave?"

"We fought. We drank too much. Things got bad. He got tired of it."

He sat on her bed and listened to her talk about San Francisco and watched her cigarette smoke drift in patterns toward the ceiling. She fell asleep, and he took the cigarette from her hand and turned the light off. He was afraid to leave her, afraid she would wake up and smoke again. He had heard stories of people who burned up in bed by falling asleep with a cigarette. He took the pack of cigarettes from her bedside and put it on the bureau. That way, if she woke up, she would have to get up and smoke them.

The week after Christmas dragged like bricks on a blank wall, one day after the other the same. The grownups had lives of their own and problems of their own, and there was no time for David. Even worse, there was no money. You could do things with money, like go to the movies and go out for dinner, you could go to Times Square or the Music Hall or Madison Square Garden. You could buy comic books or go to the Museum of Science and Industry at Rockefeller Center and watch the models of the machines, but without money there was only Bernie's apartment or Elizabeth's apartment or his mother's hotel room, and there was nothing to do there. He began to think about school, and he remembered what he had said to Humphrey on the train going back from the weekend. School was better. The masters could be counted on, and there was something to do all the time. When vacations came, everyone shouted and screamed,

"No more classes, no more books!"

"No more grubby old blue suits!"

"No more rising bell!"

"No more marks!"

But David felt differently. He always felt a funny feeling in his stomach when vacation came, and now he knew why. It was because he never knew what was going to happen next. School was safe, but vacation wasn't. Every vacation he found out something new. This time it was Bernie leaving and Molly Ariel. What would it be next vacation? He had no idea where he would go for the summer. Back to camp? He hated the stupid camp. To the beach? His grandparents weren't renting the beach house.

He was one of the first ones to arrive at Grand Central for the train back to school, and when they opened the gates, he said goodbye to Phil and walked quickly to the Lowell School car, where he found a window seat. He hadn't been there long when someone sat down beside him. It was Terry Roche.

"Listen," said Terry. "I was thinking about what you said before Christmas, you know, about helping me."

"O.K.," said David. He was excited, and he was nervous.

"My mom and dad want me to do better. They say dumb jocks don't get into prep school. And they asked me about you."

"About me? How do they know about me?"

"There's some magazine they send the parents, and you're in it. 'He's the smartest kid in your class,' my dad said. 'Why don't you get him to help you?' And I said, 'He already is.'"

Terry laughed. "So how do your balls feel?"

"Not very good," said David.

"They're not still burning after all this time!"

"Oh no, I was just thinking about how I hate vacations."

"What do you mean?"

"Nobody has any money and there's never anything to do and it's awful."

"Hold on a minute, Dave," said Terry. "Get your stuff and come sit with Griff and me. We've got facing seats with a table at the front of the car."

And so, something began on the train from New York to Framingham. David told them about Elizabeth and his mother and Bernie and Sally Dawes. "I don't know where I'm going to spend the summer," he said.

"What about this lady in California?" asked Terry.

"You mean my godmother, Molly Ariel?"

"She's rich, isn't she? Why don't you write her and ask her for some money?"

"Why don't you go live with her?" asked Griff. "I mean, if she's so rich and she sends you to school, why don't you just tell her that you want to live with her, and see if she'll take you?"

The idea scared David and fascinated him. He really wanted to write her. But he couldn't ask her for money. It was too complicated. He'd wait awhile and see what happened. There was a long time before summer, and he had other things to think about first. He looked out the window.

They were passing Portchester, where three giant rolls of lifesavers hung like green, blue and red submarines from the wall of the factory.

"Lifesavers," said Terry. "Hey, that's us."

"Lifesavers for each other," said David.

"We'll each be a different flavor," said Griff.

"I'll be cherry," said Terry Roche.

"And I'll be orange," said Griff.

David couldn't decide. His favorite flavor was crystomint, but that wasn't exactly a good name. He hated lime. What else was there? Spearmint… Peppermint…

"I know," said Terry. "You can be Butter Rum."

David didn't feel exactly like butter rum, but he liked the name. They agreed. They would have signals. If you needed to talk to someone privately you made a circle with the thumb and forefinger of your right hand. If you did it with your left hand, it just meant hi.

They would be a club. They would have meetings on Saturday afternoons during free time under the ski jump, and emergency meetings in Terry's alcove on Sunday nights. The trouble with the alcoves was that people were always opening the curtains and jumping over the walls and there was no privacy because you could hear everything in the next alcove, but everyone was afraid of Terry and they wouldn't bother him.

They started writing stories together. It had begun with Griff and David helping Terry with his English papers, and before long they were working together on a story that never ended. They would take turns, and you never knew until it was your turn what kind of a mess the hero would be in, and your job was to get him out of the mess and put him into another one for the next guy to get him out of. Finally they would tire of it and start another one. This way they could have two or three stories going. Their favorite was the adventures of Sam Shovel, and Mr. Fourier got even more excited than usual about it.

"Make a play out of it, boys, and you can put it on some Saturday night before the movie."

They did. It was their favorite Sam Shovel story in which the intrepid Sam, played by David, finds the missing diamonds hidden in a secret pocket of the heel of the dowager duchess' shoe (Griff, of course, was the dowager duchess, complete with pillows), and foils the villain, played by Terry. The play went smoothly until the climactic moment when David, leaning over to snatch the duchess' shoe and reveal the loot, heard a distinct rip in the seat of his pants, followed by roars of laughter from the audience. His now threadbare blue suit had come apart, and there was nothing left to do but end the play red-faced to the cheers of the crowd who much preferred this unexpected ending to the one the script had called for.

The club was David's joy. It got him through the bad times and made the good times better, but summer was coming fast and it hadn't helped with that. They had a special meeting one Sunday in April under the ski jump.

"You've still got time," said Griff. "Just write her a letter and tell her you want to get to know her."

"You don't need to ask for money," said Terry.

"You can do that later," said Griff.

"Right," said Terry. "Just say you want to spend the summer with her."

"Besides," said Griff, "California's neat."

# CHAPTER *eight*

*I*t was dark now, and in the fourth form dormitory at the Lowell School for Boys no sign of life; only in Terry Roche's bed there were three bodies instead of one.

"Suppose we get caught," whispered David.

"Stop worrying," said Terry. "It's the night before Prize Day. All the masters are over at Lowell House drinking with the parents."

David was never comfortable breaking rules. He started to get up, but Terry put his arm over and held him down.

"It's all right," said Griff. "Mr. L'll be drunk when he gets back anyway, and if he catches us he won't spoil your record. You're such a brown-noser, Butter Rum, he'd never give you a mark."

Griff smiled and rolled his eyes. David was silent. He knew what "brown noser" meant, only he didn't know what it really meant. The students who got Primus or Secundus ratings were always called brown nosers. So were the Student Council members. So David was a brown-noser. He knew that. It was why that eluded him. Why "brown nose"? Why not something else? There was a song the students sang in the shower room - "He's got a brown ring around his nose, and every day it grows and grows." They would stop singing if a master came into the showers.

That's the way life was. If you knew, you knew. If you didn't, it was better not to ask. You'd just make yourself look stupid by asking. Eventually you would find out.

"Guess what?" David said.

"What wisdom, oh wise one, do you have to offer?" said Griff.

"I'm going to California for the summer," he said.

"Yesterday you said you weren't," said Terry.

"I lied. I was mad at Molly Ariel, so I lied. I'm not going to her house. She's sending me to my father's."

"Zounds," said Griff in his best knight errant voice. "I am filled with amazement."

"It wasn't really a lie," said David. "I told you guys I wasn't going to Molly Ariel's and that was true. I just didn't tell you the other part."

The letter had completely thrown him. When he wrote to his godmother in April, he counted on her asking him for the summer. He had made up his mind that it would happen. Never in his deepest dreams did he imagine she would send him to his father. Why?

"I don't even know what he looks like," said David.

"Well, he might be neat," said Terry.

"Perhaps you will be blessed with the gift of flight," said Griff.

"Can the knight errant stuff," said Terry.

"Well, I would love to fly," said Griff.

David wasn't sure how he felt about it. Molly's letter had told him he was to take the train to Bridgeport where he would be met by Mrs. McCarver. She would take care of him for a few days and then drive him to LaGuardia Airport where he would take a United Airlines flight to San Francisco. Mrs. McCarver would give him his ticket, and his father would meet him on the other end. The letter was typed on gray paper with MOLLY ARIEL in block letters printed across the top. It was signed, "Affectionately, Molly."

"Who's Mrs. McCarver?" asked Terry.

"Oh, she lives next door to where I used to live when I was little." said David.

All that seemed so long ago. He tried to imagine staying at the McCarvers and seeing his house next door with someone else living in it. He liked Mrs. McCarver. She was kind of fat and jolly and smiling, and used to invite him in for apple juice, but they only had one radio that he could remember and it was in the living room right next to Mr. McCarver's chair. He would never be able to listen to his favorite programs. Mr. McCarver probably listened to the news and those programs where people talked all the time about current events. It was so boring. But it was only for three days. Three days couldn't be that bad.

Somewhere a door slammed.

"Quick," said Griff, "before he gets up the stairs," and he was gone, like a flash, three alcoves down.

David headed for the bathroom. That was always safest. If anyone caught you, you could just say you were going to the bathroom. In the door, a quick stop at the urinal, and back to bed. It wasn't a rocking night. In fact the rocking had stopped when the club was formed. It was more the sleeplessness that comes from excitement. Tomorrow was Prize Day and tomorrow night he would be sleeping in a strange house, and then he would fly to California to meet his father.

He thought about Molly Ariel. She didn't make sense. If she didn't want him to come for the summer, why was she sending him to school? Her letter didn't say anything about why. It just said, "You'll be spending your summer on your father's ranch in the Sacramento Valley." Maybe she didn't like children. Maybe she didn't have any place where children could stay. Maybe it was Mr. Ariel, maybe he didn't want her to have him there. He couldn't piece it together. Why didn't she come to see him at school or in New York? If she was sending him to school, she would want to see what he looked like. Nobody was making her. There was no law that she had to send him, and if she decided to stop, then where would he go? Who would he live with? Maybe Mr. Armbrister would keep him at his house. And his father? Why his father? David's mind flew like a diving bird, darting in and out of the treetops, soaring up and then down, first on one person, then on another. Elizabeth and the baby Alexander, born in April, whom he hadn't seen, and his mother, in the hospital again, Elizabeth said, but a different kind of hospital, one to help her with her problem. It was upstate, Elizabeth said, and would be cooler and good for her. Be sure to write, Elizabeth said. "Mommy is very sick and needs your love. Just a few lines will mean a lot to her." That's why they're sending me to my father's, he thought. Bernie is gone, Elizabeth has a baby, and my mother is sick. Still he didn't understand Molly Ariel.

In the morning he was bright again, and he marched proudly up to the stage, twice this time, with the threadbare blue suit, to receive Prester John for scholarship and the Adventures of Robin Hood for two years of perfect punctuality. Dan Humphrey winked at him from the front row where the graduating seniors sat, and Terry and Griff gave the club sign as he worked his way past them to his seat. So far so good. Two years to go.

And then the train to Bridgeport and the strange bed upstairs at the McCarvers with a view from his window of the old house, but no mother working in the garden planting flowers, no Elizabeth swinging her books on her hip, no Marion Fisher across the street. He thought of the cave and whether any of his food was still there, but he had lost his heart for it. If he found it, what would he do with it anyway?

He spent most of his time reading the sports pages of the newspaper which Mr. McCarver had brought home from work the night before. The star players were back from the war, and Ted Williams was having a great year. In fact, the Red Sox were having a great year, and Mr. Hackett had been so excited he could hardly contain his mustache. David liked the Yankees, but they just kept losing to the Red Sox, and Joe DiMaggio was hitting under .300 for the first time in his career. He was hurting, the papers said, and just didn't seem to be himself. David studied the box scores, and read the accounts of the games over and over.

Then, at long last, the morning and the new drive, unfamiliar, down winding parkways and across the Whitestone Bridge to the airport, and the heart pounding and the stewardess taking his hand and leading him onto the plane and Mrs. McCarver waving and the door shut and the engines, four of them, slowly turning, then faster and faster and the seat strapped closely, the boy chewing furiously, and the plane moving faster and faster down the runway, and then up into the air and the breathtaking sight of New York City from the sky, the buildings like toys, and the boy flying in his heart too and the plane going and going and the boy wondering about his father.

"You'll recognize him," Elizabeth had told him on the phone. "He's tall and thin and very handsome. His hair is almost white now. It just went from blond to white. He sent me a picture, which I keep in my wallet. Give him a hug for me, David, a big hug. I still miss him."

"Will he know me?" the boy asked himself. "Will he know what I look like? Will I walk by him at the gate?"

The turbulence brought him from reverie, and over the cabin door a sign flashed on: PLEASE FASTEN SEAT BELTS. He was frightened, and his hands trembled as he grabbed for the two pieces of his belt. The stewardess walked by easily and smoothly and her hands clipped the belt together in a simple click. His heart beat furiously with each bump, and inch by inch the Hershey bar and the peppermint lifesavers and the Juicy Fruit gum rose and he reached for the bag in the pocket of the seat in front of him, and then it all came up, and he didn't know which was worse, the sickness or the embarrassment, and afterwards he held the bag in his hand and all over the plane little lights were going on and bells ringing and the stewardesses walking up and down the aisle collecting bags, and he couldn't understand why anyone would want to fly.

The plane reached Chicago at noon. It was due in San Francisco at six with a refueling stop in Cheyenne, Wyoming. The stewardess worked on him:

"Flying isn't all bumps, David. What happened this morning wasn't normal. We ought to have a smooth flight from here on, and you can see the Rocky Mountains from the air and the great Salt Lake."

A sailor came and sat by him and cheered him up.

"This ain't bad, buckaroo, you oughta see a destroyer go up and down in a storm at sea. You just gotta tough it out and think of something else."

From his pocket he brought out a little machine with a handle on one side and three windows. You pulled the handle down and tried to get three bars or oranges or bells in the windows. The sailor explained to him: "In Reno, Nevada, they got these things all over the place — in hotels, in gas stations, train stations, everywhere. And you put in nickels or dimes or quarters, and play them. They call 'em one-armed bandits. This here's just a toy, but it works like the real ones. You keep this, buckaroo, and when you get older you can tackle the big machines."

The sailor was neat. David laughed and the color came back to his cheeks, and he told the sailor the story of his life and why he was going to San Francisco.

"Hey, that's great, buckaroo. Maybe this's your big break. Maybe your dad's a neat guy and you'll like him and settle down there. The West is a great place. I'm getting off in Cheyenne and goin' home to my daddy's ranch."

"Gonna be a cowboy?" asked David.

"You might say so, buckeroo."

David hated to see him leave. The sky in Cheyenne was darkening, and it looked like bad weather for the run over the mountains to San Francisco. He'd felt safer with his friend beside him. Now there was just a fat man in a brown business suit who read the newspaper and didn't talk, the boy began to feel scared again, and soon the bumping started, and he remembered the words of the sailor, but it didn't help, and the bells began to ring again, and the plane bumped its way through the storm up and down so hard that David thought the wings would be torn off, and then the nausea and the bag, and his face pale and sweaty, and his hands trembling. This time it didn't stop. It seemed like the storm lasted all the way to San Francisco, and he was sick again and again, and finally he could not hold back the tears. He vowed never to get in an airplane again, that is, if he lived, and he couldn't understand why his father made him do this. By the time they landed in San Francisco he was so tired that he would have gone home with the first man who came along.

He recognized his father right away, standing at the gate with his white hair neatly combed, a blue sports shirt open at the neck, and brown, freshly-pressed slacks. David hesitated for a moment, then put his head against the older man's chest and let himself be held.

"Pretty rough flight, David?"

"It was awful. Please don't make me fly back."

"Don't worry. Come on, we'll get your bags and go into town."

Town was San Francisco, my birthplace, thought the boy as they drove in the dark toward the city. The next day he fell in love with it, with the steep hills and the green and yellow cable cars and the clean, sharp buildings, and the mystery of Alcatraz out in the bay from whose walls no prisoner was ever known to have escaped. They stayed at the Mark Hopkins on top of Nob Hill, and in the evening after their day of sightseeing they drank cocktails at the "Top of the Mark." The Golden Gate stood tall and straight and then disappeared into the fog of Marin County across the bay. David had never seen anything like it.

His father talked:

"When your mother and I were young we'd come up here and sit at this table with Molly Ariel, she was Molly Burton then, and whatever beau she was courting at the time."

"What was she like, Molly Ariel? Did you like her?"

"Everyone liked her. She and your mother were the most popular girls in San Francisco." He laughed. "We were her chaperones. In those days, David, a young woman and a young man weren't allowed out in the evening without a married couple to chaperone them. So, since your mother and I were married, we ended up as the official chaperones for most of the young kids. Molly was one of them. She had a lot of charm."

"Will we see her this summer?"

"I don't know. I hadn't thought about it."

David hadn't thought about it either. He was having fun; it was nice to have a father and a birthplace. They lay in their beds in the hotel room with the thick blue carpet and the curtains billowing out and the lights of the city twinkling like stars and David told his father about the Founder's Medal and Terry Roche and Griff. It was nice having a father.

In the morning they left and drove inland across the mountains to the Sacramento Valley. It was late June and already the hills were brown and the small streams dried up from lack of rain. It was so different from the East, with its lush green grass and the great maples and oaks shading the lawns.

His father talked.

"We live on a ranch. You'll see. It isn't like the city. There's not much to do unless you learn to help milk the cows and move the irrigation pipes. Jimmy and Sarah are too young to be more than a nuisance, but I imagine you're old enough."

David said nothing. He tried to imagine, but he couldn't make any pictures. He really had never been around animals, and he didn't know what to expect from them.

He found out soon enough.

There were three cows, two of them brown and white, and one black and white.

"Their names are Bessie, Tessie, and Lessie," said Jimmy, who was blond and seven.

"Lessie?" asked David.

"I think it was supposed to be Lassie, but the kids like the sound," said his father.

David and Jimmy and Sarah, who was four, stood in the barn and watched their father milk. He sat on a stool with his head on Lessie's flank, the pail under her swollen udder, his hands firm but gentle on her teats, the milk squirting into the pail in the regular one-two rhythm of his squeezes.

"You can't pull or jerk," he said. "It'll hurt her. Then she'll kick the bucket over, or you."

David tried it, placing his fingers around the teats and squeezing. Nothing happened.

"Harder, David, with a downward motion."

He tried it again, piecing together his father's words in his brain. Down from the top, the index finger first, then the next, and so on, moving the milk downward. Still nothing happened. Then he did it again, hard. Boom. The left foot of the cow lashed out, and the pail went over. David fell backwards off the stool. Jimmy and Sarah loved it.

His father was not a patient teacher. If you got something right the first time, that was great. If you didn't he only grumbled and walked away. After three days David gave up on milking. He tried moving pipes in the alfalfa field. That lasted until he saw the first rattlesnake, gray and white, sliding through the sun, dividing the grass like a thin wind. He ran for the house and called Diane.

Diane was in the kitchen peeling potatoes. She was a tall blond woman with blue eyes like his father's and light skin and freckles. She had big shoulders and strong hands and could milk the cows as well as the men, but she stayed in the house during the heat of the day because the sun burned her. Jimmy and Sarah both looked more like her than their father. They had her skin and her high cheek bones.

When he told her about the snake she just laughed. "You city kids are all alike. You see a snake and you think it's the end of the world. I grew up here. Snakes are like spiders. You respect 'em and you kill the bad ones, but you can't let 'em run you off. Wear your heavy boots, David, and call your dad or one of the men. They won't hurt you if you don't panic."

But he couldn't make himself go back. He stood at the edge of the field, watching the men walking through the alfalfa, changing the irrigation pipes from one section to the next, and he imagined the snakes lurking there in the high grass waiting to strike. He saw the spread of the mouth and the white fangs, and he felt the lightning strike, the pain, and the poison spreading.

"It's your imagination that scares you," his father said at supper.

"David's a scaredy-cat," said Sarah laughing.

"I wouldn't be scared," said Jimmy.

"You would too," said Sarah.

"Would not," said Jimmy.

Diane and his father carried the dishes from the table into the kitchen. David could hear them talking.

"He's just a little coward," said Diane. "He's a little city boy, afraid of everything."

"That's not his fault," said his father. "He's never been on a farm or a ranch. He's got to learn. He'll be better."

"I sure hope so," said Diane. "He drooped around here like a baby calf without its mother all afternoon. He's gonna drive me bananas if he doesn't find something to do."

They came back in with dessert. David pretended that he had heard nothing. After supper he walked down to the barn and talked to the cows. He liked them, especially the two brown and white ones. He couldn't milk them but he liked to talk and watch their faces and rub their foreheads with his hand.

Suppose cows had brains like people, he thought. Or suppose horses or elephants had brains like people. What would the world be like? If you were a cow, and you had a brain like a person, would you just stand there and let somebody milk you? Would you, Tessie? I mean, wouldn't you want to do something else? If you had a brain like a person, would you be able to talk instead of mooing? If he could be any animal he wanted, he would be a tiger...no, an elephant...no, something fast like a wild stallion or a black panther.

Later, on the way back to the house, he saw the boards piled against the side of the garage, and as he lay in bed waiting for sleep to come, thinking about tomorrow, and how tomorrow would just be today all over again, it came to him that he could use the boards. He would build something.

After breakfast he got Jimmy and Sarah.

"We're going to have a clubhouse," he said proudly. He sent them to the garage for hammers and nails and he picked a spot in the yard behind the slide out of the way of the path the grownups used from the garage to the house. Then he went to the pile and pulled out four wooden fence posts.

"We'll use these for the corners," he said, "and then we'll nail braces across, and then tack the boards to the braces."

He wasn't sure if that was right, but it seemed sensible. After all, he had never built a house before. In fact he had never really built anything. Shop wasn't one of his best subjects at Lowell. He took it, like everyone else, for an hour a week, but all he'd ever made was a birdhouse and a two-shelf bookcase. And what you did with those was follow a pattern and cut out the pieces and glue them together. Building from scratch was something new. He dug the fence post holes and he and Jimmy and Sarah buried the fence posts and then nailed the braces to them front and back and both sides and started tacking on the boards.

"It's not very big," said Jimmy.

"Well, we don't have a very big club," said David.

"What's a club?" asked Sarah.

"It's a place where grownups aren't allowed," said David.

"Oh," said Sarah.

David remembered. "Oh" was good.

At lunch they were on their best behavior. Diane couldn't figure it out.

Why are you so nice to each other today?" she asked.

Jimmy looked at her seriously. "We're making a club," he said.

"Oh, I see," said Diane.

They worked all afternoon, and by five o'clock it was finished. Just big enough for the three of them to crawl into and sit down. But it was a clubhouse, and there was a ceiling and three walls and an old curtain over the front for a door.

"We have to have a name for our club," said David.

Suddenly he heard his father's voice, harsh and deep, outside.

"Get out of there this minute. Hurry up. Jimmy, Sarah, get out of there."

The younger children left quickly, but David waited, uncertain of the meaning. Then he heard the thud of his father's boot on the side and felt the boards caving in around him, the sides falling away, the ceiling on his shoulders, and his father's face, stern and angry, rising above the rubble of his creation.

"It's a snake trap. A goddamn snake trap. Don't you know any better? What the hell's the matter with you? A boy your age. Everytime you walk in a place like this you're just inviting a rattler to take a bite out of you. They always look for someplace to get out of the sun."

"But I made it," the boy cried. "You didn't have to knock it down."

"Get into the house," his father said.

"You didn't have to knock it down," the boy cried, louder this time. "That was cruel. I hate you. I HATE YOU."

And he ran at the man, striking out at the blue work shirt with his fists as hard as he could, scratching and biting with his teeth into the flesh of his father's chest, screaming, I HATE YOU, until he felt his father's hand on the side of his head, and everything turned black.

When he woke up he was in his bed. His shoes were on the floor, and no one else was there. He sat up slowly, remembering, ashamed that he had let his temper get the better of him. His mother would not have been happy with him. Mr. Armbrister would not have been happy with him. He would have to learn better.

He sat up, cleared his head, and walked into the living room. Diane sat on the sofa, reading. She looked up, startled. "I didn't hear you," she said.

"Where is everyone?" David asked.

"Your father took Jimmy and Sarah to the store for shoes. I thought you'd both be better off apart for a while."

"Cooling off time," David said.

Diane put her book down. "Come on over and sit down," she said. "I won't bite you." She patted her hand on the blue cushions of the couch. "Come on."

He sat next to her, but not too close.

"Look," she said. "I know I haven't been very nice to you, and I know today was rough — your house and all. It's just that we…that I…that your dad…"

David watched her eyes move down and up and over his face and down again.

"You know it's rough for your dad to be working for peanuts for his wife's father. It's rough for me to have you here. I don't know anything about you really. You're kind of, you know, different."

David laughed. "I guess I'm not much cut out for ranch life," he said.

"Nope, you sure aren't." She put her hand on his knee. "Give us another chance, will you, and we'll try to do the same. There's no money for vacation trips or stuff like that, but we'll try to find something fun for you to do. O.K.?"

"O.K.," David said.

"Good." She bent over and kissed him on the cheek, then stood up and went to the kitchen to make dinner. When Jimmy and Sarah came running in from the store, they brought him a Tootsie Roll and a pack of bubble gum with baseball cards.

"A peace offering," said David.

"What's that?" asked Jimmy.

"Never mind," said David. "It's too complicated to explain."

For a while things were better. Sometimes Diane took the kids places and let David stay home and read. She knew he loved to read. He read Ivanhoe and The Black Knight, and The Adventures of Robin Hood. After dinner he read stories to Jimmy and Sarah, and when they had gone to sleep, he came out to the living room to work on the jigsaw puzzle or play Parcheesi with Diane or his father.

One night he thought about Molly Ariel.

"Is it a long way to Molly Ariel's house?" he asked.

"What do you mean, David?" his father answered.

"I mean, could we go visit her?"

"I don't think so. I just can't take the time off."

David was pretty good at knowing when to stop asking questions. He could tell by their mood. Sometimes drinking made them happy, sometimes it made them sad or angry. When they fought, he just went into his room and shut the door and read until he felt sleepy. When they were happy, they hugged each other and kissed and promised each other that things would be better.

One night, when they were both happy, he asked, "What was my mother like?"

"She was a character. I guess we were both pretty crazy."

"Did you meet her out here?"

"Oh no. I met her in New York. At the Plaza."

"Is that where you lived?"

He finished his drink and handed the glass to Diane who walked into the kitchen with it.

"I guess you don't know much about me, do you?" his father said. "I was born in Wisconsin — Madison, Wisconsin. My father, your grandfather, was a lawyer, and then a judge. Judge Lear. Tough as nails, strict, but good. Smart. He worked for the Union Pacific Railroad. Went to Chicago a lot on business. Anyway, everybody got sent east to college in those days. I was pretty much a goof-off in school, so they sent me east to one of those places where you spent a year prepping for college, so you could pass your exams. They wanted me to go to Princeton. I was nineteen. Holidays I would go to New York and live at the Plaza with my Aunt Estelle, your great aunt."

"Is she still alive? Does she still live at the Plaza?"

"One thing at a time. Yes, she's still alive, but no, she doesn't still live at the Plaza."

Diane walked back in with two drinks and handed one to his father.

"Tell him about Maggie, Allan," she said.

It seemed funny to hear their names, to think of his mother and father as people with names like Allan and Maggie.

"I'm getting to it." David could hear his father's voice over his own thoughts.

"Anyway," his father said, "everybody had to have a chaperone in those days. Estelle was mine. They had debutante balls at the hotels during the winter and spring, and one of the debutantes that year was your mother, Miss Margaret Hope, from Savannah, Georgia. She was there with her mother. We were both nineteen. We fell in love and wanted to get married."

He laughed. "Then the shit hit the fan. The Judge was horrified. Maggie's mother was horrified. The great Southern lady from Savannah who was courting her own third husband said that we were too young, that I had to prove myself. 'A gentleman does not marry until he is twenty-five,' she said. So she packed your mother up to take her back to Georgia, and your mother threw a fit, literally threw a fit. She threw her clothes all over the goddamn hotel room and said she wasn't going to budge. So the great Southern lady called the Judge, who took the train in from Chicago, and there was a big Council of War."

"A big Council of War," echoed Diane from the next chair. She had heard the story before.

"We had lunch at the Plaza in the Oak Room, the five of us. My sweet mother had stayed at home, and your grandmother was courting Mr. E. Everett Sampson, but he was not official family yet, so there was Maggie and me and the judge and the great Southern lady, and of course, Estelle, presiding, the chaperone who had somehow failed to keep the wild, young things apart.

"It looked like the family was going to arrange a separation, and then your mother played her trump card…"

"Her trump card," said Diane.

" 'I'm pregnant,' she said. 'Not in the Plaza,' said Estelle, and the Judge frowned and the great Southern lady denied it, and Maggie said, 'I ought to know, mother.' And I was flabbergasted. It was the first time I'd heard of it. But, true or not, it worked. They shipped us off to California and got us married right away. They couldn't let this penniless black sheep with no college degree marry the Georgia belle without some source of livelihood, so they set us up in the family lumber business right here, and eight months later Lizzie was born."

"So she was right," said Diane.

"She guessed," said his father. "She couldn't have known for sure that early. Even if she was wrong, she got what she wanted."

"It was a risk," said Diane. "It might have backfired."

"Maggie was always a gutsy woman," said his father.

"David, I think it's your bedtime," said Diane.

That's the way it usually went, Diane giving the signal that it was enough, and David going back to his room to read or sleep. Sometimes, if he kept his door open, he would hear them, laughing and kissing in their dark bedroom. He heard other sounds too, the sounds of the bedsprings squeaking and Diane moaning. One night there was a thunderstorm in the middle of the night, and Sarah woke, screaming. David didn't know what to do. He went to her, but she kept crying. "I want my mommy," she sobbed, as lightning cracked outside and the thunder boomed.

He opened the door and walked into the bedroom. His father and Diane were on the bed naked, his father on top of Diane moving up and down, Diane moaning and moving her head from side to side. "Christ," she kept saying, "Oh, Jesus." David backed away. They hadn't seen him. He walked back to Sarah's room, climbed into bed with her, and held her. After a while she stopped crying.

After that he felt funny around Diane, like he knew something he wasn't supposed to know, and he was careful not to look into their bedroom when she was there. He wanted to, but he knew it was wrong, and when he caught himself watching the rise and fall of her breasts under her light shirt, he would quickly look away and try to get his mind on something else.

As the summer passed, his father became more and more irritable. Sometimes he came home from the fields, slamming his gloves in the dirt as he got out of the jeep, swearing and cursing Diane's father. "Goddamsonofabitch," he would say, as if it were one long word. "Bastard," he would mutter, as he stomped into the kitchen and poured himself a drink out of the bottle on the top shelf of the cupboard.

"You drink too much," said Diane.

"Your father's a fucking slavedriver," said the man.

"You're the one that's getting a free house," said Diane.

"He doesn't have to treat me like a fucking nigger," said his father.

"All he expects is an honest day's work, Allan," Diane said.

David learned to keep away during these arguments. So did Jimmy and Sarah. When they saw the jeep coming, they would stay outside in the back yard and play on the swing set or build forts in the sand pile until after their father had time to cool off. David liked Sarah best. She would sit in his lap, and he would read to her the way Elizabeth had read to him, and he would build her castles which she would step on and knock down, laughing and running off like an elf until he caught her and tickled her ribs and made her promise not to do it again. But it was hard with three. Somebody always got left out. With Terry and Griff it was O.K., because they were all the same age, but if David played with Sarah, Jimmy got bored, and if David played with Jimmy, Sarah cried, and sometimes it was better just to let Sarah and Jimmy play together. David could play by himself better than they could.

On his last afternoon he walked over to the river, down a dirt road through the woods and across the rocky river bed that was full in the early spring when it rained and the river flooded. For a while he flung stones into the water, looking for flat ones he could skip.

Then he took off his shoes and jeans and waded in. It felt good. His father had told him not to go to the river, but today was his last day, and he just wanted to see it. He could feel the flow of the water under his feet. He went deeper. It was up to his calves, the water pulsing hard and clean. He could see the channel in the middle. He would chance it. It wasn't that far to the other side.

He dove and began stroking, kicking hard like he had at the beach, but for every foot he made forward the current carried him two feet down. He was in the middle now and he could feel the power of the water against him. He kicked, harder and harder, and stroked, keeping his head out of the water, his eyes on the far shore. Finally he broke through into the shallower water, and stood panting and gasping for breath. He looked back to where he had started. The current must have carried him a hundred yards downstream. If he tried to swim back it would carry him another hundred.

Then he figured it out. If he walked upstream two hundred yards he could swim back and let the current carry him to the place where he had begun. Two hundred yards was like five miles. If he walked on the bare rocks, they burned the bottom of his feet, and so he walked in the water, ankle deep, but very slowly. Sometimes his feet slipped down between rocks and he would bruise his ankle bone or his heel. His feet weren't used to this. When he reached the point of departure, he had to rest and gain his strength back. Finally he plunged in and stroked his way back across, coming out a little below where he had calculated his shoes to be. By the time he had his shoes and his jeans on and had begun to walk across the rocks to where the road began, he knew he was in trouble. His watch said 5:30 and his father would be home from the fields. When he walked into the yard, it was after six.

"Where've you been?" his father asked. He was in one of his moods. He'd been drinking and his face was flushed with anger.

"At the river," said David.

"I thought I told you not to go over there."

"I'm sorry. It was my last day, and I wanted to see it."

"I suppose you went swimming."

"Yes, sir."

"Well," said his father, "you're going to be punished." He took off his leather belt. "Bend over, and put your hands on the table," he said.

It was his Lowell training that saved David. His instinct told him this was a contest and that the only way he could win was to take it, and take it without a sound. He couldn't lose his temper and he couldn't cry. He couldn't fight it, because there was a rule and he had broken it. O.K., he would take it like a man. Terry had taught him that, when he'd been paddled by Armbrister. "It was worth it," Terry had told him later, "as long as you don't say anything or slobber or break down."

So David stood there, feeling the strokes of the belt, one after the other, some on his behind and some on the backs of his thighs. And when the man finished, David looked him in the eye and walked out. Later, in the barn, he cried, not out of pain but in anger. He would write Molly Ariel. He would tell her that he was not going back to his father. He wouldn't be a Judas, he wouldn't tell her about the clubhouse or the beating. He would just tell her that he wasn't going back.

∞

He picked up the train in Sacramento, and as he waved to his father and Diane and Jimmy and Sarah from the window, he suddenly felt free. For four days there was nobody to tell him what to do. His father had given him money for his meals, and he couldn't get into trouble on a train except by getting out somewhere and having the train leave him behind. He wasn't stupid enough to do that.

He marvelled as he watched the porter convert the car into upper and lower bunks. David had a lower, and when he pulled the thick, green curtains and buckled them shut and tucked his clothes into the little net bag at the head of the bed, he felt like an enchanted being in a magic world. He kept the shade up so he could see the night stars and countryside passing by like a movie. In the daytime he would study and find out where they were going. He learned the names of the states — Nevada, Utah, Wyoming, South

Dakota, Nebraska — and he read over his father's instructions about changing trains in Chicago. He would arrive at the Union Station. He was to take a taxi cab to the LaSalle Street station and go to Track 5 for the "Empire State" to New York.

He liked being in control. He liked making decisions and taking care of himself. Decisions were hard only if what you wanted to do was different from what someone else wanted to do. Then you had to decide whether to do what you wanted or what they wanted. With adults it was tricky, because if you made the wrong decision, then they got mad. So it was better to do what they wanted, if you could figure it out. Sometimes you couldn't. It was like they expected you to know what to do without being told, and you had to guess the right answer. It was the same way at school. Your teachers asked you questions, and if you gave them the answers they wanted, then you got good grades. Sometimes you just couldn't do it, or sometimes, like with his father, David thought, he just couldn't be what his father wanted him to be. He wanted me to be tough and strong and not afraid of snakes. He wanted me to be like him, but I'm not.

The change in Chicago went smoothly, and the new train made its way along the great lakes and down the Hudson River valley to New York. David loved the familiar sight of the 125th Street Station, and he counted the blocks until the beginning of the tunnel. At Grand Central Terminal he was met by a small, white-haired lady with fierce blue eyes.

"I'm your Aunt Estelle," she said, and extended her hand. She was like a miniature in black, thin as a bird, with hat, dress, shoes, and umbrella all matching. She walked rapidly with David following behind her as best he could with his two big suitcases. Out onto 42nd Street she marched, and David learned quickly that the umbrella was not for rain, it was for hailing cabs.

"To the Plaza," she said to the driver, and off they rattled across 42nd to Fifth and then up to the magnificent old hotel.

"You'll have to check your luggage at the desk," she said. "You can pick it up afterwards."

They sat at a table for two in the Oak Room.

"Well, I hear you're not much of a rancher," she said.

"No ma'am," said David.

"Don't ma'am me, David. It bores me to death. At my age, everybody ma'ams me. Call me Estelle or Aunt Estelle, but not ma'am."

David laughed. "Yes, Aunt Estelle," he said.

"And don't 'ant' me either. I'm not a small insect with six legs. Pronounce your 'a' as 'ah'."

"Yes, Aunt Estelle," the boy said, pronouncing the "a" as she had requested.

A waiter with black trousers and an emerald green jacket came to take their orders.

"What do boys eat?" she asked the waiter.

"Hamburger, Miss Hamilton, and French fried potatoes," said the waiter, with a quick wink at David.

"Well, bring him some, then," she smiled. "I've never entertained a gentleman this age for luncheon before."

"Yes, Miss Hamilton," said the waiter. "And for yourself, Miss Hamilton?"

"I'll have the bouillabaisse, and spinach salad with oil and vinegar."

"Very good, madam." He turned and walked off slowly with great importance.

"What's bouillabaisse?" David asked.

"It's a cold cream soup with fish and potatoes. It's delicious, especially on hot summer days." She smiled. "You're not bad looking," she went on. "In fact, you're much better looking than I expected. I like your chin. It's a strong chin. Your father gave the impression in his letter that you were a weak person. I don't agree. You have your mother's eyes and nose, I can see that. How is your mother? I never see her anymore."

David really didn't know. He hadn't seen his mother since Christmas. "She's been in the hospital," he said. "I think she's better now."

"Oh, I see," said Aunt Estelle. "Well, she certainly did break your father's heart."

"How is that?" asked David.

"Every summer she came to New York, every summer. She left poor Allan alone on the coast and brought the child, your sister, east on the train, and spent two months with her mother at the beach. You can't expect a marriage to go on like that. It broke his heart. The summer after you were born, she just brought you both and never went back. They were divorced in Reno. That's as close as she came to California again. I couldn't bear to see her."

"And that's why they got divorced?"

"As far as I can see," said Aunt Estelle, beckoning to the waiter. "Bring the boy a Coca-Cola, Harold, would you please?" and then she went on as if she had never stopped, "...Of course, there were other reasons, the drinking, and your father's health, but mainly, I believe, it was your grandmother. She never could accept your father. She always thought your mother was too good for him, and she made her come east. She had great power over your mother. They were very close."

"Aunt Estelle," David began, "I was wondering..."

"Don't wonder, boy," she returned. "Just ask."

"Do you live here?" David asked.

"Goodness, no. I can't afford it. It's much too expensive — any other questions?"

"Well," David hesitated. "I don't quite understand who you are, you know, how we are related."

She laughed. "I'm your father's aunt. I'm the sister of your father's mother, your grandmother Lear."

"Thank you," said David.

After lunch, they walked back to the main desk and through the Palm Court out onto the street where the horses and carriages waited for customers. She hailed a cab, and dropped him off at the Columbus Circle subway station.

"That wasn't so bad, was it?"

"No," he answered, "I enjoyed it, and I'll call you when I come back for Christmas."

"Good," she said, and turned her cheek toward him. "Now kiss me, and get along."

Her cheek was leathery and smelled of powder where he kissed her. But he didn't mind.

By the time he'd hauled his bags down the hill to Elizabeth's he was sweating heavily. The perspiration was running down his forehead into his eyes and from under his arms to his waist. Even with his coat off and his tie untied, he felt hot.

&#8734;

The next day he went to see his mother. He really didn't want to go at all, and after breakfast he looked for excuses.

"Let's take the baby for a walk up Riverside Drive," he said.

"You're stalling," said Elizabeth. "We'll take Alex walking afterwards."

"Why don't you go with me?" he asked.

"Because, David, I live here. I see Mommy all the time. You haven't seen her since Christmas. That's eight months."

"I'm scared."

"Don't be silly. She's your mother and she loves you. You're not scared, you're just guilty. Now go on."

As he walked out the door she added, "Remember, she needs your love."

He wondered about that. Walking down Broadway, glancing in the windows of his favorite shops — the bakery with its fresh rolls and cakes, the florist with its green-tinted windows, the cigar store — he thought about love. He didn't really know what it was. "Do you love me, David?" she had asked the last time. "Say that you love me," she had said, and he wouldn't, couldn't. What was love? Being held by her and touched and smelling her breath? Sitting in her room and watching her dress and undress and talk and smoke cigarettes?

He turned into the hotel and rode to the fourth floor in the tiny elevator that bumped its way upward, the accordion-like door rattling away like a Model T Ford. She was in a different room from the one he had seen at Christmas, nearer the back on a narrow hallway near the emergency stairs. He knocked.

When she came to the door he was shocked by her appearance. It was not the gray; he noticed that before. It was as if everything had dropped. The flesh on her face had fallen, her breasts and shoulders sagged, and the skin under her arms flapped when she moved.

"Sit down, Sweetie," she said.

He looked for a chair, but they were covered with her things, old books and magazines, stockings and slips and dresses draped over the back and down the legs. She cleared him a space.

"Don't be so damned fastidious," she said. "You're worse than your father. Everything so neat and clean. Christ, you make me sick."

David was frightened. He sat on the chair and waited. He wouldn't say anything.

She sat on the bed and sipped from a glass of Coca-Cola, took a Chesterfield from the pack and quickly lit it. Then she began to talk, the cigarette hanging from her mouth.

"You know what they want to do? Come on, David. I wasn't born yesterday. I'm no damned fool. All this going to California, Estelle meeting you at the station, lunch at the Plaza Hotel. You eat it up, don't you? Well, don't you?"

"Yes," he said.

"They're buying you. All of them. Allan, Molly, Estelle — the whole bunch. They want you, and they're buying you. You're disgusted with me, aren't you? They already have you. Look at me. I SAID LOOK AT ME."

He looked at her, slowly, sadly.

"They want you. Well, you remember this. I'm your mother. And when you had all those damned operations on your feet, it wasn't they who did all the exercises with you day after day. It wasn't Allan Lear who twisted and kneaded and pulled those feet so you could walk around today in your Brooks Brothers shoes. It wasn't fancy Estelle who came to sit with you in the hospital with every operation. She didn't leave her room at the Plaza to help."

Suddenly he realized that she wanted him to cry, to break down and say I love you and hold her. He held firm, gazing steadily at her, through her, by her, out the window toward the light that flickered through the small holes in the shade.

Then she was silent and her face changed, and for a moment David saw the beauty his father had spoken of, the beauty of the girl who had played the piano and sat so straight, smiling with the men surrounding her. She was not angry any more.

"Come here, Toots, and sit by me. I won't eat you up."

Her voice was gentle and she looked at him like she was looking for her lost youth. Her eyes were bright with the memory of some forgotten evening, maybe, something before all this.

"What is it, Mom?" he asked.

"When you were little, your eyes were so bright, and your fingers danced. I'd sit you on top of the piano while I played, and watch your fingers leap to the music. I never read a note. Always played by ear, singing and watching your eyes and fingers. Do you remember that?"

"No," he said.

"What do you remember?"

No answer.

"Come on, Toots. Talk to me. You've got to remember."

"I remember the hospital," he said gravely.

"Good things. You've got to remember good things. Look at me. I don't want you to remember me like this. I was beautiful. We were happy for a while. You and little Elizabeth and I."

He didn't remember that. Except for Gretel and the green Plymouth.

"I remember the car," he said, " and you driving me to the beach, and swimming, and the waves."

"And me playing the piano?"

"No."

He was honest, at least. He would not tell her what he did not remember even though he knew that she wanted him to. He knew about grownups and how there were things which they wanted to hear and things they did not want to hear, but somehow he could not lie to her.

"I'm going to die," she said flatly.

He did not answer.

"I said I'm going to die. A year, two years, I don't know. I can't last much longer. I've gone sick inside, David, and I'm going to die, and I don't want you to remember me like this. Do you understand?"

"Yes."

There was a silence while she lit another cigarette.

"It's because of that weekend, isn't it?"

"What?"

"It's because of that weekend when you came down from school and I didn't meet you. You've been cold ever since. That's why, isn't it?"

"I guess so."

He wanted to leave now, and go out into the August sun, to the beach, to the country, to school, somewhere away from this.

"What did Phil tell you?"

"That you couldn't be trusted."

"Oh Jesus, that smug bastard. Your mother can't be trusted. I can just hear him. Oh, David, David, David. I'm your mother, don't you understand that? You can't just stop loving someone because they can't be trusted. Everything's so nice and neat up there at that snotty school. But life is messy, Honey. Do you understand?"

"Yes," he answered.

"You're almost thirteen, David. A teenager. You can't hide from the world all your life. You can't spend all your time just being careful and pleasing people with money. I'm your mother. You can't just throw me away."

He knew that she was right but he also knew that he did not know what to say to her or what to do for her. He was a boy and it was not fair, he thought, that he should have to do this.

"Do you know what I live on? Do you know what I eat and drink? Do you know how I feel in this crummy room in the middle of the night when my stomach hurts and I want a drink so bad I can cry and there isn't any, and what it's like to be alone? Do you know that? Do you ever think up there at that rich school of yours about the telegram you're going to get some day? 'Mother dead.' Well, think about it. I haven't got long, Toots."

She got up and slipped off the house coat and began, as he remembered her doing before in the other hotel, rummaging through the clothes on the chair, on the bed, in the closet, hunting the right dress, then finding it and slipping it over her head, then down across her hips.

"Zip me up, will you, Toots?"

She turned and smiled.

"It's nice to have a man to zip you up. I can never reach back there."

Suddenly his head cleared.

"Can I take you to lunch, Mom?" he asked.

"Why, yes, that would be very nice, she smiled. "I thought you'd never ask. Now go downstairs to the lobby and buy me a pack of Chesterfields while I put my face on."

The restaurant wasn't the Oak Room at the Plaza, but it was nice, and it was dark and quiet with red-checkered tablecloths and pictures of the baseball players on the walls, DiMaggio and Williams and Musial, Bob Feller and Peewee Reese.

"You know what I'd like to do more than anything in the whole world?" he said.

"What?"

"I'd like to go to Yankee Stadium and see Joe DiMaggio play. He's my favorite."

"Why?"

"Because he's from San Francisco and he has bone spurs in his heel. Everybody in California loves him. He used to play for the San Francisco Seals, and they always have articles about him in the paper, how he plays even though he's hurt. His heel is like Achilles'. It's like that's his weak spot. It sort of makes him like me. We both were born in San Francisco, and we both have Achilles' heels. Anyway, he's super, and I want to see him play."

She laughed. "I love to hear you talk, and smile. You're always so morose around me. It scares me. Don't be so serious all the time, O.K.?"

"O.K."

"Now tell me about your summer."

He told her some of it, leaving out the part about the house and the river. He didn't want her to know these things. "Daddy told me about meeting you and the great Council of War and how you got married."

"You mean the great pregnancy alarm?"

"Yes, were you really?"

"Probably. I wasn't sure, but it was worth the chance."

"Why did you and Daddy get divorced? He said it was because of your mother."

"That's him, all the way. He could never stand her. Used to call her 'the great Southern lady.'"

David laughed. "He still does."

"Your father's a big talker," she said. "He always was. He read a lot, he was smart, and could talk about anything. He could never hold a job, though. It drove me crazy. He had a swelled head. He thought he was God. He could never take orders from anybody. After a few months or a year, he'd start coming home and bitching about how everybody over him was stupid and didn't know what they were doing, and then he'd get transferred to another division, and things were O.K. for a while, and then it would start again. I took Lizzie back East for relief. He drank too much. We both drank too much."

"And now?"

"Now what?"

"Do you drink too much?"

"I'm on the wagon. Can't you tell? No drink on the table. That's where I was in June, at one of those places you go to dry out. They call 'em hospitals, but they're just drying out places for sots."

"And will you always now? I mean, always not drink?"

"I don't know. It's hard, Toots, real hard, and it doesn't much matter, anyway. It's too late. I've got something wrong inside. It hurts like hell, sometimes. Next week I go to Bellevue for tests, then an operation, maybe, and then…we'll just have to wait. Let's talk about something else."

When the meal was over, his mother tried to take the check, but he put his hand over hers like he had seen men do in the movies. "I'm taking you to lunch," he said proudly, and he pulled a ten-dollar bill from his wallet and handed it to the waiter.

# CHAPTER
*nine*

*A*ND THEN IT WAS TIME for school. David was happy, no he was more than happy, as he walked down the ramp at Track 32 with his suitcases in his hand. He looked at the initials M.H. on his leather bag, and he said to himself, "I'm leaving, Maggie Hope. I'm going to school." He had been to his father's, he had visited his mother, and now it was finally time to go back. He was a Fifth Former, one of the older boys, and he was going to school.

In the Lowell School car all was chaos, parents saying goodbye, boys chasing each other down the aisles. David remembered the first time he had taken the train and he laughed at how young he was, how scared. From the other end of the car he heard a whistle and then saw a tall blonde head rise above the others. It was Terry, and next to him, his brown bowl of hair flopping in all directions, was Griff. They had saved him a seat.

On the way up they talked, talked about their summers, Griff's in Bermuda. "Alcatraz in Technicolor," he called it. "There's nothing to do there."

"What about you, Butter Rum?" Terry asked. "Did you get to see her?"

"Who?" asked David.

"Molly Ariel, stupid," said Griff.

"No," said David.

Bit by bit they dragged the story of the summer out of him, and then they voted, solemnly, two to one, that he had to write Molly Ariel.

A week later, David showed them the letter.

*Dear Molly,*

*I am writing to thank you for sending me to school. The summer was O.K., but I don't want to go back. My father is nice and Diane is nice, but I would rather go to you. We just started a new year, and I will do my best. Do you ever come to New York? Maybe we can talk at Christmas. Should I go to Elizabeth for Christmas? It is very crowded there, and I don't think Phil likes me to stay there. I need money for clothes. My stuff is wearing out, and I don't know what to do about it. I am sorry to bother you with all this, but I don't know who else to write.*

*Love, David*

Two weeks later the answer came back:

*Dear David:*

*Thank you for your letter. I will be in New York for three days from December 20-23, and will be staying at the St. Regis. Come to me then, and we will do your shopping and discuss next summer. Keep up the good work.*

*Affectionately, Molly*

He was so excited he could hardly stand it. In fact he was so excited he almost forgot about Mickey Saperstein.

"The reason he's so smart is because he's a Jew," said Terry Roche.

Mickey had come to Lowell as a fourth former. He was small and wiry, dark-skinned, with glasses and curly, black hair. And he was smart.

David didn't like him, and it bothered him that he didn't like him, because David wanted to be fair. He knew about prejudice and what had happened to the Jews during the war. In The March of Time they showed pictures of the Jews in the prison camps when the war ended and the American soldiers opening the gates and the bodies in rags like skeletons with dirty sheets on. "That's what prejudice can do," Mr. Armbrister had said. "A Lowell boy is fair; he does not discriminate because of race or religion."

Still David did not like Mickey Saperstein. Maybe it was the withered arm, the one arm thinner and shorter than the other and the miracle of Mickey playing second base on the baseball team and catching the ball in his glove on the right hand, flipping the glove up with one motion and catching the ball in the same hand and throwing it to first, the withered arm useless, and his batting mostly with the one good arm. It made David mad. Here was David with two strong arms and strong shoulders from the crawling when he was little who couldn't hit and couldn't field and loved baseball with a love that surpassed everything.

Or maybe it was Mr. Parilli liking Mickey being the best student in science.

"It's 'cause he's a Jew," said Terry Roche. "That's why Parilli likes him. He's got that Jew smirk."

"Jews are always good in science. Look at Einstein," said Griff.

"Parilli's out to get you," said Terry. "He doesn't want you to win the Founder's Medal."

"That's not true," said David. "It's just that I'm no good in science and Mickey is, and I'm no good in baseball. Mr. Myers likes me, and Mr. Parilli likes Mickey. That doesn't mean he's out to get me."

David was uncomfortable in science. After class Mickey would walk up to Mr. Parilli's desk and smile and Mr. Parilli would smile and they would talk like they were old friends or something. David didn't know what was going on, and Terry Roche would nudge him on the way out of class.

At the end of the fall term Mickey got a 98 in science and David an 89. David beat Mickey in Latin and English and math, but Mickey was so strong in science that his overall average was a half point higher than David's. For the first time he was second in his class, and he sulked about it all the way to New York, until Griff gave him the solution.

"Tell her about it," he said.

"Tell who what?" said David moodily. He was looking out the window waiting for Portchester to come.

"Tell Molly Ariel, she'll know what to do."

"No, she won't," said David. "She'll just be mad at me because I'm not first. She sends me to school because I'm smart. If I'm not number one, maybe she won't want to send me anymore. Then what will happen?"

"Well, maybe Mrs. Rossiter will adopt you," laughed Terry Roche.

"I sure wouldn't mind that," said Griff. "That would beat the Beethoven blues."

David blushed. The whole school loved Mrs. Rossiter. She had soft, brown hair that curled under at the sides and white teeth and laughing eyes. She directed the choir, and David sang his heart out for her. He would watch her hands move and her lips make the words as she directed, and he could see the soft movement of her breasts under her blouse. That would be all right, he thought, being adopted by Mrs. Rossiter.

"Look at David blush," said Terry. "He looks more like cherry than butter rum." And soon they were laughing and tickling each other under the ribs and standing to cheer and give the club salute as the train passed the Lifesaver factory at Portchester. He would worry about Mickey Saperstein later.

∞

The lobby at the St. Regis was soft and elegant. From the moment that David passed through the revolving door to the suck of rubber he was in a magic world. At first he could hardly see at all. The sun had been so bright outside that he had to stand still and close his eyes for a moment. When he opened them he could see blue and gold uniformed bellboys carrying bags toward the elevator. How old did you have to be to be a bellboy, he wondered. He needed money, but there wasn't much you could do to make money when you were twelve. He was almost thirteen. Maybe Molly would know. He walked to the desk and asked for her room number as she had instructed him to do.

"Eight thirteen, sir," the man at the desk said.

How strange to be called "sir." The masters were "sir" and his grandfather. He stopped in front of the elevators and looked at himself in the mirror. His overcoat was too short and frayed at the cuffs. He took it off and looked again. The familiar blue suit and red tie seemed strangely out of place here, as if this Sunday uniform of the Lowell School could not live outside its own environment without calling attention to itself as some kind of monster. It seemed ugly and awkward with the pockets crumpled at the edges and the food-stains which Elizabeth had tried to wipe off still damp from the rag she had used. Molly would think he didn't know how to take care of himself.

The elevator was silent as it rose to the eighth floor. He could only tell it was stopping by the little flutter in his stomach as the floor pressed against his feet. How different from the elevator at his mother's. He got out, and the memory of the day he had run away from school and hidden in the bushes by his house came back to him. He had been sent home to get something, some form that was required. He lived only two blocks away, and he had come across the street to the front door and frozen, terrified that his mother would be mad at him for forgetting the form. He couldn't go back to school; he couldn't knock on the door. So he hid, in the bushes by the front door, stayed in the bushes all day until it was time for school to be out, and then knocked on the door as if nothing had happened, as if it had been a normal day. And how, standing in the hallway of the St. Regis, he felt the same fear, the same terror that had gripped him on that other occasion.

He stood in front of the door to Room 813. Suppose he didn't like her, or suppose, even worse, that she didn't like him? It was the new-ness of the thing, the strangeness of it, the not knowing, which terri-fied him, and so he stood for a long time, and then finally knocked.

Molly Ariel opened the door and stretched out her hand. He

shook it. It was a strong hand, firm. There was no foolishness about her, no crying or fussing, or talk about love or kissing and getting lipstick on his cheek.

"Sit down, chum, and let me look at you," she said.

He sat in the chair next to the table by the window. She sat on the bed.

"I bet you're hungry," she said.

"Yes," he answered.

She was short, like Elizabeth, with her brown hair cut close under the ears, her skin tan from the California sun, a simple beige dress with a gold pin. She took a long cigarette from her purse.

"I've never seen that kind," he said.

"It's a Fatima. It's got more Turkish tobacco than other brands."

"Do you like smoking?"

"It's a filthy habit, but I like it. Yes, I do like it."

Everything she said was straight. It made him feel like nothing else mattered.

"You need some clothes," she said. "I'll take you to Brooks Brothers after lunch."

They ate in the dining room of the hotel. She would not let him order a hamburger.

"You can have a hamburger any time. You need to develop a taste for different food."

While they ate, she talked.

"I guess you're pretty confused about things, eh, chum?"

He nodded and swallowed a bite of his eggs benedict. She had said he would like them when she ordered for him. The memory of eggs at school had touched him for a moment, and he was scared, scared he would disappoint her. But when he tasted them, they were good. She had been right. The yellow sauce was delicious.

"I think you're old enough to understand some of this. Do you want me to try and explain it to you?"

Another nod. Another bite.

"Let me start with Bernie. I knew your mother wasn't well enough to take care of you, let alone herself, so I just gave Bernie a certain amount of money to pay your school bills and buy your clothes. When he left, I decided to try your father. We had a long talk last spring and he agreed to take over the bills and have you out for the summer."

"But why didn't I come to you?"

"I wanted you to be a part of your own family."

"But why?"

"Because it's right. A person ought to have a blood family. I wanted someone in your family to be in charge of you. I would just work behind the scenes."

"Do you have children of your own?"

"No. My husband, Jack, has two children by his first wife. They live with her in the wintertime and come to us at the ranch in the summer. In fact, Jessie is just a little older than you, and Bert a little younger.

"Can I come to you this summer?"

She looked at him and smiled. "Yes, I think so, chum."

He told her everything, while they ate and while they walked and shopped, about the Lifesavers and Elizabeth and Phil and the baby and the summer at his father's. He told her about Mickey Saperstein.

"Of course you hate him," she laughed.

"But why?"

"Because he's competition. He's a rival. That's all right. You don't have to like him. Just respect him. Be fair."

"And if he wins?"

"Then take him by the hand and congratulate him."

"And would you be mad?"

"If he beat you out?"

"Yes."

"Why should I?"

"I don't know. I just always thought I had to win."

"For yourself, if you like, David. Not for me."

He hadn't thought of it that way before.

"You like the competition, don't you? It keeps you going, gives you something to work for. That's fine. I'm very proud of you. Just do your best."

"How can I beat him if he's a Jew?" David asked suddenly. "Jews are smarter. That's what everybody says."

"David, that's nonsense, complete nonsense. Jews do well, because no matter where they go in the world, they are outsiders. In our country clubs, we have signs that say, 'No Jews Allowed.' They work harder, because that's their road to success. That's where they get their security. They succeed, because they work harder, that's all."

He liked her. Of course, he knew he would like her, but she was special in just the right way. He thought about it, sitting in the subway on the way back to Elizabeth's, his boxes from Brooks Brothers piled on the empty seat beside him. "She's — what's the word — safe." Maybe it wasn't the right word. What he meant was that she made him feel safe. She was hard, but she was fair. He had asked her about money:

"I won't let you starve and I won't let you go ragged," she'd said. "But if you want extra spending money, you'll have to work for it."

Starting in the fall he was to have an allowance. She would pay the school bills, and he was to have fifty dollars a month for clothing and expenses.

"If your socks wear out or your underpants or shirts, you can't wait for me or Elizabeth or your mother to take you to the store. What we bought today will get you through until the fall. Then you do it yourself, ok, chum?"

He liked it. It was good to be independent, he thought. The only hard part was being careful that you didn't get gypped and making sure that the money lasted. If you spent it all at the beginning of the month, there wasn't any left over for later. You had to save for the hard months like December and June. Christmas was the worst problem. Thinking up presents for people and trying to pay for them. It was already the 20th — "Three Shopping Days Till Christmas" all the signs shouted — and he hadn't bought anything for Elizabeth or Phil. Alex was no problem. He didn't know what Christmas was yet, anyway. He could get him a stuffed animal or something. But he felt funny coming home with the boxes and bags from Brooks Brothers and nothing for Elizabeth. He should have asked Molly what to get her.

He got off at 116th Street and walked up the stairs into the wind that whistled down Broadway.

When he came into the apartment, Elizabeth was crying. "Thank God, you're back," she said. "Keep an eye on Alex until Phil gets home. I've got to go the hospital right away. It's Mommy."

"What happened?"

"I don't know. They called me from the hotel and said she'd been taken in an ambulance. They found her unconscious in her room. It could be serious, or she might just have passed out."

"From drinking?"

"Yes, from drinking."

She wiped her eyes and blew her nose and looked in the mirror. "God, I look awful." she said.

"I thought she'd quit drinking," said David.

"She did, for a while, but she couldn't keep it up. God, it's just one thing after another."

She put on her coat and gloves, and tied a scarf around her head. "Give Alex a bottle about five. It's in the icebox. Warm it up, but not too hot. Squirt it on your hand first to see. Change his pants when he wakes up. You're a good kid." And she was out the door.

He knew he should feel sad about his mother, and he did, but he didn't want to see her — it scared him to think of what she might look like. And so he was glad to have Alex as a distraction. He was almost nine months and crawling like mad. David got down on all fours with him and they followed each other around like puppies from room to room. David piled blocks on top of each other, and Alex knocked them down, laughing. Even changing his pants wasn't too bad unless it was real runny or he'd sat in it and smushed it around. If it was in one piece, you could just flush it down the john and throw the diaper in the hamper.

Phil came in at six and Elizabeth a little after. She looked pale and tired.

"She's O.K., but for how long they don't know. Something about the kidneys. She'll be there three or four weeks for treatment. Then convalescence. She's pretty doped up right now. I'll go back tomorrow."

"Can I go, too?" asked David.

"You have to be thirteen to visit. No kids. They're worried about kids catching whatever's going around the hospital. Next year, Sweetheart. You can go next year; I'm sure she'll be back."

She went into the next room and lay down. David could hear her crying.

"I wish I could do something," said David.

"You are," said Phil. "Just your being here means a lot to Lizzie. She needs to get out and shop. She needs help with Alex. Just be here, that's plenty."

It was a funny Christmas. Elizabeth was teary and jittery. David liked it better when he was alone with Alex. He walked the baby in his stroller a lot up and down Broadway and Riverside Drive. David kept him wrapped up in his snowsuit and blanket. They shopped for gifts and David talked to the baby as if he were a grownup. Mr. Horowitz in the delicatessen thought he'd gone crazy.

"The kid don't understan' nothin'," he said. "Why you keep talkin' to 'im like that? You bonkers?"

"He helps me decide," said David. "Watch."

"Here are some pickles, Alex. Would your mom like pickles for Christmas?" Alex frowned.

"See, she doesn't like pickles."

"Yeah, but the kid don't know dat."

"Watch!" David held up a box of imported cookies.

"Does your mom like cookies?" asked David, with a big smile. Alex clapped his hands.

"See?" said David. "I told you. I'll take the cookies."

On the day before Christmas, Elizabeth got back from the hospital early. "Let's go buy a tree," she said.

So they bundled up Alex and set off down Broadway and looked at trees. There were only a few left. They were scrawny, and Elizabeth picked at them, and then started to cry.

"They're so ugly," she half sobbed.

"Come on, Elizabeth," said David. "You take Alex home and go lie down. I'll find a tree."

She wiped her nose. "It's not the trees, David, you know that."

"I know," he said. "You go on. I'll find one."

He wanted that. He liked that, having something to do, having some task to take his mind off it, somewhere to go away from Elizabeth and Alex and his mother, yet not away, not alone, only something to do to take his mind off of it. He saw the sign — IRT. SUBWAY. Then he thought of it. Of course. He slipped into the subway and took the local to 96th Street, and then the express to Columbus Circle. He walked the three long crosstown blocks alongside the park to the Plaza. He stopped at the door of the Oak Room, and looked around. There he was, the slow waiter who spoke like an Englishman.

"Excuse me, sir," the boy said.

"Yes?" replied the waiter, without seeming to exert himself.

"Do you know my great aunt, Miss Estelle Hamilton?"

"Of course. And you are the gentleman with whom she lunched late last summer. Mr. Lear, I believe."

"How did you know?"

"She speaks of you frequently, young man."

"Can you reach her? I mean, can I? I need to telephone her."

The waiter disappeared and came back with a number written on a piece of paper.

"Thanks. Thanks a lot," said David. "See you at lunch, soon."

He thought he saw a trace of a smile on the waiter's face.

"The hard part," he explained to Aunt Estelle at the lunch the next week, "was getting it home on the subway. I always seem to end up traveling in rush hour, and people kept pushing and shoving and breaking branches."

"But it was Christmas Eve," added Aunt Estelle.

"It certainly was," said David.

"And did it make Elizabeth happy?"

"Oh, yes, she cried and then laughed and cried some more and put the tree up in the corner and hugged me and asked me where I'd found it. I just said it was a secret. Thanks. I really appreciate what you did."

"I think it was rather clever, the way you found me. Harold told me about it."

"I didn't know his name was Harold."

"Oh, yes. I've known him since the old days, when I lived here."

She dropped her napkin, and David got up quickly, picked it up, and handed it back to her. Suddenly there was a look of alarm on her face. "Your shoes," she said. "I must give you some money to buy shoes. Your clothes do look better than they did this summer, but you mustn't wear dirty tennis shoes to luncheon."

David laughed and laughed. "Those aren't dirty tennis shoes, Aunt Estelle. Those are white bucks. They are the fashion. In fact, you can't wear them clean. Everybody would laugh at you and step on them, and get them dirty. Only nerds wear clean white bucks."

"Oh, I see," she said. "It's like hamburgers and french fries. It's what boys do."

"That's right."

"Well, I must say, I don't approve. Young people dressed better in my time."

∞

In the spring David was thirteen. He got pimples on his face, and fell in love with Mrs. Rossiter. Of course almost everyone was in love with Mrs. Rossiter, but David knew that his case was different.

Music class was twice a week in the basement under the big schoolroom. To the left, as you walked in the door of her classroom, there was a small window, high up on the wall, too high to see out of, and under the window, the record player. All fifth and sixth formers took music, and what Mrs. Rossiter did was to play examples of what Mr. Armbrister called "good" music from Bach to Stravinsky. You got through half of it the first year and the rest of it the second. Everyone liked music, because, no matter how awful Bach and Brahms or Sibelius were, you got to look at Mrs. Rossiter. Looking at Mrs. Rossiter was the favorite occupation of Lowell School boys.

She wore loosely fitting blouses with scooped necks. She would stand by her desk in the front of the room talking about Schubert's "Unfinished" or Beethoven's deafness or Mozart being so young, and she would point to the chart behind her with all the composers on it, with their births and deaths and thick lines to show how long they lived. Then she would pick up the record she was going to play, walk to the record player, bend over facing the class and put the record on. Now, David's seat was the most strategic in the room. Alphabetically the L's put him in the first seat in the second row, right in front of the record player. At first David didn't look. He wrote in his notebook or watched his feet or closed his eyes.

"I've been watching you," said Griff Ryan.

He and Terry Roche, being R's, sat at the other end of the row, too far to see.

"You're missing the show," said Terry Roche.

"What show?" asked David.

"Don't give me that crap," said Terry Roche.

David blushed. He knew, of course, what Terry was talking about. He just didn't know how to handle it. It was like seeing his father and Diane in bed the night of the thunderstorm. David wanted to look at Mrs. Rossiter's breasts as she bent over the record player, and he knew he would like looking at them, but something told him that it was wrong for him to look, and that if Mrs. Rossiter caught him or even worse if someone else caught him and told her, then he'd get in trouble and she wouldn't like him any more. So he started looking just a little but never letting on to anyone that he did, taking a quick glance as if he were moving his head from her desk to look out the window, or dropping his pencil and peeking at her as he bent to pick it up.

He loved Mrs. Rossiter and he wanted more than anything else for her to like him. David did everything he could with her. It was his third year in the choir, and he had been in the girls' chorus in The Mikado and Trial by Jury. But this year David would try out for a male part for the first time — the hero, Ralph Rackstraw in H.M.S. Pinafore and if he didn't make Ralph, then he would be a sailor. But he was worried. His voice wasn't working right. He could no longer reach some of the high notes, and there was a hoarseness in the low notes. When he tried out for Pinafore, Mrs. Rossiter took him aside.

"David," she said, "I think you better rest your voice a while."

He was frightened. He could feel his heart beating under his shirt, and he knew that if he spoke his voice would crack.

"Don't look so sad. You're just growing up. It happens to everyone. When you get to be thirteen or fourteen your voice starts getting lower, and for a while you sound like a sick frog."

He smiled, and she touched him on the shoulder with her hand.

"Why don't you drop out of the choir for the rest of this year and skip the operetta? By fall you'll probably be a baritone."

It hurt him terribly, and the worst part of it was he couldn't talk to anyone about it. Not even Griff and Terry. They'd just laugh. She was fair and she was right, and he did sound like a sick frog — that wasn't the point. It was that he wouldn't get to be with her. No choir practice, no operetta practice, and he'd have to sit in the pews with the rest of the school in the church. He'd never sat in the pews, not since his first few weeks at the school as a third former. He'd have to sit alphabetically with the fifth form L's. That was more than halfway back, and on the opposite side from the organ. He couldn't even see her from there.

That was March. One day early in April she asked him to stay after class.

She sat in the seat next to him, smoothing her skirt with her hands and looking worried.

"You seem different, David. Are you upset about something?"

He wanted her to hold him.

"What is it, David. Are you upset about something?"

"Oh, no." he said. "It's just..."

He could feel the tears beginning, and he didn't want to cry.

"It's the singing... I never..."

"You never what, David?"

"Never...get to...see you anymore."

There — he'd blurted it out.

"Everybody...goes to choir and to practice and...I never..."

"Oh, I see," she said.

There was a long pause. He wiped his nose with the back of his hand, and felt kind of stupid.

"I have an idea," she said. "You can be my assistant. Since you can't sing, you can just turn pages in church and help me with things for the operetta. Would you like that? It isn't very exciting, but you'd still be part of the show. O.K.?"

He wanted more than anything in the world to throw his arms around her and say thank you over and over.

"Yes," he said. "I would like that very much."

She reached out and touched him on the cheek. "Now, scoot," she said, "and wipe that frown off your face."

It was heavenly. All of April and May he had a chair right next to her in the church, and he turned pages, and helped find props for the show, and ran to the village to buy cough drops when her voice was hoarse. She smelled of lilac, and he dreamed of her at night. She would take him home to her house. There was no Mr. Rossiter, Terry Roche said. He was dead or they were divorced. Nobody really knew, and David certainly wasn't going to ask. She would take him home, and he would have his own room for the weekend, with clean sheets and soft blankets and curtains billowing, and she would come in and kiss him goodnight, and go downstairs and play the piano until he went to sleep. No, he wouldn't mind being adopted by her.

Mr. Parilli liked to tease him about it. He confused David, ignoring him at times and beaming big hello's from his barrel chest at others, catching him in the hall on the way to operetta practice and talking to him, David knew, just to keep him from getting there.

"And where is Butter Rum off to so fast tonight?" he would boom, standing in the doorway of the staff room with his bull neck and thick legs spread wide. He had played football at Boston College, and Terry Roche said that if he hadn't hurt his knee his senior year he might have been an All-American.

"I'm going to operetta practice, sir."

"Aaah, I see," the big man would answer with a knowing wink toward one of the other teachers in the room. "And how is your — uh — throat feeling tonight, young David? Won't be able to sing...have to stand next to Mrs. Rossiter."

David would blush and not know whether to leave or try to

say something. If he left, Parilli could call him back and make him stand there forever. If he said something, it would come out wrong. Parilli liked to be funny, and people like Mickey Saperstein, who could make wise remarks, or Terry, who was a big athlete, did fine with him, but David was just confused.

"Go on, go on." Parilli would say after a while and turn back into the room, and David would run all the way to the gym for practice, half looking over his shoulder to see if the man was following him.

Then Mickey took up the teasing, snickering and making dirty remarks. They were walking back from baseball practice one afternoon, Mickey from the varsity field and David from the field below where the fifth and sixth formers who hadn't made the varsity practiced.

"Here comes Debbie's darling," said Mickey to one of his friends.

"Lay off, Saperstein," said Terry Roche.

"Stop protecting him, Roche," said Mickey. "Why don't you let him stand up for himself?"

David kept walking. He tried to ignore him just as he tried to ignore Parilli. It was the only way. If he got involved he'd get mad. And if he got mad then he'd lose control like he had in soccer or like he had with his father. That's what Mr. Myers had been trying to teach him, not to let his temper get the better of him, to walk away and calm down. But Mickey wouldn't let him. Even in the locker room, as they undressed for showers, Mickey kept after him.

"She's a whore, that's all she is. Everybody knows that."

"She is not."

"That's why her husband left her."

David reddened with anger.

"Take it back," he said.

"Shove it, Lear," the other boy said, turning away.

David grabbed his shoulder. Mickey wheeled suddenly.

"Take your hands off me," he said.

"I will if you take it back."

"She's a whore," said Mickey.

Then David hit him in the nose, drawing blood, and Mickey

hit him back in the stomach, and they were hitting and clawing and wrestling on the floor of the locker room, David crying with rage and other boy laughing triumphantly, his glasses broken, his nose bleeding, his withered arm raised above his head.

He sat on the long leather sofa in Mr. Armbrister's office watching the headmaster.

"It's your Achilles heel, this temper. Don't you see, David? You can't let people goad you into fights. You're number one. You're at the top. They want to bring you down to their level to make you think dirty thoughts, to cheat and steal and fight. Do you ever steal magazines or candy from the drugstore in the village?"

"No, sir."

"Do they ask you to? Do they dare you to?"

"Yes."

"And what do you think?"

"I think I'd like to try it, but I'm scared to."

"But you only want to try it because they want you to. Debbie Rossiter doesn't need your protection. She needs your strength, your self discipline, your best effort. It's easy to be like the others. It's hard to be yourself."

"Yes, sir."

A pause, then, "The fight will cost you five marks and loss of town privileges for the rest of the year."

"Yes, sir."

Outside the office Mickey was waiting.

"What'd you get?" he asked.

"Five marks and restricted to school grounds," David answered.

"Me too," said Mickey.

They started back toward the schoolroom, then hesitated.

"Listen, David," said Mickey. "I'm sorry. I mean I didn't know about your mother and all…well, I wouldn't have teased you about Mrs. Rossiter…Mr. Armbrister explained."

David wondered what Mr. Armbrister had said, what Mickey

meant by "your mother and all." It was strange how you could be so mad at someone one minute and then get over it so quickly.

"Truce?" asked Mickey.

"Sure," said David.

They shook hands.

"I'm sorry I hit you."

"I'm sorry I teased you."

It was all right now. They would never be friends like Terry and Griff were or like Mickey was with Chip Epskin, who was the short-stop on the baseball team. But they would be friendly enemies, rivals. Maybe they'd had to have their fight before they settled down to the real business.

"My godmother says it's because we're competing for the Founder's Medal."

"Yes, that's what my dad told me."

"Well, the fight didn't help either of us," laughed David.

"No," said Mickey. "How about you picking a fight with some-one else next time?"

Prize Day was gloomy for David. For the first time in his years at Lowell he didn't win anything. His marks had ruined his general average, so he didn't win anything for behavior. Mickey beat him out for the highest scholastic average in the fifth form, and Mr. Par-illi had ruined his perfect punctuality record only three days before.

David had lingered uncharacteristically in the bathroom to in-spect his face. There were pimples just below his eyes on either side of his nose and blackheads in the small cleft between his mouth and chin. His hair looked terrible. No matter how he combed it, it seemed as if he was going bald. Finally he had hit upon an idea: He would change the part to the other side and comb his hair over the receding place where the old part had been. Good, he thought, as he moved the comb from the left to the right and started making the line forward. Only he was left-handed, and his left hand didn't reach over to the right side of his head very well, and so he tried it with his right hand, and because he wasn't used to using his right hand, the line came out crooked, and he had to do it again and again. And suddenly it seemed very quiet, and he realized that he was the last one left in the dorm. He'd be late. He took off down the stairs two at a time, full speed, down and around, down and around, and hit the main floor outside the staff room.

"Gotcha, Butter Rum," came a familiar voice.

He froze. It was Parilli. And there was no way to get out of it.

"You know there's no running allowed in the building."

"Yes, sir, but I'll be late."

"You should have left earlier."

"I know, sir, but…"

He could hear Armbrister's gong from the dining room. Three more marks for running, a lateness, and the end of his punctuality record.

The Lifesavers had their final meeting of the year on the New York train. Griff's family had moved to the Bahamas and he was flying from New York. Terry was going to the Jersey shore for a couple of weeks before he went to camp. David was going to Elizabeth's, and then would take the train to California. Molly Ariel had promised he wouldn't have to fly.

"Will you see your father?" asked Terry.

"He's moved to Phoenix, Arizona," said David.

"I wonder what it's like there," asked Terry.

"It's so hot you can water the flowers with your sweat," said Griff. "You can fry an egg on the sidewalk in July."

"It doesn't matter. I'm not going there, anyway," said David.

"But don't you want to, just a little bit?" said Griff.

"No. I just want to go to Molly's," David answered.

He felt funny about his father. It was as if he wanted to like him and didn't like him, and felt bad that he didn't like him. He felt guilty. Maybe he should stop at Phoenix on the way home. Maybe there was a train from San Francisco to Phoenix that would get him home. He'd have to look at an atlas and figure out the route.

"What about your mom?" asked Terry.

"I don't know if I'll see her. Sometimes I do and sometimes I don't. Christmas, she was in the hospital. Elizabeth went to visit her, but I couldn't go, 'cause you have to be thirteen."

"She's in the hospital a lot," said Griff.

"I know," said David.

They talked about drinking and grownups and smoking and vacations, and football and Mr. Parilli and Mickey and Mr. Armbrister and Mrs. Rossiter, and after a while they grew pensive and quiet. In Grand Central Station they went their separate ways.

"So long, Orange."

"Bye, Cherry."

"Keep it cool, Butter Rum."

They were gone. David looked for his mother in the crowd as he always did, not expecting her, not even knowing if she knew that he was arriving. The school sent Molly Ariel the notices about vacation, and she would tell Elizabeth or Mrs. McCarver or whoever she wanted to be in charge. His mother couldn't be trusted, as Phil had said. It was sad, he thought. He picked up his suitcase and followed the signs for the shuttle to Times Square. Across town. One stop. Then FOLLOW GREEN ARROWS FOR WEST SIDE SUBWAY. Then the Broadway local or express to 116th Street, and the walk down the hill to the apartment.

It smelled when he went in the door of the building. It always smelled like something stale or fish frying or grease, and he was sweating now under the armpits from the walk with the heavy suitcases. He walked up the flight of stairs to 2A. Elizabeth wasn't home. Maybe she was at the grocery store or in the park with the baby. David opened the door with key that she had mailed him — "in case you ever need to get in and we're not home."

All at once he felt trapped. School had spoiled him with its space to run and play. Here in this two-room apartment that was no bigger than one of his classrooms three people had to live, four if David was there. Elizabeth and Phil had talked of moving into a bigger place with an extra bedroom and a real kitchen, but they couldn't afford it. Money confused David. It was as if he was rich and poor at the same time. Here were Elizabeth and Phil who could never go out even to the movies because they had no money and David going to his rich man's school, as his grandfather called it, with his Brooks Brothers suits and striped ties and button-down shirts, and his mother in a seedy hotel room four blocks down

Broadway, if she was not in the hospital. Molly Ariel was rich. Why didn't she give Elizabeth money? If David stayed at Elizabeth's, who paid for the groceries? Why didn't his grandmother and grandfather give her mother money or give Elizabeth money? He never saw them anymore. They were always in France or in Florida. Life was pretty stupid if you thought too much about it.

# CHAPTER
## *ten*

*M*OLLY ARIEL MET HIM at the train in her gray Bentley. It was the most beautiful car he'd ever seen, long and sleek with a dashboard of polished wood, instruments and dials everywhere, and soft leather upholstery. The road from San Francisco to Santa Cruz, where Molly lived, was winding, but the Bentley took the curves at sixty-five without even a squeal of the tires. With the windows closed you couldn't hear the engine.

"It's the best car made," said Molly. "I wouldn't own a Rolls. It's too flashy."

David loved her. Oh, he never said, "I love you, Molly," or anything like that. He couldn't wait to tell Terry Roche about the Bentley. "I wouldn't own a Rolls," he could hear himself saying, "It's too flashy." She drove with two hands on the wheel and a cigarette hanging from her mouth, her gray skirt hiked over her knees, her legs already brown from the California sun. David caught glimpses of the blue Pacific out the window as the Bentley swept silently around the curves.

Just north of Santa Cruz she turned and climbed into the hills. He was disappointed. He wanted the place to be on the water, near the beach so he could swim and ride the waves. Deeper and deeper she drove into the trees and then up a steep, winding, narrow road, up and up, until the trees thinned and there were brown fields and fences with Black Angus grazing. A left-hand turn, then the thwunk of tires as the Bentley crossed a cattle guard.

"We're home," she said.

That was nice, thought David as he got out. At school everyone always asked him where he lived, and he never knew what to say. Usually he said in New York with his sister, but he didn't really live there. It wasn't like there was a house and a yard and a family. Now he could say, "In California, with my godmother, on her ranch."

The house was gray like the car, long and curving in a crescent moon around the shape of the gravel circle on which the car stood. All the rooms had windows in the back overlooking the ocean. They hadn't left it after all, only gone high above so that every morning he could wake and look out his window past the giant Douglas firs down to the coast and the sea beyond. The whole place stood on the edge of the world, he thought, and dipped down into the sea.

From the driveway you could see three separate houses, the business section where Jack Ariel had his office, the middle section with the kitchen, dining and living rooms and Jack and Molly's bedroom over them, and to the right the children's section where David would live with Jessie and Bert.

They ate their meals together on the redwood terrace between the kitchen and the office. It never rained, and even if there was fog along the coast below, they were too high for it, and usually the sun had burned away the mist by the time they got up. It was like a magic kingdom sometimes, with the fog shrouding the rest of the world and the sun here above the clouds.

There was a rhythm to their days, a regularity that David came to cherish. Breakfast at nine, then mornings in the barns, grooming the favorite Black Angus bulls who were going to be shown at the state and county fairs in August and September. That was Bert's job, and he taught David carefully where to stand and how to brush. Jessie's department was horses. Some days David worked with her, bringing them hay and cleaning out their stalls with shovel and hose while they romped in the corral outside. In the afternoons the three of them could ride up and down the dusty roads and into the cool woods on winding trails through the trees.

Their usual costume was blue jeans, boots, and cowboy shirts that came off as the day got hotter. Jessie, who was fifteen, wore a halter to cover her breasts. David couldn't take his eyes off them. Bert, who was thirteen, but a year ahead of David in school, just laughed. "It's all right. She doesn't mind. She just thinks of herself as a guy with tits. She'd like to take her shirt off like us, but Jack and Molly won't let her."

David and Bert became great friends. Bert was like Griff Ryan. He was a natural-born comedian, making faces at the cows and coming up with one-liners that left David in tears. He also shared David's love for drama. In the evenings in their room they would work out plots for plays, and once a week on the redwood terrace they would perform them for Molly and Jack and their friends, using the garage as a dressing room and Jessie, if they could get her to cooperate.

"You're both obnoxious," she would say, "and your stupid plays are juvenile."

"Gasp, gasp," Bert would choke. "Get me a dictionary. Help!" And he would stagger off, holding his throat to look up "juvenile" in the dictionary. It was his way of pretending not to be smart.

In the end Jessie usually gave in, though sometimes she played men's parts because she was the tallest and Bert loved to dress up as a girl with socks inside his shirt and a scarf over her head. His specialty was the Charley's aunt character — a guy dressed up as a girl who has to change back and forth quickly. He loved the voice changes and the costume changes, and if his pants came down under his skirt when he was a woman, it just made it funnier.

David's favorite times were his talks with Molly. Jack went away on business a lot, and there would be evenings after dinner on the terrace when Molly liked to sit and smoke and watch the sun dip into the Pacific. Jessie and Bert usually went off to visit their animals. Then David and Molly would talk, as they had at the St. Regis, about school and grades, money and families and loyalty.

"Things shouldn't come too easily," she said. "If they do, you get soft and forget how to work. I'm glad you weren't number one this year. It'll make you respect the task more.

"Watch out for social pressures. They can swallow you up. You don't want a prep school like Andover or Exeter or Groton or Deerfield. They're too rich, and everyone goes to deb parties. You'd spend your whole year's allowance in a month trying to keep up with them. You need a place that's got values you can live by.

"We live out here to get away from the city and the people. The city's always there, if you want it. We can be in San Francisco in an hour or two, and Jack keeps an apartment there for business. The city can eat up your money, your time, and your energy. I like to garden, and I like to travel. I don't like seeing the same people over and over at cocktail parties."

One night he asked her about his mother.

"For a long time she was my best friend. The M and M girls, Molly and Maggie. We even looked alike. Then it got too complicated. Your father and I got thrown together every summer, when your mother took your sister back East. Toward the end we didn't see much of each other."

"But what was she like?" asked David.

"She was very beautiful and bright as a whip. She and your father had too much money and not enough discipline. When they went broke, her mother would bail her out or the Judge would send your father money. They could never face reality."

"What about my father?" he asked another time. "Will I see him again?"

"Do you want to?"

"No."

"Well, don't. We tried it last summer, and it didn't work."

"I somehow feel that I ought to, you know, like it's my fault we didn't get along."

"No, it's just his life. He's drinking too much and he's very irritable. Maybe later, if he stops drinking, you'll get along better."

"Why do people drink so much?" he asked.

"To escape," she said. "Because they hate themselves."

"My mother says I should never drink."

"You might be able to. Some people can drink socially and some can't. If you can take one or two drinks and stop, then you're all right."

He never tired of asking her questions. He liked her answers. They made sense to him. There were some adults you didn't ask questions, because you knew from the start you wouldn't like what they were going to say or you could tell by the looks on their faces that they didn't want to be bothered. But Molly was different. She made you feel important.

Next to Molly he liked the ocean best. It was strange. It had called to him from the day he arrived, beckoning from the back of the house. It was the first thing he saw in the morning and the last at night, and sometimes after lunch he would sit in one of the rocking chairs on the deck behind the living room and just watch the rhythm of the waves in the distance. He knew that when he grew up he would want to live near the sea. He couldn't imagine living some place like Kansas where he would be thousands of miles from the ocean.

What he couldn't figure out was how to get to the ocean. No one else seemed to care much about it. Bert had his Black Angus and Jessie her horses. Jack Ariel was in San Francisco half the time, and when he was home he seemed to prefer skeet and trap shooting to anything else. Molly gardened and read books and drove cars. After a while it became an obsession with him. He cherished the foggy mornings and the bright days and the crisp, cold nights, and the smells of the pines when they rode into the woods, but day by day as the summer wore on, he thought more and more about the ocean. He wanted to mention it to somebody, but he was afraid.

"That's me, through and through," he thought. "Wonderful. I'm such a chicken. I talk about anything except what I care most about. Why?"

He tried to figure it out. It was because, if he didn't talk about it, they couldn't say no. That was it. He couldn't stand it if someone said no to the thing he wanted most, so he just didn't mention it. But it was stupid. How was he going to get to the beach if he never asked?

What saved him was B.D. Day. B.D. meant Birthday Day, and it also meant Bert and David Day. How it happened was simple. Jessie's birthday was in July, and it was one of Molly Ariel's rules that on your birthday you could choose what you wanted for dinner and what you wanted to do. Jessie, of course, chose to go to the horse show in Monterey, which David and Bert had to do whether they liked it or not, and on the way home in the back of Jack's pick up truck, Bert got an idea.

"Listen, David," he said. "Molly likes to be fair. Right?"

"Right," said David.

"And since your birthday and my birthday aren't during the summer, it's not fair for Jessie to have her day and us to have nothing. Right?"

"Right," said David.

"So, we just have to ask Molly for a special day. We'll call it Bert and David's day."

"B.D. Day," said David.

"B.D. Day. Wow, that's great," said Bert. Then there was a long pause. David didn't know whether to say something or not.

"I got it. I got it," said Bert. "If Molly says yes, then we have to think up what we want to eat and what we want to do. Right?"

"Right," said David.

"So what do you want to do?"

And that's how they got to go to the beach. It was simple. Molly had to take them to the beach, if she agreed to let them have B.D. Day, and if she was fair, she couldn't say no. And, of course, she didn't, except what David didn't know was how cold the water would be. It wasn't like swimming in Connecticut or New York. It was nothing like his grandfather's. It was like numbing yourself so you could stand it. You just eased into the water bit by bit and got each part so cold that you couldn't feel anything, and then it didn't hurt any more, except it was still fun, and the lift of the waves as they brought him crashing into the sand of the shallows was wonderful.

After they swam, he and Bert walked up and down the beach and looked at the girls. David was quiet. He loved the smell of oil on their bodies and the way they lay on their stomachs with the straps of their halters undone, but he felt funny talking about it. Terry and Griff and Bert could say all those words.

"Wow, look at those tits," Bert would say, and David would

look, but he couldn't say the word. Girls were complicated. It was better to stay away from them. Maybe that's why they had different schools, because if you were there with them all the time, you'd just think about them instead of studying. At the Casino they ate hot dogs and french fries, and carried some back to Jessie, who wouldn't go walking with them because they were so "disgusting."

Later they swam again and then walked to the bath house to shower and change. In the shower room they sang as they soaped themselves, and David looked down at his feet. Suddenly he realized that nobody had looked at him in a funny way or laughed or made some remark. In fact, he couldn't remember the last time anyone at school had made fun of his feet. He had forgotten about them.

That night they cooked steak on the grill and ate corn from the garden.

"Omigod," said Bert, dropping his fork and gasping.

"We're eating Eric. I can't stand it." He stood up and wiped his eyes with his napkin, then placed his hands over his heart, and began to recite:

> This is the most unkindest cut of all, that we
> should do this to thee, gentlest of all bulls.
> Mine eyes do cloud with tears and no perfume
> from Arabia can wipe out this blot upon my heart.
> I come to bury Eric, not to eat him.

"Boo! Hiss!" Pieces of napkin came flying at Bert.

"Actually, it's not Eric," said Molly Ariel. "I think it's that one we didn't like, the one with the narrow head."

"Toadstool," said Jessie.

"What a relief," said Bert, sitting down. "I couldn't stand the thought of eating Eric."

Afterwards Molly talked to David.

"Elizabeth's moved," she said, "to a larger apartment in the Bronx."

"In the Bronx?" The name Bronx brought forth images of hoods in black leather jackets, gangs on the street, broken bottles in the gutter, Italians and Negroes and Puerto Ricans.

She got a New York City map and showed him where it was.

"Wow," said David. "It's right near Yankee stadium."

"That was a quick change," said Molly.

"It's only seven or eight blocks from Yankee Stadium. I can walk there," said David.

He did. The apartment was on 165th Street. The day after he got back he took his glove and walked up the hill to the Grand Concourse and down to 161st Street where the Stadium stood, flags flying, naming the cities of the American League.

The Yankees were playing Cleveland. It wasn't the hated Red Sox, whom David would have liked to have seen best of all-the Yankee Clipper, DiMaggio, against Williams, The Splendid Splinter. That would have been terrific, but Cleveland was next best, Cleveland with Bob Feller, the fastest pitcher in the league, Rapid Robert, who nobody on the Yankees could hit except DiMaggio.

David sat in the upper stands, high, high behind home plate. The players seemed so small down below, and the beautiful green field so large. And there out in center field next to the 461 foot sign were the famous monuments to Babe Ruth and Lou Gehrig and their manager, Miller Huggins. Some day there would be one for DiMaggio too, he thought.

The Yankees were taking fielding practice. A coach was hitting fungoes to the infielders. He could see Phil Rizzuto, the shortstop, who was his favorite player next to DiMaggio. He was small and dark and fast and fierce and never gave up. Another coach hit fly balls to the outfielders. David scanned the expanse of green. There was Tommy Henrich, "Old Reliable" he was called, and Charlie "King Kong" Keller with his bushy eyebrows, but where was Joe? David's heart sank. Maybe he was sick, maybe he wouldn't play today.

"Ya lookin' for the Clipper?" asked the man on his left, a burly, black haired character in an undershirt, with a cup of Ballantine beer in his hand. "You won't see him 'til the game starts. He don't take fielding, He already knows how." The man laughed. "Your first game, kid?"

"Yes," said David shyly.

"DiMag, he always takes batting practice first — then he goes to the Clubhouse to change, and he don't come out 'til the very end. You'll see."

He did see. One by one, they announced the players. Each took the field as his name was called. "And batting fourth, playing center field, Number 5, Joe DiMaggio." The roar of the crowd was deafening. Everyone stood, as Joe, with perfect grace, ran with the steps of a gazelle, to center field. He was beautiful with his long legs and his muscular back, his thick black hair.

It was a wonderful game, Allie Reynolds, the Cherokee Indian who pitched so hard you could hear the bone chips in his elbow rattle as he whistled his fast ball past the batters, against Bob Feller. No one could get a run. Then DiMag came up in the bottom of the fifth.

"He's had a tough time," said David's companion. "He had those bone spurs in his heel, they had to operate on him, and he ain't as fast as he used to be. But he don't complain. He just plays, the best he can every day."

DiMaggio took two balls, and then on the third pitch he swung from his heels and smashed a line drive which just kept rising and rising until it settled in the upper deck in left field. Joe rounded the bases, while the fans cheered and cheered, and David thought it was the most wonderful thing he had ever seen.

In the seventh, Cleveland got two runs off Reynolds, and David began to calculate. DiMaggio would get another chance to bat in the ninth, if somebody could get on. He was right. "Fireman" Joe Page, the Yankees' great relief pitcher, got Cleveland out in the eighth and ninth, and when Phil Rizzuto singled to deep short, it gave Joe a chance. He stood, deep in the box, waiting for each pitch, as if he had all day. The speed of Feller's fastballs seemed nothing to him. He waited for the right moment, a 3 and 1 pitch that was out over the plate. He swung, and the ball soared toward the 461 foot sign, toward the monuments. Rizzuto was off with the crack of the bat, and the Cleveland center fielder was too. He caught the ball on the run at the warning track. Sixty-five thousand people were silent. Joe rounded second base and headed toward the dugout.

"It would've been a home run anywhere else," said David.

"If DiMag'd played in Boston," said the man next to him, "he'd a hit twenty more a year."

The fans bumped and jostled each other on the way out. They'd been cheated of victory, and now the August heat seemed oppressive, and the sixty-thousand who had been one were strangers. When David got home he found that his wallet was missing.

Phil said he had to learn to be more careful. "Carry your wallet in one of your front pockets," he advised. "They're harder to get into. A good pickpocket can get the back ones really easy in a crowd — subways, ballparks, where people bump against each other are their favorite places."

They were sitting at dinner in the new apartment, the four of them — David, Phil and Elizabeth and Alex, sixteen months now, perched in his highchair and plastering his face with junior beans and apricots.

"I want you to go see Mommy tomorrow," said Elizabeth, wiping Alex's face with one and spooning with the other. "She's very hurt. You've hardly written her all summer."

"I know," said David. It wasn't that he didn't want to write her, it was just that everything he said in his letters sounded so stupid. He would start a letter telling her what he was doing and then tear it up. He couldn't seem to say anything that would interest her. She didn't care anything about baseball or horses or Black Angus steers.

"She's on Welfare Island," said Elizabeth.

"Where?"

"Welfare Island. It's a state hospital where they keep people who can't pay. It's in the East River just below the Triboro Bridge. Take the subway to 72nd Street and the crosstown bus to the river. There's a ferry to take you over."

David said nothing.

Elizabeth kept feeding Alex. She looked at David. "I know how you feel. You want to escape it. We all do. We want to hide and pretend it's not happening. But it is, and you've got to go, just this one time. She may not last 'till Christmas."

Welfare Island was gray and gaunt, and the hot August sun made everything harder. The buildings sweltered and held the heat, and as David walked in the door to the main desk he could smell ether. He hadn't smelled ether since he was five, and it all came back to him, the doctors with the masks on their faces bending over him, and the round mask with the ether on it coming down, down over his own face. He felt faint and nauseated, and he had to sit down for a few minutes before he could summon the courage to ask for his mother. They gave him a yellow card and sent him to Elevator Three, which took him to the fourth floor.

She was in a large room with beds on both sides. When he saw her, she was sleeping. He was glad. He didn't want her to see the look on his face. She was skin and bones. The fleshiness he had re-membered from the last visit had been eaten away. Her thin arms lay outside the sheet, and he could see the black and blue marks where the needles had gone in. Her hair lay matted in sweat against her forehead, and there were deep, dark circles under her eyes. There was a water glass with a straw and a pack of cigarettes next to it on the table.

"I told you I was dying, Toots," she said, when she woke up.

He could not answer.

"Well I am. I've got cancer. The doctors never tell you any-thing. The last operations didn't do anything. They just went in and looked around and sewed me back up. Too far gone."

He tried to think of something to say but his mind would not work. He only sat there in the white chair by the bed.

"Give me a cigarette, Toots. I can't eat, but I might as well smoke. It can't hurt me now."

He picked a cigarette from the pack and put it in his mouth, then lit it. He almost inhaled, and then stopped. The tobacco tasted awful.

"Hold it for me, Toots. My hand isn't too steady."

So he sat there and placed the cigarette in her mouth and watched the ash turn red before he withdrew it. She blew the smoke out and talked slowly between puffs.

"Elizabeth doesn't know how bad it is. She thinks I'll pull through, but I won't. She's not as strong as you. Don't tell her. Hell, I might be in a coma for months. She'll keep hoping. There's no need for her to mourn until she has to. You'll be all right. You don't need me."

"Yes, I do," he said, not so much meaning it as feeling he ought to say it. "I'm sorry I haven't been a better son," he said. "I should have spent more time with you. I should have written you more often. I think I was ashamed of you. That was wrong."

"Yes," she answered. "That was wrong."

"Do you hurt much?" he asked.

"Not too much," she said. "They've got me pretty doped up on morphine. I sleep, and I wake up and talk a while, and then it begins to hurt like hell, and they give me some more and I go back to sleep. I'm O.K. most of the time. You don't have to say anything. Just sit with me."

He took her hand and held it. He was all right now. When he had first entered the ward and seen her and smelled the rot of the dying and seen the gauntness of their faces, he thought he would be sick and the nausea which had overtaken him in the lobby started again, but it had passed, and he was getting used to it. Maybe this is what the Bible meant by the rottenness of the flesh. The flesh had to rot away and you died and had another life, like Jesus said.

He hadn't thought about it before. He had never paid much attention to the lessons in church and Sunday school that had to do with dying. He couldn't imagine dying himself, but here was his mother, wasting away to nothing, becoming thinner and thinner and smelling. That's what the Bible meant by eternal life. Only the body died. Under the bruised arms and the gaunt face with its ugly dark circles and the burned-out lungs and the stomach they had cut into, there was a person who would live on. That's what his mother had meant when they talked in the hotel room. "I don't want you to remember me like this," she had said. He understood now. The beautiful part lives on. She had wanted him to remember that.

She dozed a while, then woke and squeezed his hand.

"I may not see you again," she said. "There are some things I want to tell you. Don't ever have a gun in your house. You remember that awful business with the police when I shot Bernie?"

"Yes," he said. And then, suddenly, from nowhere, there were tears in his eyes. "I'm sorry," he said softly, "I'm sorry I told the police."

"That doesn't matter now, Toots. I deserved it. I was terrible. We were so drunk, and the gun was sitting there — Bernie's pride and joy, his great shotgun. I just wanted to take him down a peg. I didn't want to hurt him. That's the point, Toots. If there was no gun, I wouldn't have done anything — maybe I would have thrown an ashtray at him and missed."

She paused to catch her breath.

"Don't ever have a gun in your house," she said again, almost in a whisper.

"I won't, Mom," he said.

Silence, and then, "Promise me something, Toots."

"Yes."

"Promise me you'll try to love somebody."

"I will."

"I mean it, Baby. There are four things in life. You've got three of them, but the fourth thing is love."

"What are the others?"

"Hush. Just let me talk. It's the privilege of the dying. Me. I'm Maggie Hope. I've always had hope 'till now. That's the first thing."

Her eyes glittered. "We were always hopers. It'll be better in the morning. We really believed that, you and Lizzie and I. The second thing is courage. You learned that from your feet. That and the third, determination. Hope and courage and determination. They're great things. They kept us all going. But you, you're afraid of love, afraid of risking it. Don't be afraid. Just don't."

He lit her another cigarette and she smoked it.

"You know what I hate most, sweetheart?"

"No, Mom."

"I hate not getting to see you grow up."

"I know."

"You're going to be something — I can feel that, Toots. I wish I was going to be there to see what that something is. Now give me a hug, not too hard, just a gentle one."

He leaned down and placed his arms around her shoulders. They looked at each other, and he started to speak.

"Call the nurse," she said. "I'm hurting now. Kiss me and then get out of here."

He kissed her on the cheek and walked to the nurse's station. On the way out he forgot to turn in the yellow card.

# CHAPTER
## *eleven*

*J*ERRY ROCHE LOOKED DIFFERENT. It was as if his body had changed over the summer. There were muscles in his thighs and calves, the hint of a mustache over his lip, and the strong shoulders were even wider. He was the captain of the football team and the president of the Whites. David was secretary of the Reds. Griff Ryan wasn't anything, but everyone loved him because he was so funny.

"Have you ever shaved?" Terry asked David.

"No, have you?"

"No." He felt his mustache with his fingers. "My dad told me that once you start shaving it grows more. I don't know what to do. I don't want to make it grow, but I want to get rid of it."

They stood before the mirrors in the bathroom at the end of the hall, feeling their mustaches and making faces.

"If you shave," said David, "you'll cut your pimples, and then you'll bleed all over the place."

"Yeah," said Terry Roche, "you can't go around them."

Griff Ryan laughed. He was smooth and fat and didn't have anything at all except down below. He didn't have pimples even.

They were happy. It was the third week of school, and the fall colors were October bright, and they were sixth formers. They had doors and walls and closets, the joy of privacy, and radios that they could play every night between suppertime and bed. They could study in their rooms instead of going to the big schoolroom downstairs, and in the mornings they could sleep later because the sixth form dorm was right next to the dining hall. They were the biggest, the smartest, and the toughest, and there was no one except Mr. Parilli to boss them around. On Saturdays they could go downtown and spend the afternoon at the soda shop, and at meals they could sit at the top of the table next to the masters.

David was at Mr. Langdon's table, and he loved it. He was in his third year of Latin.

"Latin's neat," said David.

"Why?" asked Mr. Langdon with a smile. Of course, he knew.

"Because there's a reason for everything."

"Go on."

"Well," said the boy. "You pronounce everything the way it looks, and words go in certain places and always mean the same thing. You can be sure with Latin."

"And English?" asked the master.

"English is fun, but you can't be sure with it."

"Meaning?"

"Well, like rough and through."

"Go on." That was Mr. Langdon's favorite expression. If he liked something he would always smile and say, "Go on." If he didn't like it he would frown and tap his pencil on the table. Then you knew you were wrong.

"I mean why don't we say *ruff* and *thruff* or *roo* and *throo*?"

"I don't know, David. You're right. Latin is much clearer."

The other boys usually listened. There were ten or twelve at each table, usually two from each form. Since David was the only sixth former, he could talk to Mr. Langdon all he wanted. The younger boys wouldn't interrupt.

"You're a bright young man, David," said Mr. Langdon.

David smiled. "My godmother says it's because I spend a lot time around grownups. When I'm not in school I read a lot and talk to grownups. I guess you just learn how to think about things."

He hoped the year would last forever. He was doing well, and the rage that had turned him against Mickey Saperstein the year before had burned away in the energy he gave to his daily tasks. Latin,

French, Math, English and History were his subjects. No science, no Parilli, and Saperstein had lost his advantage. If you could do Latin, you could do French. French was just the same words with different sounds, different endings. Math was clear and logical, and history was just learning names and dates.

And English. Well, English wasn't the safest, but it was the most exciting, mainly because of Mr. Pierce. He had joined the faculty during David's fifth form year, and from the day he taught his first class, he was popular. He wasn't easy. That wasn't the point at all. But he made English seem like the most important thing in the world. For him, the characters in the novels and plays they read were more interesting, more alive than life itself. He loved Shakespeare, and he had directed scenes from A Midsummer Night's Dream as the winter play. David was amazed at how Mr. Pierce made all those characters speaking Elizabethan English seem so real. He didn't get angry during rehearsal, if you did badly. He just did it over himself and showed you how to pronounce the words. He made the words come alive.

David knew he could do well in English for Mr. Pierce. He felt it inside him. And he knew he could win the medal if he just stuck to it, all the way. The thing was not to talk about it, not to get in trouble. It was based on general average. That meant studies, lateness, neatness, behavior. He couldn't get any marks. But he couldn't be a sissy either. It was a thin line. He had to be a friend, a good guy, but he couldn't get in trouble like Eric Marshall who could have won the medal the year before but got caught stealing a magazine from the soda shop on a dare from Ed Fetzer and got five marks and ended up losing it to Perry Mitchell. David and Mickey were friends now, and it was a rule between them not to mention the medal. No one else had a chance, and talking about it only made David nervous and Mickey angry.

Even Parilli was nicer. David figured it was because of his dog. It was a strange story. Parilli lived in the house at the end of the football field, and Armbrister had got the idea in the spring to build a swimming pool that they could freeze and use for a hockey rink in the winter, instead of flooding the football field. When they came back to school in September here was this swimming pool with a chain fence around it to keep the kids and dogs out. One day someone left the gate open, and Parilli's dog, a boxer named Lulu, got in and went in the pool and the water was down from the sides and she couldn't climb out, and she just swam around and around until she got tired and drowned.

Armbrister got mad, and called a special meeting of the school and chewed the school out for leaving the gate open, and everyone felt so guilty. So there was a big meeting of the officers of the Reds and the Whites and David and Terry Roche and Bailey Abbott from Marblehead, who was president of the Reds, decided the only thing to do was to get Parilli a new dog. So they went around to all the dorms without telling Parilli and got money from the kids and the dorm masters and raised enough to buy a little puppy from a pet store in Framingham. Then one day they had a special assembly, and Terry Roche called Parilli in from the master's room, and they took the puppy out of the basket with a red and white ribbon around its neck to signify the two colors, and everyone stood up and cheered for Parilli. He just stood there and cried, and after that he was a different person.

"That was a mighty nice thing you boys did for me," he would call out of the masters' room, as David and Terry walked by.

One night just before Thanksgiving he invited the officers of the two colors to his house for dinner. And they sat at the table with Parilli and Mrs. Parilli and talked about football and baseball and hockey and basketball. Parilli liked the Boston Bruins and the Celtics, the Braves and the Red Sox. Above all he liked the Red Sox. "Ted Williams," he said, "is the greatest natural hitter of all time. He has eyes that are so good he can see the seams rotate when the ball is coming toward the plate." David tried to imagine that and couldn't. As much as he loved baseball there were times that he would strike out again and again. "Watch the ball all the way to the bat," said Mr. Myers, and he did, but it still didn't help him. Hitting was a great mystery.

"This spring," said Parilli, "I'll take you boys to a game at Fenway. We can't see 'em play the Yankees, 'cause those are all sold out in advance. We can catch 'em against Philadelphia or the White Sox."

"Parilli's really nice," said David to Terry Roche as they walked back up the hill toward the dorm after dinner. "Do you think it was just the dog that made him change?"

"I don't know," said Terry. "Sometimes people think it's real cool to make jokes all the time and be wise. You remember how we were before? It was like we were afraid to be nice to each other. Sometimes something happens that, well, you know, makes you have to be nice, and then you find out it's not so hard."

"That's really true, Terry," said David.

That night in bed he thought more about it, and he realized that Parilli hadn't once kidded him about Mrs. Rossiter. That was really different. Then he remembered about the operetta. It was almost time to cast the show, and he didn't know whether to try out or not. He went over it in his mind. If she wanted me to try out, then she would have said something to me. I've been turning pages for her in church all fall. But then she never asks people to try out. I mean, you just try out and if you make it, you make it. But I don't want to try out and have her tell me I can't make it, and I don't want to not try out if I can make it. It was something he didn't even talk to the club about. It was a rule, David knew, that you were supposed to talk about everything at meetings. But there were some things — like his mother or Mrs. Rossiter — that he couldn't bring to the group. Griff would look funny at him and Terry would laugh and say something about Mrs. Rossiter's tits, and so it just wasn't worth it. You could talk about school problems and grown-ups in general and what was it Terry said? — oh, "social tics, and politics, and other kinds of tics" — but David couldn't talk about Mrs. Rossiter and his mother. So he didn't ask them.

On the night of tryouts David sat stonily in his room listening to the music downstairs. The piano had been rolled from the music room into the dining room where all the students who had volunteered waited their chance to sing. This year was The Pirates of Penzance and one by one the characters were called: The Pirate King, tall and dark, with a deep voice; his sidekick, Ruth, the nurse, who has raised the hero Frederick, now twenty-one and through with his apprenticeship, who must choose between becoming a full-fledged pirate and "going straight," as Mr. Pierce said; the major general and his daughter, Mabel, with whom Frederick falls in love. David knew the story because Mr. Pierce always told it in English class before try-outs. They had even read some of the lines that morning, because Mr. Pierce would be directing the play along with Mrs. Rossiter.

David moved from his room down the hall to the top of the stairs. He could hear better now. Terry Roche was trying out for the Pirate King. Sammy Hartwick would have to be Mabel. He was the only one who could act whose voice was still high enough to sing girls' parts. Griff Ryan would be Ruth. David was sure of that. And Ian Stuart would be the major general because he was the only one who could say the words fast enough — "I am the very model of the modern major general...I've information animal, vegetable, and mineral"...the words had to click off the tongue, and Ian's Scottish brogue was perfect.

Then David heard steps on the stairs. He jumped up guiltily and ran to his room. He did not want to be caught listening. Quickly he pulled out a book and pretended to read. There was a knock on the door.

"Come in," said David, his heart pounding.

The door opened. It was a younger boy that David didn't know.

"Mrs. Rossiter wants to see you downstairs."

"O.K.," said David, trying to sound calm.

He was so excited that he didn't know what to do first. Teeth. He had to brush his teeth. He couldn't go down there with bad breath. Toothbrush. He had to find his toothbrush. Hair. He grabbed his comb and toothbrush and towel and headed for the bathroom.

Five minutes later he was standing in front of Mrs. Rossiter, immaculately groomed.

"I missed you, David," she said. "Why didn't you try out?"

He thought quickly. "You told me my voice was changing, and I needed to rest it," he said.

"Not forever, silly," she smiled. "Come on, let's give it a try. If you can't make some of the high notes, we can change them."

She leafed through the book and handed it to him.

"Try this one," she said. It was Frederick.

She was right. There were some high notes he couldn't reach with his new voice, but for the most part he did all right.

"You look like a Frederick to me," she said, and gave him a knowing smile.

Now it was lights out and David crouched on the floor of Griff Ryan's closet so the light wouldn't shine under the door into the hall, and he and Griff read their scripts like lovers huddled over a single milkshake with two straws.

Griff laughed.

"It says here that Frederick kisses Mabel at the end."

"You gotta be kidding."

"No. Look on page sixty-eight. It says it right there."

Much rustling of pages. Then silence.

"Oh, my god, it does say it."

Griff Ryan laughed, this time louder.

"Shhhh," whispered David. "Roderick will hear us."

Griff Ryan laughed again, this time muffled in his coats and boots.

"Well," said David, "I don't think it really means it. I mean the script doesn't know that a boy is playing Mabel. It means that Frederick kisses Mabel (pause)…if grownups are playing the roles."

"Wriggle, worm, wriggle," said Griff. "You gotta do it, because it'll be great. Don't you see? It'll bring the house down. Everyone will stand up and cheer and scream. Just pucker up and lay it on him, and everyone will love you."

David laughed. Griff was right. It would bring the house down.

"I'll do it," he said. "Unless Sammy's chicken."

"Sammy'll do anything you say. He's just a fourth former."

∝∞∾

The big event of the fall term was Armbrister's lecture series: The Human Body. He thought every "well-educated young man should leave Lowell School knowing something about his own body and the bodies of the opposite sex."

"I'd like to know a lot more about the bodies of the opposite sex," said Griff Ryan.

"This lecture series is not to be taken lightly. While there is no examination, all sixth formers are required to attend, and masters will be present to mark absences."

"Lecture Four's the one I want to hear," said Griff.

Lecture Four was on the reproductive system. Armbrister had given the lectures for several years, pulling down the shades in the common room and setting up slides to illustrate his talk. The first lecture was on the skeletal and muscular construction of the body, the second on the respiratory and circulatory systems, the third on the digestive system. Lecture Four was the popular one.

"Every year," said Mr. Armbrister, "Some immature characters start laughing and making smutty jokes during this lecture. If you do you will be thrown out. This is serious business, gentlemen."

Griff bit his lip and looked at Terry. David concentrated on the slides. He learned first of all how the male and female bodies change at puberty.

Then he learned about the sperm and the ovum and how fertilization takes place, and then Mr. Armbrister went on: "In order to bring about such fertilization, the male inserts the penis into the vagina of the female and ejects the sperm into the canal. This is called the act of coitus."

"What's that, sir?" asked Ian Stuart.

"Coitus, Stuart," said Mr. Armbrister.

"You wouldn't know about it, Stuart," said Griff.

"That's not what my father calls it, sir," said another boy.

"Oh, no," thought David.

"Oh, Jesus, it's gonna hit the fan now," whispered Terry.

It was Peter Winemiller, and he had about as much sense as a pair of dirty socks after football practice. He had come to Lowell at the same time as David, because his parents thought it would help him get into a good prep school, but all he'd done at Lowell was to hold up the bottom of the class. He had red hair and greenish eyes that looked constantly puzzled.

"My father calls it screwing, sir," he said.

"That is a vulgar name. It is not the scientific name," said Mr. Armbrister.

"Oh," said Peter.

"I think he really thought 'screwing' was the polite thing to call it," said Terry.

But the fans were restless now. Mr. Armbrister went on. "After fertilization takes place the embryo grows in the womb." He showed slides of the baby growing larger and larger. Then he showed a slide of the baby just before delivery.

"How does it get out, sir?" asked Peter Winemiller.

Mr. Armbrister pointed to the pelvic area: "The cervix dilates, allowing the baby to be pushed out by the mother's muscular contractions. In difficult deliveries the baby's head is sometimes damaged during these contractions."

"That's what happened to you, Winemiller," said Griff. The place went wild.

The headmaster's pointer came down with a sharp crack on the top of the lectern. "That's enough," he shouted. There was silence. He walked toward the boys, then paced up and down in front of the first row. "This," he said, "is the most incredibly immature group of sixth formers that I have ever seen. Go to your rooms. That's all. The rest of the lecture is cancelled."

"Christ," said Terry, as they walked back to the dorm. "We missed the best part."

"What's that?" asked David.

"The part at the end about the joy of sex and how it's not just a mechanical thing."

"He never would've got through it," said Griff. "Winemiller would've asked him what sex was."

"Ryan?" There was a voice behind them. "Report to my study immediately." It was Armbrister.

David and Terry waited outside in the hall.

"Let's see if we can hear anything," said Terry. "Come on."

"No," said David. "Somebody'll see us and then we'll get it, too."

After about fifteen minutes Griff came out. He didn't say anything.

"Well?" said Terry.

"Well?" asked David.

"My mouth feels awful," said Griff. "I gotta go brush my teeth. I'll tell you about it after."

In the room he explained. "He sat me down and said what a foul mouth I had, and gave me this long spiel about how the punishment should fit the crime, and then he took me into the little bathroom next to his study and picked up the soap and made me bite it. 'Chew it,' he said. 'Chew it well, and let that be a lesson to you, boy.'"

"I thought for a while about swallowing it and pretending to be real sick and calling my father to sue Armbrister, but then I figured that wasn't too smart because I might really get sick. So I just spit it out in the sink." Then he laughed. "It was worth it."

"I still don't see how it gets out," said David.

"I know," said Terry. "Did you see how big the kid was in the picture?"

"I'm sure glad I'm not a girl," said Griff.

"You'd be a hell of an ugly one," said Terry.

∞

A few days later David was told by Mr. Roderick, the sixth form dorm master, to report to Lowell House.

"Mrs. Armbrister wants to talk to you," he said.

Lowell House, where the Armbristers lived, was three houses down from the school. The headmaster and his wife invited groups of boys to Lowell House to drink tea and "experience some culture." David had been there a couple of times before, but always in a group, once for a piano recital, and once to hear a man read poetry. But he had never been asked to come over all by himself and wondered why Mrs. Armbrister would send for him.

She met him at the door and led him into the living room. She looked the same to him as she always had, even from that first day, kind and patient, tall and cool and collected. She was always involved in everything, making costumes for the plays and operettas, baking cakes for people's birthdays, surprising even Mr. Armbrister with announcements in the dining room when he rang the gong.

"Today," she would say, "is Four Leaf Clover Day. The first one to bring me a four leaf clover gets a free ice cream cone at Taft's Drug Store." She was the best cheerleader at the football games and the first one to take care of anyone that was hurt. When Bailey Abbott broke his leg ski jumping she was the one to drive him to Framingham to get his bone set.

"We're going to miss you, David," she said. "You've been pretty special. You've given a lot to Lowell School."

"Lowell School has given a lot to me, Mrs. Armbrister," he said. He meant it. But he wondered why he was there.

"David," she said and the pause after his name he could tell that something was wrong.

"We had a telegram from your sister, Mrs. O'Donnell."

It sounded so funny. "Mrs. O'Donnell." He never thought of Elizabeth as Mrs. O'Donnell.

"It's your mother. I'm afraid she's…"

"Dead," said David. He knew. That's what his mother had said. "Remember, Toots, one of these days at school you'll get a telegram saying, 'Mother dead,' and I don't want you to remember me like this." She knew.

"Yes, David," said Mrs. Armbrister quietly. "I'm sorry."

"It's better," said David. "She was very sick."

"We know," said Mrs. Armbrister, "but it's always a shock."

"Yes, ma'am," said David. Perhaps he was supposed to cry now, he thought, and go to her and let her comfort him. That would be all right. He was supposed to grieve, to cry his heart out for his mother, and that was why Mrs. Armbrister had been chosen, because she was good in these situations. You could cry with her. She was like a mother to all the boys. But he had no tears in him.

"The funeral is on Saturday. You'll have to take the New York train tomorrow and come back Sunday. You can stay longer if you need to."

"No, ma'am, I'll be back Sunday," said David. He did not want to be around the grownups any longer than he had to.

"Would you like someone to ride down on the train with you?" asked Mrs. Armbrister.

"No, ma'am," he answered. "I'll be fine."

⧼⧽

It was not until the boy asked the question that he felt the ghost of the other trip. The school station wagon had dropped him in Framingham along with a fourth former that David didn't know. David had helped the boy with his bags and the boy asked if he could sit with him.

"It's my first weekend," he said. "I live in New Haven. My dad teaches at Yale. My name is Jeremy Newland."

"That's nice," said David. He had not been much in the mood for talk and at first the boy annoyed him. He wanted to think things out, but the boy caught him by surprise and held him:

"You're David Lear, aren't you?"

"I sure am."

"You're secretary of the Reds and you have a Primus rating, and you're Frederick."

"How did you know that?"

"I'm in the operetta, too. I'm gonna be one of the girls, you know, the daughters of the major general."

"And how do you know who I am?"

"Because we all know the sixth formers. We talk about you."

"And am I O.K.?"

"Yeah, you're nice."

"What's nice?"

"You say 'Hi,' and talk to people and don't bully them."

"Thank you."

"Say, can I ask you a question?"

"Go ahead."

He had a bright face and curious eyes. "Have you ever kissed a girl?"

That was when David did the double take. "Humphrey," he said.

"What?" said the younger boy.

"I'm sorry," said David. "No, I haven't."

"Well," Jeremy said, "Mike Winston said that every sixth former, except maybe Peter Winemiller, has kissed a girl, and I said it wasn't true because my brother's fourteen and he hasn't so I just wanted to ask you."

"You're pretty talkative, Jeremy," said David.

"My dad says I run my mouth a lot," The boy was nervous. He chattered away like a sparrow.

"Thanks for listenin'," he said when he got off. "See ya Sunday."

The train picked up speed and headed toward New York. At the back of the car the door opened, and David heard a familiar voice: "Get your Hershey bars, Almond Joys, cigars, cigarettes. Get your fresh cashew nuts. Cashews. Get your cashews."

"Cashews," said David.

"Hey, hot shot," said the man. "Vot you doin' in the train? Takin' a weekend? Vere's your crazy friends, the fat one and the big, tall guy?"

"They only let me out this time, Cashews," said David. "My..." Then he stopped. Funny, he thought. I was about to tell Cashews my mother died. "My mouth is dry, Cashews, how about a coke?"

"Sure! Comin' up. Hey, you gonna whatchacallit this year?"

"Graduate, Cashews? Yeah, I'm gonna graduate."

"Then ver you goin' to school?"

"I don't know."

"Well, you pick a good school. You wanna get a good education. You don' wanna end up like me, sellin' cashew nuts."

He wandered down the aisle. "See ya Christmas time, Cashews," said David. "Happy Hanukkah, kid," said Cashews, laughing.

⚮

He had always wanted to get off at 125th Street. After all, it made sense to walk the block to Lexington Avenue and pick up the subway there. It might save half an hour. Why ride all the way to Grand Central and then back again? He was scared. That was the simple reason he had never done it and wouldn't do it now. As the train stood in the station he looked out across 125th Street and saw the faces of the colored people. What would they do to him? This fear was stupid, but it was there just the same. They weren't going to mug him or steal his suitcase right out on 125th Street. It was probably no more dangerous than the walk from the subway stop to the apartment. Was it the strangeness that scared him, the fact that you never saw colored people except in Harlem? Once going to Elizabeth's when they lived on 115th Street, he had taken the 7th Avenue Express by mistake. When he got out of the train at 116th Street and walked up the stairs, he'd realized his mistake instantly. Everyone was colored. He was on Lenox Avenue right in the middle of Harlem. He'd hastily looked around, crossed the street to the downtown side, and taken the first train back to Columbus Circle. What was this fear of colored people? He didn't know any colored people who were bad. In fact, he didn't know any at all. There were none at Lowell. The whole thing bothered him because he wanted to be fair. It was like the business with the Jews. He didn't want to be afraid of someone because their skin was a different color. He just was. He had to change that. His mother would have wanted him to get off at 125th Street. She wouldn't want him to be afraid. "You'll have to get over that, Toots," she would have said.

Elizabeth met him at Grand Central. She was big.

"It's strange, isn't it?" she said. "Life and death. I keep thinking if it's a girl I'll name her Margaret. Margaret Hope O'Donnell. Do you like that, David?"

"You didn't have to come," said David. "I could get there by myself."

"I know. I just wanted to. I needed to get out of the house. Phil's taking care of Alex for me, so we don't have to go straight home. You want to go out and eat?"

"What about the money?"

"How much can you spare?" She looked in her purse. He looked in his wallet. They agreed to three-fifty each, including tip. He checked his suitcase, the one with the M. H. on it, and they walked through the great room with the stars on the ceiling, and he remembered the time his mother had shown him the signs. Cancer was her sign, she had said.

"We never went to the Newsreel Theatre together," he said to Elizabeth. "We were always going to do that."

"There were a lot of things we were all going to do," said Elizabeth. She put her arm through his and they walked down the long corridor with the newsstand out onto Lexington Avenue, then across 44th to Third, where the elevated railway ran. There were always cheap restaurants on Third Avenue under the El.

They sat in a small Italian place called Donatello's. It had candles in Chianti bottles on the table. It was small and dark, and served spaghetti for $1.95 a plate.

"Phil and I used to come here when I was living in Westport. I'd take the train in and meet him here. That's how I got to know the Village. He'd take me down there afterwards and we'd hear jazz at the Village Barn or Condon's or someplace like that."

"Did you drink?" asked David.

"Are you kidding? I can't touch it. It makes me sick."

"That's good," he said. "I'm glad."

They ate and talked, and he told her about school and Griff having to eat the soap and what a jerk Peter Winemiller was.

"I thought about you during the lecture," he said.

"Why?"

"About the baby. It's so big? How does it get out? Doesn't it hurt a lot?"

"Yes, it does. But it's exciting, too."

"I wouldn't want to be a girl. I wouldn't want that."

"But it's life inside your body, David. There's nothing like that. It's what keeps me going. When Mommy died I thought that if it weren't for Alex and little Margaret inside me, I wouldn't want to go on living. And you…I'd go on living for you."

She started to cry, and David was silent while she wiped her eyes and blew her nose. People were watching them. Suddenly David said, "You don't think…"

"Think what?"

"That you and I…you know, with the baby and all, you don't think they think…"

"Oh my God," she said, and began laughing. "Wouldn't that be hysterical? Come on, I'll hold your arm as we go out, and call you Dear. That'll give them something to think about."

Shannon's Funeral Home was three blocks from his grandparents' old apartment. The three of them — Elizabeth and Phil and David — had ridden the D train from the Bronx, David and Phil in their dark blue suits, Elizabeth in a black dress of their mother's, her blond hair strangely bright. They seemed out of place on this Saturday morning, rattling down the hundred and twenty blocks to Columbus Circle among blue-jeaned workers and teenagers in corduroy pants and Army jackets. David felt like they had death written all over them.

When they got to the home they were ushered into a waiting room to the right of the entrance hall. Their grandparents were already there. David hadn't seen them in two years. His grandfather looked just the same, hearty, pink-skinned, robust. He took Elizabeth by the hand and led her over to their grandmother, who was seated in a chair, crying. She looked terrible. David had never seen anyone look like this, not even his mother. Her appearance frightened him. She was sick, but it was a painted sickness. Whatever was wrong with her she tried to cover with rouge and lipstick, powder and eye makeup. The powder only accentuated the illness. Her eyes were dark hollows, and her cheeks sunk. She was like paintings David had seen in art class.

"You look well, David," she said hoarsely.

"Thank you, Grandma," he answered.

A man with slick hair and a dark gray suit came in.

"We are ready for you now," he said. He led them into the hall and then opened a door on the other side. It was a small chapel with five rows on each side. They were to sit in the front row. His grandfather led his grandmother in and Phil took Elizabeth. David followed.

Then another door opened and a different man rolled in the casket. David was not prepared for this. Somehow it had never occurred to him that this might happen. He knew there would be prayers and readings from the Bible. He knew they would say something about life after death and that Elizabeth would cry, but he did not know that they would have to look at the body. He turned his head away and saw others in the first two or three rows across the aisle. He did not recognize them. Perhaps they were friends of his mother's or relatives he had never seen. There was a woman with gray hair and next to her a boy a little older than David, in back of them a couple and then two or three men. He wanted to turn his head and look to see who was behind them, but he was afraid to.

The service began. The man who had called them from the waiting room prayed for the soul of Margaret Hope Petersen. David wondered where Bernie was and if he knew. He kept his eyes closed. The casket was pretty close, but as long as they were sitting or kneeling he couldn't see inside. Still, it was better to keep your eyes closed. "Jesus Christ," said the man, "has overcome death," and he read from the scripture, "O Death where is thy sting? O grave, where is thy victory?" David thought of graves and bodies falling into them. He could imagine being in the box in the ground, he could not imagine eternal life. What was it like? What did your body look like? Would his mother be somewhere in Heaven looking down at him? Would she know everything he did and thought? If the body was in the grave, then how would he recognize her when he got to Heaven? How could you know somebody without their bodies?

"Let us rise, now," said the man, "and pay our respects to the dead."

Elizabeth handed David a flower. She was crying quietly. "Put it on her hands as you walk by," said Phil.

He didn't want to do this. His brain kept saying, "No," but somehow his legs followed Elizabeth and Phil, his heart pounding, his eyes wanting to turn away, but the very force of the others moved him, kept his face riveted on the casket, and he looked despite himself. It was not her. That was his first impression. It was as if they had done to her what his grandmother had done to herself. They had painted her. It was like a bloated doll dressed in his mother's clothes, a bloated doll with red lips and rouge and powdered cheeks, and the hands folded over the breast, eyes closed, the lifeless figure of mockery. He placed the flower on her hands, and followed Elizabeth out. He was angry. It was wrong. It made him sick. He walked down the hall and out the front door into the sunlight. He breathed deeply and sat on the steps. When he was a father he would not do this to his children. He would not have them paint the body and bring it in for them to look at. If the spirit was gone, why bring in the body? Why make people look at it? It was barbaric.

They went to Schrafft's for lunch, the five of them and the woman with the boy. David remembered her now. She was the woman who used to play bridge at his grandparents', and the boy was her son. They were cousins. Everyone ate and talked softly. David wondered what they would do with the body, where it would be buried. Afterwards, on the street, they said good-bye. His grandparents were going to France. His grandfather had retired, and he said it was much cheaper to live abroad. The cousins were moving to Cleveland. Elizabeth was tired. She was almost seven months pregnant, and her feet were swollen. She needed to get home and lie down.

∞

Jeremy Newland got on the train at New Haven. David looked up from his book and smiled. The kid was a character. He jounced down the aisle and tried to throw his bag on the overhead rack, but he was too short and the bag just came down on his head.

"Whoops," he said.

"Let me help you," said David

Jeremy started talking right away. "I sure had a good time, did you have a good time? The best thing about bein' home is the ice-box. You can snack any time you want and sleep late and not have to do things by the bells. I sure hate to go back. Don't you hate to go back, Lear?"

"No," said David. He was tired, too tired to be polite.

"No?" said Newland. "Did I hear you right?"

"I like school," said David. "Bad things don't happen at school. I just went to my mother's funeral, and I don't feel like talking, O.K.?"

There was a very long silence.

"Lear?" It was a different kind of voice, smaller and softer.

"Yes?"

"My mom died, too, about a year ago. That's why I go to this school 'cause my dad can't take care of me alone. I never told anybody before. I was embarrassed.

Now it was David's turn to be silent.

"Newland," he said after a while, "do you know anybody that talks about their families?"

Newland thought for a moment. "Not really," he said.

"I don't either," said David.

"Maybe that's why we're all at school," said the younger boy.

"That's right," said David. "Maybe everybody's got some reason to be at boarding school, and no one wants to talk about it. Everyone's got somebody divorced or dead or sick. I've never thought about it like that before."

Even with Terry and Griff, David didn't talk much about his family, only enough to say where he was going for vacations. And he didn't know anything about their families. Griff lived in the Bahamas because his father worked there. He was like an ambassador or something. David couldn't remember. Terry kind of moved around. His father was in the Army. He was at a fort in New Jersey for a while, and then got moved to one in Massachusetts. "You're ashamed of me, Toots," his mother had said. That was the problem. Everyone was ashamed of his parents, and no one wanted to talk about them. Then David had an idea. It was the best idea of his life. It scared him, and he wasn't sure if he could bring it off, but if he could...

"Newland," he said "you're terrific."

"I am?" said the boy, surprised.

"Listen," said David. "I'll tell you about my family if you tell me about yours."

"And you won't tell all your friends what I tell you?"

"Not if you won't tell yours what I tell you."

"Swear to God?"

"Swear to God."

They talked all the way to Framingham.

# CHAPTER
*twelve*

$\mathcal{T}$HE PRIZE DAY CEREMONIES at the Lowell School took place on the first weekend in June. They were divided into two parts: on Friday evening the finals of the public speaking contest and the presentation of athletic awards. Then on Saturday morning Mr. Armbrister gave out the other awards and the sixth formers received their diplomas from Mr. Henry L. Proctor, the President of the Board of Trustees. As the last event, Mr. Richard Granger Lowell, the great-grandson of the founder, presented the Founder's Medal.

David had been thinking about the public speaking contest ever since the trip back from his mother's funeral. The procedure in the contest was simple. Each class had a competition, and the two winners from each class spoke in front of the school. Then Mr. Armbrister picked five finalists to speak on Prize Day. David had made the finals twice before, but had never won the award. He was a good speaker, clear, forceful, well-organized, and that was enough to get him to the finals, but he always felt outclassed by two or three of the other finalists because of their topics. "Ben Franklin, Man of Many Talents" just wasn't original enough.

Fifth form year he had struggled for months trying to find a topic, and the one he found seemed perfect. He read an article in National Geographic about a man who had been swallowed by a whale and had survived. David was thrilled. He could lead into it with the Jonah story and talk about how nobody believed it and then give a modern proof that Jonah could really have been swallowed. He would make it vivid, as Mr. Pierce always suggested. He would put in lots of description of how the man felt inside the belly of the whale. When "A Modern Jonah" was given in front of the school, everybody loved it. The younger kids ooh'd and aah'd, and David got the loudest applause of the ten semifinalists.

When he gave it on Prize Day, he came in fourth.

"It was because HLP almost barfed," said Terry.

The incident occurred during one of the choicer descriptive passages: "Down, down he went, sliding smoothly into a great cavern. The stench was impossible. Great masses of half-digested fish seethed in bubbles of digestive juices. He knew that he would die if he could not get out. Already he could feel himself choking, gasping for air in the foul cavern."

At that point David turned to look at Mr. Proctor. It was a mistake. The Chairman of the Board was green and his lower lip hung open as if he'd had a stroke.

"I thought it was great," said Griff. "You may have lost the prize, but you made a lot of friends."

"So what're you going to do this year?" asked Terry.

"I don't know," said David.

That was the problem. He wanted to do something about the school and how they were all ashamed of their families and shouldn't be. But it was risky. If he did it in class and Mr. Pierce didn't like it, he wouldn't make the semifinals. If he did in front of the school and Mr. Armbrister didn't like it, then he wouldn't make the finals. Besides, it was a good speech for the parents. He'd have to write two speeches, one for the first two rounds, and then save this one for the finals. That was it. He wrote "Joe DiMaggio, the Achilles Heel of Baseball" for the school. He told the story of Achilles being dipped in the ancient river, immortal except for the spot on his heel where his mother held him. He told of the arrow which struck and killed Achilles in his one vulnerable spot, and how DiMaggio, with his bone spurs, was like Achilles, a great wounded hero, who played through pain and never complained despite his handicap. The Red Sox fans booed, but Mr. Armbrister liked it. "You've the Lowell philosophy down perfectly, lad. Good job."

Then he began working on the other secretly. He showed it to no one, not even Terry and Griff. They would all think he was going to give the baseball speech.

Now it was the night for the speech. First, the athletic awards, and Terry Roche, marched proudly to the stage three times for the football trophy, the baseball trophy, and the cup for the best all-around athlete at Lowell. He winked at David, who sat on the stage with the four other finalists. Then came the speeches. David went third.

"Our third finalist," said Mr. Armbrister, "is David Lear. His subject is 'Joe DiMaggio, the Achilles Heel of Baseball.'"

David stood at the podium, looking out at the students in the front rows and the parents behind them. His hands shook as he held his note cards.

"Mr. Armbrister," he began, "Mr. Proctor, parents, guests, and students at Lowell School. My subject is different from the one announced by Mr. Armbrister." A murmur went up from the students. No one had ever done that before. There was no rule against it, it was just terribly risky to change topics at the last minute.

"I would like," said David, "to talk about something that is more personal and meaningful to all of us. I'd like to talk about families." Another murmur.

He went on slowly, telling the story of his trip to New York for his mother's funeral and his discussion with Jeremy Newland. And at the name, Newland, he turned and nodded his head to Jeremy, who was sitting in the chair next to the one David had vacated. Jeremy was the fourth speaker. "I realized," said David, "that none of us had ever talked to each other about our families and that, perhaps, the reason was that we were ashamed of them. Why are we all here at Lowell School? Isn't it because we all have problems in our families? Isn't it because our parents need help and send us here because of that? Is that something to be ashamed of? No. It is not.

"Our families, more than other families, need our support. They need our help. When my mother was dying in the hospital, she told me there were four things I needed to learn: hope, courage, determination, and love. She said that I knew something about the first three. God knows, Lowell School teaches us something about the first three, especially courage and determination." In the rows of blue-suited students in front of him, he could see smiles and he could hear laughter. He turned to look at the headmaster. He was smiling. He understood. "Oh yes," David said, "we know determination. But what do we know about love? Nothing. When my mother was dying in the hospital, she asked me to make a promise to her. She asked…"

That was when the tears came. Suddenly his voice broke and he couldn't go on. He went back and tried again, but after "Promise" the voice went, and he just stopped and sat down.

For a long time there was silence and nobody knew what to do, not even Mr. Armbrister. Then someone in the audience started to clap, and then a few more, and soon everyone was clapping, loudly.

After the speeches, the judges huddled while Mr. Armbrister and Mrs. Rossiter played a duet for two pianos. The public speaking award was presented to Jeremy Newland for his speech on "Our Real Enemies: The Russians." His father was a professor at Yale, David remembered.

David did not feel bad about what had happened. He knew after he had broken down that he could not win, and he understood that if he had known in advance that he would break down, he never would have attempted the speech. But he was glad he had done it, and he felt clean inside. His mother would be proud of him.

As they were walking back to the dorms, Mrs. Rossiter came up to him. "David," she said, "that was wonderful." She put her arm around him and hugged him. He could smell her perfume and hear his heart beat like crazy.

"Listen," she said. "How would you like to go to the Mother and Son Dance with me? I know it's not the same, but I could be…well, her understudy. How about it?"

"Wow," he said. "That'd be terrific."

"Good," she said. "I'll meet you there in half an hour."

The Mother and Son Dance took place in the dining hall after the awards. You could only go if you had a "mother." It didn't have to be your real mother. It could be an aunt or a cousin, and even a grandmother. If you didn't have anyone coming you couldn't go unless you got someone from the school like one of the master's wives to be your "mother." But you couldn't ask. They had to ask you. David had hoped that Elizabeth would come or maybe even Molly Ariel. He hated to graduate without anyone being there. But Elizabeth had written that the new baby was too little for her to go away and leave, and Molly Ariel was going to be somewhere with her husband for a sports car race. They both loved car racing and this was one of the big events of the year. She would see him when he got to the ranch. So when Mrs. Rossiter asked him, he had all but given up hope of getting to the dance.

He raced back to the dorm to change. Terry and Griff were already there.

"Guess what?" he said.

"What?" they said in unison.

"Mrs. Rossiter's going to be my mother for the dance."

"Fantastic," said Terry.

"Let's trade," said Griff.

Terry's parents were there, and Griff had been invited earlier that evening by Mrs. Roderick, their dorm master's wife. She was a thin little woman with frizzy brown hair who sounded like she had a cold all the time.

"Tough luck, Griffo," said David, and walked off to his room to change. He had to decide what to wear. Blue suits were mandatory for the awards and speeches, but you could wear anything for the dance. The rich guys like Bobby Hershey, whose father made Hershey bars, had tuxedos. Some people had light colored suits, and some wore sports jackets. He wanted to look his best for Mrs. Rossiter. She had brought him through the winter, the gray and painful winter. Out his window he could almost see it again.

When they had started rehearsals after Christmas for the operetta, David was exhausted. The vacation had taken its toll. Vacation, he thought. What a strange word. In Latin it meant empty. To vacate, to leave, to empty out. That's what it was, an empty time. Mr. Langdon was right. The Latin meanings of words were clearer than English. The vacation had emptied him. Elizabeth was depressed and cried a lot. She was getting ready to have the baby, and it tired her to be on her feet for more than a few hours a day. David tried to help by taking care of Alex but the weather was bad. It was windy and cold or it would rain and sleet, and they couldn't go walking. Besides the neighborhood was no good. At the old apartment there was the park on Riverside Drive, and the shops on Broadway near Columbia. But the only thing good about the Bronx was Yankee Stadium, and that was useless in the middle of winter.

And then there was the money problem. Nobody had any money. The music business was bad, and David felt guilty about eating their food and not contributing anything. So he decided to get a job. He walked down the street from shop to shop, asking. Finally he found a grocery store on 163rd Street that needed a delivery boy, someone who could carry packages to the old ladies who lived in the apartments up on top of the hill and were too old to go out. They would pay him thirty-five cents an hour plus tips. He figured it out. If he gave Elizabeth and Phil a dollar a day, he'd have a little over a dollar left for himself. Then he could go out. He couldn't stand being cooped up in the apartment night after night. He was almost fourteen and he could go to the movies by himself and get around on the subway system as well as Phil. But without money he was stuck.

So for two weeks he trudged down Morris Avenue and up the hill to the Grand Concourse as far as north as 170th Street. Lots of people called because the weather was bad. It was cold work. David's gloves had holes in them, and his boots leaked. He had never really worked before, and he had never before felt the kind of tiredness that comes from plain physical exhaustion. Sometimes someone would invite him in for a cup of tea or hot chocolate. He was very grateful. He would take off his gloves and put them on the radiator in the kitchen.

"You're not from around here," they would say. "I can tell from your accent."

That's what they always said, no matter where he went. In California they said it. In Boston they said it. In California there was one accent, in Boston another. There was a Bronx accent. But David didn't really have an accent at all. "When I grow up," he thought, "I'll write a book about this, about always being from somewhere else."

Most of the people were nice. They gave him a dime or fifteen cents tip. Some of them were scared. One old lady made him leave the bag outside the door and wouldn't open it until he'd gone down in the elevator. She kept staring at him from behind her chain while he waited for her to give him the money. He wasn't allowed to return without the groceries unless they paid. She didn't tip him. He went to Mrs. Livanos almost every day. She was the Greek lady who lived on 165th Street down toward Jerome Avenue. She was a widow, and she liked to talk. "The men," she would say, "they eat too much, drink too much, work too hard, and leave us all widows. Thatsa why they's so many old ladies up here." Then she would give him tea and cake and call him a nice boy.

On Christmas day he worked for a florist downtown. Aunt Estelle had gotten him the job. They always needed an extra hand to deliver flowers on Christmas. He liked that, because it was mostly riding on the subway. The florist gave him tokens and told him where each place was. The nicest thing was that everyone had paid in advance and so people were either surprised or just plain glad to see him.

Tired as he was, he was happier out of the apartment than in it. There were two bedrooms, Elizabeth and Phil's at the end of the hall and Alex's next to the bathroom. David slept on the couch beside the piano in the living room and kept his clothes in the suitcase in the corner. He liked to sleep late but he couldn't because Alex woke up early and came in and jumped on him, and even though Elizabeth tried to keep everybody quiet, it was much easier if he got up.

At night Phil liked to work on his music. He needed the piano. He did his copy work at the desk in their bedroom, but he needed the piano for arranging. Then David would go in with Alex or sit with Elizabeth in the bedroom, playing cards or reading. He really was happier out. If he timed it right he could go to the movies at seven and be back at ten in time for bed. There were double features at the Stadium Theatre on 161st, and there was a Loew's on 167th.

Phil and Elizabeth wouldn't let him go downtown at night. It was too dangerous, they said. But on Saturdays and Sundays, if he wasn't working, he could go to Times Square to the Paramount or the Roxy or the Rivoli. Those and the Radio City Music Hall were the best. They had a movie and a stage show, and if you got there before one o'clock you could get in for fifty cents. You could see Louis Armstrong or Frank Sinatra or Tommy Dorsey, and at the Music Hall there were the Rockettes, who danced in unison, fifty beautiful legs moving like a single limb-not one out of place. He hated to come out of the shows in the afternoon into the light of day, into the sun which blinded him or the gray drizzle which reminded him of where he really was.

He liked going at night better, even though it was more dangerous. He worked out a routine. First of all, he never wore good clothes. If he looked like he lived in the neighborhood, no one would bother him. Secondly, he never looked at anyone. Sometimes he would hear footsteps behind him and want to turn around and look to see if he was being followed, but he wouldn't let himself. He just walked slowly, acting as if he wasn't worried. He knew if he started to walk fast or run or if he turned around that would only make it worse.

In the theatres he sat by himself. He always kept at least one seat between him and the next person, especially if it was a man. If it was crowded, he tried to find a nice looking family to sit next to. Once the movie started it didn't matter. He was in another world. He loved the movies. "It's your alcohol," his mother had said. "You're a movie junkie." It was real for him. He believed everything he saw unless it was really stupid. He believed Westerns and mysteries and sea adventures. He believed in Captain Bligh and Sir Francis Drake and Billy the Kid and Jesse James. He believed in all the generals and admirals from the war and the soldiers who died fighting against Germany and Japan. He never said, "This is Gary Cooper or Tyrone Power." When the movie started, he forgot the name of the actor. And when he came out into the dark, it was almost as if the dark were part of the movie world itself.

But he couldn't go too often. Vacation lasted three weeks, ten days before Christmas and ten days afterwards. He had to buy Christmas presents and shepherd his money. Also he hated to ask too many times. "Is it all right if I go to the movies?" he had to ask Elizabeth or Phil. If he asked too often, they would say it was bad for him.

So he had empty places to fill. He read, and he memorized his lines for the operetta, and he thought. There was plenty of time to think. He tried to figure out about his mother. The Bible said that "whoso believeth in me shall never die but shall have life eternal." But did his mother believe? He tried to remember. They never went to church when they lived in Westport and when he had visited his mother in New York they never talked about God or Jesus. But that didn't mean she didn't believe. Maybe she kept it to herself. He couldn't imagine her not existing. A person, a soul, can't just not exist any more. She must be somewhere, but where, and in what kind of body? He dreamed about her. He would see her in strange places where he'd never been or she would be driving off in the green Plymouth somewhere, like down the street in front of Elizabeth's. He would speak to her, but she didn't answer. It was like she wasn't allowed to talk to people. He wanted a message, a sign, he wanted her to say something that would let him know she was still alive somewhere.

So, when he got back to school he was exhausted. He was glad the vacation was over, glad to be back among his friends, but he didn't have any energy. Rehearsals were in full swing for the operetta, but he couldn't get into them the way he had expected to. He knew his lines and where he was supposed to go, and he listened to what Mrs. Rossiter said, but it wasn't fun.

One day they were practicing the trio, the scene where Ruth and the Pirate King tell Frederick that because he was born on February 29 he is legally only five, since he has had only five birthdays.

"The important thing here," said Mrs. Rossiter, "is for each of you to act out your own emotions. You mustn't be influenced by the emotions of the others. The Pirate King is pleased. He's got Frederick where he wants him. Ruth is happy. She likes Frederick and wants him to stay. Frederick is shocked. He can't believe the story he's being told."

They practiced it twice. It was terrible.

"You're too mechanical, David," said Mrs. Rossiter. "You're wooden. You've got to loosen up and move. Let your emotions out."

They did it one more time. It was still flat. Mrs. Rossiter told the Pirate King and Ruth to leave. She wanted to talk to David.

"Come on down and sit with me a minute, David," she said. She swung one leg over the piano bench and straddled it like a horse. David came down the steps from the stage and sat facing her. Then, without any warning he started to cry and put his head against her breast. She put her arms around him and held him.

"It's all right," she kept saying. "It's all right. Just cry it out. You can't keep everything inside all the time."

After a while he stopped. She gave him a tissue, and he blew his nose.

"There's nothing wrong with crying," she said, smiling. "Men are such fools. They think they're being manly by not showing their emotions. All they're doing is making ulcers. Now, let's talk about what's wrong."

He told her about vacations, about his mother, about living at Elizabeth's and Phil's, about the movies.

"And friends?" she asked. "Do you ever go to a friend's house and play? Just mess around?"

"No."

"Well, that's part of the problem. You haven't had any chance just to enjoy your childhood. When you go home, you're a little adult. You talk to adults, you work, you read, but you don't play. The reason you're so tired is that you worry all the time about adult problems. You need to just be a kid sometimes."

"That's what Mrs. Armbrister always tells me."

"I know," said Mrs. Rossiter. "We women are trying to save your life. At this rate, you'll be a little old man by thirty."

David laughed. She kissed him, lightly on the forehead, then got up and walked over to her purse, which was on the floor behind the piano. She got out a cigarette and lit it.

"I didn't know you smoked," said David.

"We're not allowed to around students," she said. "So don't say anything. I figure this doesn't count."

He watched her from the piano bench as she walked across the floor to the gym door and opened it. She stood in the doorway, her back against the door frame, taking puffs on her long cigarette and blowing the smoke into the dark outside. Then she threw the cigarette into the snow and came back. She was beautiful.

"You know, David," she said, "drama is a good vehicle for you. In drama you can get rid of yourself by being someone else. Your biggest problem is self-consciousness. You're worried about what you'll look like. You're not David up there. You're Frederick or the Pirate King or whatever character you're playing."

She sat down again on the bench. "You don't have to be self-conscious with me. I want you to have a good time. Moping isn't going to bring your mother back or make life any easier for your sister. If you're happy, you'll be more good to them, and to me. If you need to talk, if something's on your mind, just tell me, and you can stay after rehearsal. You can even cry if you need to, but starting tomorrow night let's perk up a little, O.K.?"

"I will," he said.

"Go on, now," she said. "Get out of here before I start crying."

He half ran, half tripped across the gym floor and just as he got to the door he turned back to look at her. He walked straight into the door jamb, and rebounded into the snow outside. As he walked back to the dorm, he could hear her laughing.

❧

Now it was Prize Day Night and David stood in front of the mirror tying his tie. He had selected gray pants, a blue shirt and a red and white striped Lowell School tie. He would wear his light blue cord jacket. That was his favorite. Terry and Griff burst into his room and threw him on the bed, pinioning his arms on both sides of his head.

"We're going to spray you with pickle juice," said Griff.

"We're going to give you halitosis," said Terry.

"We're going to hypnotize you and pour the spirit of Peter Winemiller into your veins," said Griff.

They let him up. "Let's go," said Terry. "At this rate the dance'll be over before we get there."

The dining hall had been specially arranged for the occasion, the tables removed and the chairs placed around the walls for those who weren't dancing. There was a punch bowl on a table near the kitchen door, and, at the far end where the head table usually stood, a four-piece band played waltzes and fox trots. Dancing wasn't new to Lowell School boys. They had required dancing classes once a month as fifth and sixth formers, and they had all learned from a Mrs. Van der Graft from Worcester the rudiments of the box step, the waltz and the fox trot. The more advanced students occasionally attempted a South American number.

Mrs. Rossiter was standing by the punch bowl talking to a group of fathers. She had on a blue gown, ankle length, with thin straps, and wore gold high-heeled sandals.

"Christ," said Terry as the threesome walked in.

"See you guys later," said David.

"I guess I'll go find Mouse-face," said Griff.

David danced with Mrs. Rossiter. "You're looking good," she said. David couldn't talk. He had to concentrate on the steps and listen for the beat of the music. He had memorized the dances by reading the book with the pictures of the little black feet on them. The hardest ones for him were the ones that went backwards.

"You're working again, David," said Mrs. Rossiter. "Don't try so hard. Don't think so hard. Do whatever you feel like, and I'll follow."

It began to get easier. "That's good," she said. "I could feel your spine soften."

"Mrs. Rossiter?" he said hesitantly.

"Yes?"

"Can we...I mean...sometime before the dance is over...Can I talk to you for a minute...can we?"

"Yes," she said.

He didn't get to dance with her very much. People were cutting in. So he danced with Mrs. Armbrister and Mrs. Pinckney and Mrs.

Roderick and Mrs. Langdon. He even danced with Terry's mother who was very tall. The rest of the time he sat on one of the chairs near the punch bowl and practiced his speech. He wanted to say the right thing to Mrs. Rossiter, to say good-bye and thank you. He didn't want to be sappy.

When it was close to the time for the dance to end, she walked up to him. "I think I need a cigarette, Mr. Lear," she said.

He stood up and walked out with her. They went across the street and sat on the cannon in front of the church. She took a cigarette from the thin, gold purse she carried. Everything he had practiced went out of his mind.

"Where will you be going to school next year?" she asked him.

"To Wicker," he answered. "My godmother arranged it with Mr. Armbrister. He said it was a good school for me. He didn't want me to go to a school like Andover or Deerfield where everyone had lots of money. He thought I would be uncomfortable there."

"Wicker's a good school," she said.

"I'm a little scared," he said.

"New things are always scary," she said.

"I'll miss you the most," he said suddenly. "You got me through."

She put her arm around him. "Thank you," she said. "It works both ways. You've meant a lot to me."

"You don't suppose we could write," he said.

"I don't think so," she said. "It's better to let go. Live where you are. Don't hang onto the past."

She crushed her cigarette into the grass and stood up. Then she took him in her arms and held him tight. "You'll be all right, David," she said. "You have a way of bringing out the best in us. Just keep doing that. You'll make it. Someday we'll hear from you."

They walked to her car. "Get on back to the dorm before you get marked late," she said. She got in and started the engine. He wanted badly to lean over and kiss her, but he couldn't. He couldn't say or do anything but watch her drive away, and walk back to the dorm.

The dorm was in an uproar. Nobody could sleep. Nobody even wanted to. There were trunks in the hall, and duffel bags on top of them. There were piles of trash, bodies in towels and underpants racing in and out of doors, radios blaring, and the sound of showers running. Bobby Hershey was chasing Ian Stuart down the hall, snapping a towel at him. David went into Griff's room. Terry was lying on Griff's bed and Griff was trying to pack.

"We oughta have a public burning," said Griff.

"Of what?" asked David.

"Blue suits," said Griff. "I never want to see this thing again."

"Better be careful, Griff," said Terry. "You might have to wear blue suits at Groton."

"Never," said Griff. "I checked it out when I read their stuff."

"Do you remember," said David, "the morning you put Winemiller's pants up on the flagpole?"

"That was great," said Terry. "Nobody noticed for two hours."

"Then Armbrister came running into math class. 'Roach,' he said. He could never pronounce my name right. 'Get those pants down immediately.'"

"Remember when I missed two pages in the dress rehearsal?" said David, "And didn't even know it 'til afterwards?"

"You were too busy looking at yourself in the mirror to know what you were doing," said Terry. That was the night David had worn his costume for the first time, the bright red jacket with gold epaulets, the dark blue pants with the yellow stripe running down the side.

"Do you remember when we did our play?" said Griff.

"Do you remember when we formed the club?"

"Do you remember the time some bastard put some kind of pepper in my after shave?" said Terry.

"Who, us?" said Griff.

"I don't remember," said David.

"You guys almost busted the club up," said Terry.

"Well, we couldn't do it to each other, 'cause neither of us has anything to shave," said Griff.

They danced around the real subject. David knew it. Finally he said: "When are we gonna see each other again?"

"We'll have a reunion, in New York," said Griff.

"Sure," said Terry. "We'll go to that dinner they have for all the alumni."

"But you don't live in New York. Besides you're going to Deerfield."

"I'll just come down," said Terry.

"We'll stay with you," said Griff.

"On my sister's couch?"

"I forgot," said Terry.

"We'll find some place," said Griff.

"I gotta go pack," said Terry.

"Me too," said David.

They drifted off. There was no way to finish the conversation.

David lay in the dark and waited for morning to come. First it would get gray so you could see the shapes of things, and then the color would come, the blue of the sky and the green of trees and grass. It would be Prize Day. They would walk in pairs across the lawn to the gym for the last time. The streets would be lined with cars. Afterwards the parents would load up the luggage and the school bus and the station wagons would carry the New York party to the train in Framingham for the last time, and Frankie would pronounce each of their names as they stepped down from the bus for the last time. "Davido," he would say, and then it would all be over. He couldn't imagine that. It was like death, like his mother being no more. How do you just finish something? He would come back and visit and talk to Mr. Armbrister and Mr. Langdon, to Mrs. Rossiter. Of course, he would come back and visit and stay in the room at Lowell House that was reserved for alumni. Mrs. Armbrister would bring him breakfast and he would visit classes and walk in the halls and look at the pictures of the operettas from every year in the school's history. He would look at the boards in the halls where the names of the winners of the Founder's Medal were engraved, and perhaps he would see his own name there. He tried not to think about that too much. He knew it was wrong to want it that much, and he knew that if he didn't win it he would have to be a good sport and congratulate Mickey, and he would do it, but not easily, for there was that in him that hated to be anything but first. To Terry it didn't seem to matter. He did everything so easily that he never seemed to try. Griff was a laugher. Maybe that's why they were such good friends because they were so different. David wondered if he would like himself as a friend. Probably not. They wouldn't have any fun. He wondered about Wicker. Would he have trouble making new friends there? It had taken him two years to find Terry and Griff.

He slept a while. When he woke he could see blue and green. He got up and went into the bathroom. Ian Stuart was there. Suddenly David spoke to him on an impulse:

"That time I kicked your shoe into the mud puddle, third form year. I'm sorry I did that."

Ian looked over from his basin. "I had for-r-rgotten that," he said. "We were ba-abies then."

"That's true, isn't it?" said David. They had all changed, staggering in one at a time, sleepy-eyed, to shave their budding mustaches, check their pimples, straighten their ties, comb their hair. Nobody talked. It was as if they were all thinking the same thing and no one knew how to say it, so they chose to say nothing. They didn't even tease Peter Winemiller.

To David the awards ceremony seemed to last for hours. There was the awarding of prizes for punctuality, neatness, and deportment, the scholarship awards for each form, and the address by the President of the Board of Trustees. Then each sixth former went to the stage to receive his diploma. Finally it was time for the Founder's Medal. Mr. Armbrister spoke:

"We come now to the final event of our awards ceremony, the presentation of the Founder's Medal, the highest award that Lowell School has to offer. It is given to that member of the sixth form who has the highest general average. Before presenting the award to this year's recipient, I should like to make a few remarks."

He paused for a moment. "The motto of the Lowell School, as you all know is Poteris Modo Velis, — You Can If You Will."

There was a brief round of laughter from the students.

"I know," said Mr. Armbrister, "that the laughs I just heard came from those of you who have listened to me say this many times before. But my reminder is especially appropriate today. This year's award goes to a young man who has proved the worth of that motto in a very special way, a young man who according to all theories of the specialists in psychology, according to the tests of the specialists in education, should have done very poorly at Lowell School, a young man who has never, in the midst of all his personal difficulties, stopped believing in himself and his capacity for success. To this young man, I say, on behalf of the faculty of Lowell School, we wish you every success in the years to come, and we are very proud to have had you here with us. I am proud to present the Founder's Medal to David Johnson Lear."

He felt a surge of joy and a brightness inside him he had never known before, and when he stood to begin his walk to the stage, he could feel a lightness in his legs, as if he were drunk. For a moment he didn't know if he could make it. Then a voice behind him shouted loud and clear, "Go get it, Butter Rum," and a wave of laughter shook the gym. He turned and looked three rows behind him, and there they were, Terry and Griff, making the club signal in front of the whole school with the biggest, goofiest grins David had ever seen. Dumb, wonderful Terry, wonderful, brilliant Griff, David thought as he turned to go up the stairs to the stage. Armbrister would kill them for that, but they didn't care.

David walked up the steps and bowed his head. It was different from what he had thought it would be. He was standing there, and Richard Granger Lowell was placing the Founder's Medal around his neck, and he didn't really care any more, not the way he had even moments before. He was proud, and he knew that he would have been angry if Mickey Saperstein had won, but right now all he could think about was Terry and Griff. They loved him, and didn't care what Armbrister or anybody else would say. That was the real point. David raised his head, and shook hands with Mr. Lowell. He turned and shook hands with Mr. Armbrister.

"Congratulations, lad," said the headmaster. "This is a fine day for Lowell School."

"And for me, sir," answered the boy, but his mind was still working on something else. He walked down the steps, and began to move toward his seat, but when he came to his row, he did not stop. He did not turn in. He just kept walking, quietly, at the same pace, to the back of the room and out the door into the sunshine. If Terry and Griff could do it, he could do it. He needed to be alone, to think, to find out more about this person with this medal hanging around his neck. In five minutes or ten, he would be surrounded. He walked up the hill to the street and crossed to the empty church.

He opened the door and walked down the aisle, then up the steps to the altar. He knelt on the gray stone, looked at the gold cross and closed his eyes. There are parents out there, he thought, and aunts and uncles and brothers and sisters. And when the ceremonies are over, they will take Terry and Griff and Peter and Ian and all the rest and hug them and tell them how proud they are. And all I have is this stupid medal around my neck and no one…

He took the medal from his neck and placed it in his pocket. He had wanted Elizabeth more than the medal, and he hadn't known it until now. He had wanted Elizabeth and Molly Ariel and Mrs. Rossiter. He had wanted someone to love him and care for him, he wanted someone to hold him, but it wasn't to be. He remembered the day he had taken the train to New York to visit his mother and what it had done to him. He would not cry like that again. He would not need like that again. He would be strong. He would take care of himself. He would go to Wicker and learn how to live, one day at a time. Perhaps he would never have someone to love him as he needed and wanted to be loved, but he could not control that. He could not do anything about that. Perhaps he would never again have friends like Terry and Griff who would stand up and shout for him in front of the whole school, but he knew now what friendship was and what it might cost, and he would not be afraid of it as he had been before. He would do what he could. "Poteris modo velis," he laughed.

He took the medal from his pocket and hung it round his neck, then walked outside to meet the others.

Tony is a native of San Francisco who received his undergraduate degree from Princeton University and his Ph.D. from Harvard University. He is the former chairman of the Department of English at Davidson College in North Carolina, and is the author of four books of poetry, the most recent of which is *The Man Who*, and the author of a sequel to *Leaving Maggie Hope*, *The Three Great Secret Things*.